THE
BAKER
AT SEASHELL
COVE

ALSO BY KAREN CLARKE

THE
BAKERY
AT SEASHELL
COVE

Karen Clarke

bookouture

Published by Bookouture in 2018

An imprint of StoryFire Ltd.

Carmelite House
50 Victoria Embankment
London EC4Y 0DZ

www.bookouture.com

ISBN: 978-1-78681-365-7
eBook ISBN: 978-1-78681-364-0

For Mam, with lots of love

Chapter One

'Meg, come and look at this!'

Tracing Sam's voice to the kitchen, I found him hunched over his laptop at the breakfast bar, a half-empty breakfast smoothie at his elbow. It was putty-coloured, with lumps of banana where it hadn't blended properly. More of a lumpy than a smoothie.

'What is it?' I said, though I'd guessed from his excited tone it must be cycling-related.

'It's the itinerary.' The posh voice he put on clashed with his faint, milky moustache. '"Paris to Geneva,"' he read out, his hazel eyes skimming the screen. '"Four days in the saddle, riding across stunning French countryside, through medieval towns, crossing through the famous vineyard regions of Burgundy and Champagne, culminating in the crossing of the beautiful Jura Mountains."'

I suppressed a sigh as I crossed the black-and-white chequered tile floor to join him. I'd heard so much about his upcoming cycling challenge that I felt as though I ought to know the itinerary by osmosis, but there'd been some last-minute tweaks and it had only just gone online.

'Sounds amazing,' I said, because I didn't begrudge him doing the challenge, it was just that training had taken up most of the year and nearly all his spare time, and I'd heard an awful lot about saddles, road surfaces, body-to-power ratios, lactate thresholds, and the benefits of windproof cycling jackets. 'I wouldn't mind going to Geneva.'

'Hmmm,' he said, still reading as I hoisted myself onto a shiny American-diner style stool at the breakfast bar, gripping the edge to stop myself slithering off. They were horribly impractical while wearing a silky robe. 'I doubt I'll see much of it.'

It wasn't the right response, but I knew he was 'in the zone' and when Sam was 'in the zone' he found it hard to focus on anything else. Even me. I was sure he'd have noticed if I'd spoken in Italian, or shaved my hair off, but since I hadn't changed much in the fifteen years since we'd met, there was no real need for him to drag his eyes from the screen.

'I'll print it out, so you've got a copy.' He was radiating the sort of excitement normally associated with children on Christmas Eve, no doubt seeing himself sailing across the finish line, contorted over the frame of his bike in the aerodynamic position that played havoc with his back.

'Let's have a look,' I said, leaning over, but a bolt of early sunshine had brightened the screen to a blank and I couldn't see a thing. We were in the grip of an August hot spell and my robe was already starting to cling.

'Just a few more days and we'll be in Paris.' By 'we' he meant his fellow cycling club members, who'd signed up for the challenge at the beginning of the year.

'Yay,' I said with a smile, wondering what I'd be doing while he was away, apart from worrying about whether I'd still be at the bakery when he came back.

'I'm going to post our progress on the Pedal Pushers Facebook page every day, so you'll be able to picture where we are.'

'Lovely,' I said. It might have been nice to be there in person, but the trip was members only, and I couldn't have gone anyway with the bakery up for sale.

'Oh, and Mum's emailed another link to a company that does personalised wedding invitations.' This time I was sure Sam was avoiding my gaze deliberately. Beverley's email links were reaching crisis point as she attempted to organise every aspect of our wedding. She'd already persuaded Sam to book Studley Grange for the ceremony, and while I hadn't argued because… well, Studley Grange *was* gorgeous, if insanely expensive, her suggestions were becoming ever more outrageous. I'd already declined some rhinestone studded invitations, as well as a scroll inside a bottle, complete with sand and shells as being too over the top, but Sam had clicked on the link and was saying, 'At least these ones are reasonably priced.' He picked up his glass and attempted to swirl the sludge inside around. 'Three silver hearts underneath our names and the venue, and whoever gets an invite scratches them off to reveal the wedding date.'

I couldn't stop a tiny groan escaping.

'Yeah, I'm not keen on the gambling element,' he admitted, to my relief. 'What about a customised typography of our story?'

'A *what?*'

'How we met, that kind of thing.' His eyes zoomed over the screen, and I appreciated that he was at least making an effort to think of something besides his cycling challenge. 'Our first date, first kiss, things we love to do together.' He knitted his sandy eyebrows. 'Could be fun,' he said doubtfully.

'I'm not sure,' I stalled. I had to be careful what I said, as Beverley was easily offended, and Sam preferred the path of least resistance when it came to his mother. 'Most people already know we met at school, and that our first kiss was in your dad's shed which smelt of petrol.'

'Ah, you remember.' He slapped a hand over his heart. 'I still associate the smell of fuel with you.'

'Idiot.' I smiled, in spite of myself. 'And I'm sure they won't care that our first "date" was babysitting your little sister.'

'Oh, I don't know, it was quite dramatic.' He finally planted his gaze on mine, and I fleetingly wondered what he saw. The same as always, I supposed: shoulder-length wavy hair (champagne-blonde, according to Mum), pale-denim eyes (Mum again), generous curves, and probably a shiny face, thanks to the rising temperature. 'Especially the bit where we lost her playing hide-and-seek, and ended up calling the police.'

I shuddered, recalling the episode as though it had happened yesterday. 'I'm not sure your parents will want reminding,' I said, remembering Neil and Beverley shooting home in a panic to find two squad cars outside their house, the inside swarming with officers, and a helicopter circling overhead. Luckily, the noise had woken three-year-old Sadie, who'd hidden under her duvet and fallen asleep. We hadn't even thought to look in her bed. 'And we don't really do things together, apart from Sunday lunch with your family.' It was true. Not in a bad way, we just had different interests. Sam's were cycling and – less frequently these days – fishing, and I loved baking and… well, baking.

'We go to the cinema sometimes' – I couldn't remember the last time – 'and I'm home for dinner every evening, and we do a jigsaw together every Christmas.' Sam had adopted a jokey manner, which meant he was 'handling' me. 'That's more than most couples manage.'

I supposed he was right. 'Ah yes, the Christmas jigsaw.' I tried to match his jolly tone. 'But it's not exactly white-water rafting, or… I don't know, salsa dancing.'

'You'd hate white-water rafting, you don't even like getting your face wet in the shower, but we can take up salsa if you like.' Getting off his stool, Sam began to strut up and down, popping his hips from side to side while holding an imaginary partner. I couldn't help laughing. With his athletic frame – shown to advantage in tight-fitting cycling gear – he could easily pass for a dancer.

'You're right, we do plenty together. I just don't think it needs putting on a wedding invitation.'

'OK, I'll let Mum know.' Sam reached for his drink and I almost gagged, watching him drain the glass. I'd never liked bananas. 'She thinks we need to get a wiggle on, that's all, so that people can book accommodation.'

'We've got ages yet.' I slid off the stool and moved across to the kettle, keen to draw the conversation to a close.

'January will come around quicker than you think.' He rinsed his glass and placed it in the dishwasher. 'She's just trying to help, Meg.' He swung round and, for a second, I thought he was about to comment on my apparent reluctance to let his mum get so involved, but instead, he said, 'And you're positive you don't want an owl as a ring bearer?'

I gave him my toughest look. '*Very* positive.'

Beverley had come across a website a few months earlier called Flying the Knot, which had promised a beautiful ring-bearing barn owl to 'elegantly and gracefully' fly our wedding rings along the aisle. I'd almost wept with laughter – until I realised Sam was considering it. In truth, I'd still been reeling from the suddenness of his proposal. Although we'd been together for years, Sam had always been a bit vague on the subject of a wedding – even after Beverley reminded him that it had been my dream, at sixteen, for us to be married with a child on the way by the time I was thirty.

One minute we'd been chugging along as normal, me working in the bakery at Seashell Cove, Sam training hard for his cycling challenge, weddings apparently the last thing on his mind, and the next he'd booked a night at a spa hotel in Exmoor, and after a couples' massage that he'd complained was too 'light-fingered' and a meal that took ages to arrive, he'd proposed in our four-poster-bedded room, and suggested we start trying for a baby that very night. Unfortunately, nothing had happened in that department over the next few months, despite tests showing there was no reason why, so we'd put starting a family firmly on ice until after we were married.

'The owl was one of Mum's sillier ideas,' Sam acknowledged, startling me back to the moment. I was clutching a mug and staring blankly at the boiling kettle. 'Especially as you don't even like birds that much.'

'Not close up.' Grabbing a teabag with a pair of tiny silver tongs, I flashed him a smile. 'I'd scream the place down if an owl went rogue and attacked everyone at the wedding, like the one we saw on the news.'

He smirked. 'Do you remember when a pigeon landed on your head in Trafalgar Square, and you did a little wee?'

Of course I remember. It wasn't long after you came back from Edinburgh, where you met someone else despite swearing you wouldn't, and phoned to break up with me. I banished the thought, not sure why it had popped up when it was ancient history. Sam had been at university, and when his relationship with Andrea – an aspiring model – had ended a year or so later, he'd come back to me.

Actually, he'd returned to Devon because his dad was in hospital, which was where we'd bumped into each other again, and where he'd declared he still had feelings for me, and I'd been so happy that I hadn't probed for details about his break-up. I didn't want to know whether he'd said I love you to someone else.

'Thanks for that reminder,' I said, pouring boiling water into my mug. 'It was only a tiny wee, but not my finest moment.'

'Oh, and Mum's been on again about you not wanting to take my surname.'

I tried to keep my voice light. 'I always said that I'd never become Meg Ryan.'

'She thinks most people won't remember there's an actress with that name.'

'Is she kidding?' On safer ground, I took the milk he was holding out and splashed some into my tea. 'Everyone in the entire world remembers *When Harry Met Sally.*'

'And you don't want to be double-barrelled?'

'Meg Larson-Ryan doesn't exactly roll off the tongue.' I glanced at the hot-dog-shaped clock on the wall above our reconditioned 1950s stove. 'I should get ready for work.'

He lifted his eyebrows. 'It's not really work though, is it?'

'Oh, Sam, not this again.'

'Just saying.' He glanced at his watch, and I could tell he'd already moved on in his head, even as he was speaking. 'You're paid to work at the café, not to look after the bakery.'

I shot him a glance over my mug. 'That's where I bake my cakes, Sam, and I do get paid for those.'

'Not very much,' he said, with the faintly censorious tone that made me want to throw my teabag at him. 'You need to find a full-time job.'

'You know that I'm holding out for someone to buy the bakery and take me on.'

Sam was scooping things into his backpack now, not really focused. 'Whoever buys it will probably turn the building into something else.'

You hope. For some reason, it niggled him that I was still holding out for a job there; that I'd suggested us putting in an offer, even though we could barely afford the wedding Sam had insisted on funding ourselves.

That was on top of our mortgage and bills, and his cycling challenge, which had cost more than he'd bargained for.

I opened a Tupperware box and lifted out a slice of cherry and almond tart to have for breakfast. 'We'll see,' I said mildly.

'You could always ask for more hours at the café.'

I'd already told him there were no more available hours, but decided not to remind him as he came over and bent his head to mine. He was nearly a foot taller, and had nice lips – full and kissable – but a trace of banana on his breath made me turn my face, and his lips grazed my cheek.

Backing away, he grabbed his helmet and crammed it over his thick blond hair, and I saw him checking out his quads in the glass-fronted oven door. They were impressively honed, since he'd taken to cycling to his office in Kingsbridge every day as part of his training regime, and I supposed I couldn't blame him if his eyes flicked down from time to time to admire his thighs and calves.

'I'd better go,' he said. 'Negotiating world peace can't wait any longer.'

I smiled at the little joke. Sam was a quantity surveyor, a job he'd got used to explaining as 'costing the construction of buildings' if anyone asked.

'Be careful out there.' He was one of those cyclists drivers tooted at, and I worried that one day he'd get run over.

'You too,' he said, looking vaguely appalled as I crammed a mouth-watering combination of buttery pastry and soft, almondy sponge into my mouth. 'I'll see you later.'

When he'd gone, I scooted across to the window, brushing crumbs from my cleavage, and as I watched him lovingly grip the handlebars and mount his bike, I wondered whether it was normal to feel slightly jealous. It was a long time since I'd been lovingly gripped and mounted.

Chapter Two

My spirits drooped at the sight of the For Sale sign outside the Old Bakery; a daily reminder of how little control I had over its future. Like the butcher's next door, it was a quaintly old-fashioned, two-storey building with a bow-fronted window and whitewashed exterior, and I simply couldn't imagine the street without it.

I still missed the owner, Mr Moseley, and the way he'd say, 'Here's Meg, come to bake the world a better place,' every time I walked in. He'd been at least seventy-five when I'd started work there six years ago, but he wouldn't hear of retiring. The job had been his life, and his father's before him, and nobody could imagine him sitting in his cluttered flat upstairs with his feet up, reading a newspaper all day. He'd come down every morning, until three months earlier, when I'd arrived to find his cleaner, Carol, weeping quietly in the kitchen, and a kind-faced paramedic had revealed that Mr Moseley had passed away peacefully in the night.

'Looked just like he was sleeping,' Carol had said, buttoning her coat with shaky fingers. 'I wouldn't be surprised if he's left the bakery to you, Meg. He thought the world of you.'

I hadn't been able to deny a swell of hope. Mr Moseley *had* taken a shine to me, and been like a grandfather in some ways. He'd tried to teach me how to make his signature loaves, despairing at my heavy handedness and lack of perseverance when I could bake cakes 'like an angel', but he'd trusted me with a set of keys, and hadn't minded me coming over in the evenings sometimes to bake after everyone had gone home.

But it turned out Mr Moseley hadn't even made a will, and his estranged brother, Lester, wasn't interested in the bakery, opting instead to put the building on the market.

Luckily, I still had my keys, and access to the kitchen until the place was sold. Lester – who lived in Spain, and hadn't even shown up to his brother's funeral – had given his permission through the agent dealing with the sale, who'd pitched up at the bakery to look around, and found me up to my elbows in flour in the kitchen. 'He's agreed you can act as caretaker and keep an eye on the place,' he'd said, and I'd got a bit teary with gratitude. I hadn't told Sam I'd been using the money I earned at the café, and for making my cakes, to cover the cost of using the kitchen, and to pay for the delivery of fresh ingredients I ordered every week.

As I pulled the car round the back of the bakery and got out, Big Steve emerged from the butcher's, a camera slung round his neck. When he wasn't working at the bakery at Tesco's in Newton Abbott, he liked to indulge his love of wildlife photography. 'No interest yet?' he called.

''Fraid not,' I said, thinking, as I always did, how much like a typical baker he looked with his cuddly frame and plump smiley face, topped off with a shock of curly brown hair. He'd probably looked the same as a child, and wouldn't change much as he aged, but I guessed he was in his late thirties. 'Sure you won't put in an offer?'

'Wish I could, believe me.' He pushed his curls off his forehead. 'On my salary, I can't even afford a place of my own to live.' He jerked his eyes to the flat above the butcher's, where he lived with his brothers. 'Plus,' he added, 'it would probably finish off the old man.'

His dad had nearly disowned him already for not joining the family business, struggling with the fact that his youngest son was a vegetarian and loathed the sight of meat. Luckily, Steve's brothers had taken the reins at the butcher's shop when their father retired.

'Ah well, happy baking,' he said, moving with a light step towards the corner of the building. 'Let me know if you'd like some loaves to pop in the window for show. I could make a few if you don't mind me using the kitchen. The oven in my flat is a *leetle* bit temperamental.'

'Will do,' I said, smiling. If only Mr Moseley hadn't been so territorial in his kitchen. Big Steve would have been a great asset, and things might not have gone downhill as Mr Moseley made fewer loaves, and his eyesight started to fail.

As I let myself in through the back door, goosebumps peppered my arms. I'd driven the ten-minute journey from Salcombe with the car windows down, glad of my sleeveless dress, but wished now that I'd thought to bring a cardigan.

In the past, Mr Moseley would have already been there for hours, proving the dough and baking the first batch of bread, ready for the early customers. The kitchen would have been warm and fuggy from the heat of the ovens, the door propped open in summer, and while I got busy serving, he'd start on another round, including his famous 'doorstopper' scones. Around nine o'clock, his long-time assistant, Martha, would arrive to take over serving so I could bake my repertoire of cakes, and mouth-watering aromas would drift from the building, drawing people like magic. Often, there'd be a queue outside, and Mr Moseley's furrowed face would light up with satisfaction.

'That's what I'm talking about,' he would say, before disappearing back into the steamy kitchen.

But that was before his eyesight deteriorated, and Martha retired to Scotland, and he started buying in part-baked bread to warm up in the ovens. Business had tailed off, despite the occasional request for a celebration cake, as regulars began buying their baked goods from the nearby supermarket.

Sighing, I pushed my hair inside one of the little white hairnets Mr Moseley had always insisted we wear, and pulled on my 'Star Baker' apron (Mum's nod to my love of *The Great British Bake Off*), before switching on the ancient but efficient ovens.

Everything about the small kitchen was old-fashioned (or 'vintage' as my friend Tilly would call it), from the original red-brick walls, to the cream-and-terracotta tiled floor and frosted glass panes in the window, but Mr Moseley had been rigorous about cleanliness, and all the equipment worked.

After washing my hands and cleaning the surfaces, I lined up my ingredients on the wooden worktable. As well as making another cherry and almond tart, I wanted to try a chocolate and raspberry cream cake recipe I'd seen in a magazine, and adapt it by adding some lemon zest, and layering the top with toasted flakes of coconut.

Anticipation unfurled as I weighed out the flour to make the pastry for the tart. I didn't take any chances when I was baking for the café, though I had a knack for guessing quantities correctly, like some people could play music by ear.

Mum said I took after my granny, who we'd lived with until I was seven, and my earliest memory was of cracking eggs into a ceramic bowl, her gentle hand guiding mine, while the scent of a baking cake still whizzed me back to Saturday mornings in her kitchen in Plymouth, cartoons blazing from the television in the living room.

'Baking was her way of showing love,' I'd heard Mum say to someone outside the church after Granny's funeral – she'd collapsed on her way to buy eggs one winter's morning and never came home. I hadn't understood what Mum meant because Granny had shown love in all sorts of ways, which is why it had been so tough to accept she'd gone, and why Mum had sold the house ('too many memories') and taken us to Salcombe, where she'd holidayed once when her father was still alive.

But I'd grown to understand that when someone took their first bite of something I'd baked and got that look on their face, it was as if I'd given them a gift; that a cake baked with love could lift feelings, make a day better, or even create an emotional connection.

Sam still remembered the Maltesers-smothered chocolate cake I'd made for his sixteenth birthday, and said to this day it was the tastiest cake he'd ever eaten. I couldn't imagine a day that didn't feature flour. Apart from anything, it kept me focused. Devising new recipes, mixing and measuring, rolling and kneading, meant my mind stayed away from trickier issues – like the wedding, and the bakery being for sale, and Sam's cycle challenge, which meant he'd be away for the week from Monday—

A noise like an old-fashioned doorbell made me jump. The sound of a text arriving. Normally, I kept my phone close by, knowing Mum would be in touch, and the fact that I'd left it in my bag was a worrying indication that baking-as-meditation wasn't working as well as it usually did.

Sighing again – did I usually sigh this much? – I rested a sieve of raspberries on the side of the mixing bowl, dusted my hands on my apron and reached for my bag.

This is Milo! Isn't he adorable? X

I stared at the attached photo of a yawning baby with wisps of black hair, and tiny fists bunched beside plump cheeks. I was worried she'd taken to snapping pictures of random newborns, until I remembered her friend Kath's daughter had given birth a few weeks ago.

Gorgeous x I replied, my stomach clenching. Mum was so desperate to be a grandmother, it was as if she thought that talking about babies and showing me pictures would magic one into my tummy.

This could be you next year! Another photo, this time of Milo cradled in his mother's arms. Freya was smiling piously, wearing full make-up and an expensive looking top, her long, salon-red hair a glossy sheet. We'd tried to be friends, because of our mothers, but hadn't found any common ground.

Don't hold your breath! I replied, adding smiley faces to show I was being playful, wishing Sam hadn't broadcast our intention to start a family in the first place, assuming it would be as simple as clicking his fingers.

Mum had gone into excited overdrive, just as Sam's mum had about the wedding. It was as if becoming a mother-in-law and grandmother had been her sole aim in life, and she had been sorely disappointed when I broke the news that we'd put starting a family on hold.

I've got a new treatment for you to try!

I groaned. This was Mum's latest attempt to 'help' me conceive in the future; torpedo-sized supplements that tasted like dirt, courtesy of the health food company she worked for.

I've got a cake in the oven, talk to you later! X I replied and switched off my phone to avoid any more pictures of Milo and his photogenic mother. Freya's Instagram feed was probably flooded with cute, filtered images and multiple hashtags, but knowing her from old, I suspected the baby was more of an accessory than a living, breathing human being that would need taking care of for at least the next eighteen years.

Swinging my attention away, I switched the radio on, tuning it to a station playing popular songs from the nineties, and ten minutes later slid a couple of tins of cake mixture into the oven, and decided to make some buttery, crumbly shortbread to take home later.

The kitchen had warmed up nicely, and I propped the door open with the mop bucket. I grabbed a bag of flaked almonds to toast for the tarts, which were cooling on the side, and hummed along to an All Saints version of 'Lady Marmalade'. Using a chopping knife as a makeshift microphone, I did some pelvic thrusts as I belted out a couple of verses, and had just got to *Voulez vous coucher avec moi… ce soir*, circling my hips in time to the beat, when someone exaggeratedly cleared their throat behind me.

I spun round, heart seizing with shock, and the knife flew out of my hand, heading straight at the man in the doorway.

'Whoa!' He ducked, shooting one arm up to shield his face as the knife landed with a clatter by his feet.

'I'm so sorry.' Panting with shock, I rushed to pick it up as All Saints continued to sing *Would you sleep with me tonight* in French. If only I'd been caterwauling to something less suggestive.

'It was actually pretty good, until the moment you tried to kill me.'

'I didn't… I wasn't…' I backed away, clutching the knife, knowing I must look deranged, wishing the man had been anyone but Nathan Walsh, the agent tasked with selling the Old Bakery. 'I was about to chop some nuts,' I fibbed, switching the radio off.

Nathan comically widened his eyes. 'In that case, I think I'll stay over here.'

'Not those kind of nuts.' Flustered, I shot behind the table and tipped out the almonds, which clearly didn't need chopping. I wished he'd let me know he was coming, so I could have… *what?* Nipped through to the downstairs toilet, put on some lipstick, and whipped off my hairnet and apron? Nathan Walsh held the future of the bakery in his hands, I reminded myself. Just because he'd agreed to ask Lester Moseley if I could continue using the kitchen, and had swung by a couple of times since to see how I was doing, didn't mean he was interested in what I looked like.

'I sing occasionally with friends at the Smugglers Inn,' I said, arranging the almonds in a pile, then scattering them again, praying my cheeks didn't look as hot as they felt. 'Only karaoke, nothing special. Just for fun, when we've had a few drinks. I'm no Barbra Streisand.' *Great reference, Meg. Very current.* 'In case you hadn't noticed.'

'It was better than my Mick Jagger.' Nathan leaned his shoulder against the doorframe, and slid his hands in the pockets of his light-weight trousers. 'No one gets any satisfaction when I start singing.'

Trying to picture it, I smiled.

He grinned back, and I felt a leap in my chest as I took in his olive-green eyes, and perfectly straight nose and teeth. His toasty tan was showcased by a cream shirt with the sleeves rolled up, and his short beard and wild brown hair added to his attractiveness.

'Sounds like you need to update your act,' I said in a sisterly tone.

'More like I need to ditch it.' His smile grew. 'Something smells good.'

'That'll be the sponge for my chocolate and raspberry cake.' The timer went off and I moved to the oven, fumbling a little as I stuffed my hands into oven gloves. 'You should pop to Maitland's Café sometime and try it.'

I'd told him the first time we met that I worked there part-time, as well as supplying their cakes, which was why I'd hoped to carry on using the kitchen at the Old Bakery until it was sold.

'Maybe I will,' he said, and this time there was no mistaking the look in his eyes when they fastened on mine, or the flutter of excitement that erupted beneath my ribcage.

It had happened the first time we met, when I'd dusted off my hands to show him around the bakery, and he'd told me he was fascinated by old buildings and liked to explore their history.

'I've been thinking about writing a book on the subject, but I don't know if there'll be much of an audience.'

It had surprised me how easily we'd fallen into conversation, and how much I'd enjoyed it, considering I'd planned to be cool and efficient, and when I got home that evening I'd kept replaying our conversation and found myself hoping to see him again.

The second time he came over I'd been baking a chocolate fudge cake, and he told me the building had once been a post office run by a smuggler's son, before it was bought by Mr Moseley's great-grandfather and turned into a bakery.

I hadn't told him I already knew the bakery's history. I'd been too fixated on his face and how animated he'd looked while talking. Like Sam, when he'd finally mastered removing a gilet from his jersey pocket, putting it on and zipping it up, whilst riding his bike no-handed without slowing down.

Snapping back to the moment, I put down the cake tins, slipped off the oven gloves and reached into my apron pocket, where I kept my engagement ring when I was working, in case I inadvertently baked it into a cake.

Unlocking my gaze from Nathan's, I slipped it onto my finger and said brightly, 'Did I tell you, I'm getting married next year?'

Chapter Three

'What's up?' Gwen greeted me, after I'd transferred my chocolate and raspberry cake to a wooden stand and brought it through to the counter. 'Is that future mother-in-law of yours still trying to get you in white on your wedding day?'

Her laughter, a series of wheezy rasps, was hard to resist. 'I'm fine and no, she's given up on white,' I said, smiling. Gwen was the manager of Maitland's Café and a massive hit with customers, who considered it a privilege to be insulted by her.

'Why do you look like a bulldog chewing a nettle, then?'

'I'm a bit warm, that's all,' I lied, failing to banish the memory of Nathan's face after I'd told him I was getting married. Had I imagined a flash of disappointment before his smile reappeared, and was it a coincidence that he'd made his excuses to leave immediately after? More pressingly, why did it matter? I'd only been out with one man apart from Sam – after he'd dumped me for Andrea – and that had only lasted a month, so it was unlikely I'd be attracted to a virtual stranger when my wedding was only a few months away. Even if the stranger was interesting, kind, and good-looking.

'I wore purple Doc Martens on me wedding day, and a studded collar wiv me dress, which weren't white, I'll tell you that for nuffink,' Gwen was saying, her cockney accent bringing to mind East End gangsters and Pearly Queens. Her short, burly figure didn't lend itself to images of swirly, girly gowns, so it wasn't hard to imagine her as a punk bride. 'Not that I weren't a virgin, mind.' Her tone turned steely, as though I'd called her a slut. 'I saved meself for me wedding night, which weren't easy as I'm a red-blooded woman, but I wanted me first time to be special, know what I mean?'

It was difficult to imagine Gwen in any intimate clinch, other than a headlock. 'Of course,' I said faintly.

'Waste of time, mind you,' she carried on, seeming unaware – or uncaring – that a short queue of customers was agog to hear what was coming. 'Turns out I'm allergic to whipped cream. Got a nasty rash all over, and spent most of me wedding night at an 'ospital outside Rio, trying to get diagnosed.' Scanning the delighted faces of her audience, she said, 'And you lot can drag your minds out of the gutter. I'm talking about the whipped cream we 'ad for dessert at the wedding reception.'

There were shaking heads and peals of laughter, and I wondered whether Gwen was even telling the truth. I knew from her cousin, who'd worked at Maitland's for years before retiring, that Gwen was divorced, but she'd never talked about her marriage before.

Intrigued, I waited until she'd taken a couple of orders and turned her attention to the coffee machine. 'How long were you married?' I said, oddly nervous to be treading on personal territory. 'If you don't mind me asking.'

'Long enough,' she said, raising her voice over the hiss of the steamer. 'In the SAS 'e was. 'E didn't 'ave no time to be a proper 'usband so I left him. Broke 'is 'eart.'

Unsure whether or not she was teasing me – I couldn't read her as well as I did most people – I said, 'I'm sorry to hear that. Was he The One?'

'Oh, I geddit.' She aggressively sprinkled chocolate powder over two foamy coffees. 'You're 'aving doubts about young Samuel.'

'Of *course* I'm not.' I grabbed a cloth and wiped 'Lemon and Blueberry' off the board on the wall too vigorously, removing 'Cake of the Day' as well. 'And his name's not short for Samuel, it's just Sam.'

'Well, if you don't want to marry Just Sam, you should tell 'im before fings go any further.'

'I *do* want to marry him.' I put down the cloth and turned to look at her. 'I just wondered whether your ex was The One, even though it didn't last.'

'S'pose 'e was, being as I 'ain't met no one else since.' She cocked her head. 'Wouldn't 'ave married 'im if I didn't love 'im, but I s'pose there were signs it wouldn't last.'

'What signs?'

''E were never there, for a start, always off on some mission, and 'e couldn't talk about 'is job, which drove me mad.' She seemed about to say more, then nodded at the board. 'Better sort that out,' she said, and I plucked some chalk from the drawer underneath the counter. 'So everyfink's 'unky dory with you and Just Sam?'

'Everything's fine.' I concentrated on the chalkboard, gratified when both waiting customers ordered some chocolate and raspberry cake. It was a good job I'd made two, in the end. The café was busier than ever now the summer holidays were underway, and the weather was so glorious. Once the customers had taken their plates to the only available table, I decided to change the subject.

'Have you heard from Lydia and Ed?' I asked Gwen. The café owners were away on holiday in Greece – the first time they'd been abroad since their honeymoon, more than thirty years ago.

'Not since their last postcard, but Cassie's outside, if you want to 'ave a word.' Cassie was their daughter, and came in on Mondays to sketch cartoon-style likenesses of customers, who booked in advance because her drawings were so popular. 'Not now, we're too busy,' Gwen added, as if I'd been about to leave. 'Get the rest of that cake sliced up and give Tamsin an 'and before she blows a gasket, and that goon of a waiter spills somefink on someone.'

Tamsin, the young waitress, was clearing tables, strands of blonde hair escaping her loosely coiled bun, while Dominic, the café's latest recruit, eyed her longingly, liquid dribbling from the spout of the teapot he was holding.

Looking past them, I spotted Cassie on the terrace, her sketchpad on her lap, drawing a woman with full-blown blonde hair and a pout, like Marilyn Monroe.

Smiling, my spirits rose again when I saw Tilly outside the white picket fence, back from one of her guided walks along the coastal path, chatting to a couple of elderly men in identical safari-style shirts.

One of the highlights of the past year had been reconnecting with my two best friends from high school, after more than a decade. Cassie had been in London, working for an event planning company, while Tilly had relocated to Vancouver with her parents after school. When Cassie lost her job four months ago, she'd returned to Seashell Cove and was now in demand as an artist, while Tilly was back living in Ivybridge where she'd grown up.

Our friendship had resumed with surprising ease, the only shadow being Sam, who hadn't said much but gave the impression he thought Tilly was a bad influence. I guessed it was because she was single, and did what she wanted, and had been mildly scathing about Sam at school, and about relationships in general.

'She still drifting about, living off her parents?' he'd asked when I told him she was back and had found me at the bakery.

I'd leapt to her defence, as if we were teenagers again. 'She's not drifting about, she's still into interior design,' I'd said. 'She's really talented, Sam.'

He'd smiled with his lips closed and his eyebrows raised, to indicate mild disapproval. 'She can afford to treat it as a hobby though, unlike the rest of us.'

Sam's work ethic was one of the things that defined him, and he didn't approve of parents supporting grown-up children capable of holding down a job. As the first person in his family to go to university and get a degree, he'd supported himself by tutoring maths to struggling students, and he was proud that I'd worked full-time since leaving school, and helped to support my mum when she'd been out of work for a while.

When he found out I fancied Joey from *Friends* (my all-time favourite TV show) he'd taken a surprising amount of offence that had nothing to do with looks. 'Isn't he the one who's oversexed, under-educated, and always out of work?' His teenage crush had been Sporty Spice.

'Looks like Cassie's sold another painting,' I said proudly to Gwen, noticing a gap on the wall where Cassie's artwork hung, alongside some watercolours by an artist she'd recently discovered. 'She'll be turning down work at this rate.'

'Making up for lost time.' Gwen's raisin-like eyes slid past me to the half-open door leading to the staff area.

'What is it?' I spun round and saw a black and white cat slope out of the office and settle itself on a purple velvet cushion in the passageway. 'Shouldn't Dickens be in the office?' I turned to see Gwen's normally thunderous face melt into a slushy smile.

'Aw, me likkle darlin,' she cooed in an unsettling falsetto. 'Oo's mummy's best likkle boy?' Fixing her with his remaining eye, Dickens miaowed in response. 'I wuv you too, my sweetie, and Mummy will get oo some biscuits in a minute.' It was obvious Dickens was the love of Gwen's life – *not* her ex-husband. She'd adopted the one-eyed tomcat after a cat-café day that Cassie had organised, and they'd been inseparable ever since. 'I like to keep 'im where I can see 'im, out of 'arm's way,' she said, as if catnappers lurked around every corner. ''E 'ain't doing no 'arm.'

'You know I'm allergic.'

'You'll be fine as long as you don't touch 'im, and you can take an antihistamine.'

I couldn't really argue with that, and didn't bother trying.

Determined to push my troublesome thoughts away, half-wishing I could rewind to when Tilly had just returned, Sam had recently proposed, and I was still working at the bakery, I switched my attention to the customers flowing in, the scent of sun and sea mingling with the rich aroma of coffee.

As I took orders and made tea, I tuned out of the conversations going on around me, and lapsed into a daydream where Nathan called in to the bakery to tell me there was a buyer, and not only did the new owner want to resurrect the business, he wanted me to manage it.

'He'll be very hands off because he lives in the Outer Hebrides, so it'll be entirely in your hands,' said imaginary Nathan, trailing his gaze across my face, a scattering of chest hair visible where his shirt buttons had pinged undone. 'He's giving you carte blanche to do what you want with the place.'

'Oh my god, Nathan, you don't know how much that means to me!' Awash with emotion, I leapt into his outstretched arms and we danced around the bakery kitchen, our eyes locked together, our breathing uneven, our bodies radiating heat. Suddenly, his lips were hungrily exploring mine, and his hands had pressed me against the hard contours of his body…

A strangled squeak shot out of my mouth.

Gwen's head jerked round. 'Cut yourself?'

I was holding a teaspoon, so it was highly unlikely, but I could see she was struggling to understand the cause of the noise I'd just made. 'Spilt some boiling water on my foot,' I managed, wiggling it for effect. I was close to the hot water dispenser, so it was just about plausible.

'You should wear boots and combats like me.' She eyed my sensible loafers and the navy, knee-length skirt I wore with my short-sleeved Maitland's shirt. 'You're asking for trouble, coming in half-dressed,' she said, as if I was in hot pants and flip-flops.

'I don't suit trousers, and steel toe-capped boots in this weather would make my feet smell.' I wasn't focused on what I was saying, the feeling of Nathan's lips on mine as real as if we'd actually kissed.

Gwen's eyes shrank. 'Go and 'ave your break,' she said, snatching the teaspoon off me and lobbing it into the sink. 'TAMSIN!'

Tamsin scurried behind the counter, her grey eyes round with fright. She still wasn't sure of Gwen. 'Sorry.' She put down a tray rattling with empty coffee cups and plates. 'What do you want me to do?'

'If you don't know that by now, there's no 'ope for you,' Gwen said, not unkindly, and I left them to it, glad of an excuse to shoot outside and clear the blur of images still crashing around in my head – hair, lips, skin… Nathan's eyes, his arms… *oh god.*

I paused for a second and looked past the tables at the curve of golden sand and clear, shimmering water in the cove below without really taking it in, before checking that Cassie was alone now, at the furthest table. I hurried over and plonked myself on the chair opposite, not caring I was in full sunshine and likely to burn.

'Hi, Meg.' She smiled up at me, smoothing a strand of her glossy chestnut hair back into her ponytail. It had faded from the purple shade she'd worn when she lived in London. 'I fancy another iced tea, but am too lazy to go and get one.' Her smile melted away. 'What's happened?'

'Something weird.' My limbs felt loose, as though they might detach, and the blood was roaring in my ears. Even my voice sounded strange. 'I've just had a sexy daydream.'

Chapter Four

As soon as I'd said it, I wanted to snatch the words back, but it was too late.

'Well, there's nothing wrong with that.' Cassie looked at me as though I'd turned into a Dementor from *Harry Potter*. 'Although, hats off to you, if you're still daydreaming about Sam after… what is it? Fifteen years?'

'I'm not talking about Sam.' I pushed my fingers through my hair, as if the action might settle my seething thoughts. 'That's what's so awful.'

'What is?' Shoving her sketchpad aside, Cassie leant forward. 'I don't understand.' Her silver-grey eyes were wide and concerned.

'I know it sounds ridiculous,' I said. 'I'm hardly Taylor Swift…'

'What's Taylor Swift got to do with it?'

'I'm just saying, this sort of thing only happens to people like her.'

'What sort of thing?' Cassie's eyebrows puckered. 'Meg, you're not making any sense.'

'I know, I'm sorry, I…' I took a deep breath. 'It's just there's this man, Nathan Walsh, the agent handling the sale of the bakery. I don't know if I mentioned him,' I knew I hadn't, 'but he has this way of looking at me, and I keep thinking about him, and when I told him this morning I was getting married—'

'Wait.' Cassie held up a hand, and I fleetingly registered that the stress-induced eczema she'd had on her return from London had finally healed. 'He didn't know until this morning that you were getting married?'

'We've only met twice before.' I squinted and blinked as the sun reflected off the mosaic-topped table between us, and shunted my chair so the parasol offered some shade. 'I take my engagement ring off when I'm working, so whenever we've met I've not been wearing it, and the subject didn't come up, so—'

'Hang on.' Cassie's hand went up again. There were pencil smudges on the heel of her palm. 'You've been meeting this man at the bakery?'

'Only on business matters.' My indignation was somewhat misplaced, considering my fevered daydream moments earlier. 'Mr Moseley's brother hired him, so obviously he had to come over and look around the bakery, take photos for the website, that sort of thing, and we sort of clicked and ended up talking. But only about work.' I was self-justifying, even though there was no judgement on Cassie's soft, round face, only an eagerness to understand. 'We didn't talk about personal stuff; he might have a wife for all I know.' I hoped he didn't have a wife. 'But there was this…' I paused, not wanting to make it real, but unable to stop now I'd started. 'This *feeling* between us, like an undercurrent.' Heat drenched my face. 'I can't explain it.'

'I think I know what you mean.' A gleam had entered Cassie's eyes, and I knew she was thinking about her boyfriend. Another highlight of her return had been getting together with Danny Fleetwood, an old crush from our schooldays. He'd gone out of his way to win her over and succeeded, despite some stiff competition from a banker she'd met in London. 'But Meg, what about Sam?'

Before I could answer, Tilly appeared, a jug of iced tea in one hand and three glasses in the other. 'Compliments of Gwen,' she said, placing them on the table before pulling up a chair. 'What were you saying about Sam?' She sat beside me, hunching her narrow shoulders. 'Tell me about his proposal again, I could do with a chuckle.'

'Don't be mean,' I said, grateful for the interruption. 'The way I told it made it sound a lot less romantic than it was.'

'It couldn't have *been* much less romantic.' She grinned cheekily, unaware of a man at the next table appreciating her long legs. Encased in faded jeans, they seemed to go on forever, and with her covetable cheekbones, crop of dark hair and wide green eyes, she could easily have been a model. 'At least he got down on one knee,' she prompted, already chuckling as my mind flashed back to Sam in our hotel room, at eye level with my belly button, holding out a small, satin-padded box.

'It was bad timing,' I admitted. After squealing 'YES!' I'd leaned down for a kiss, just as Sam stood up to relieve pressure on his bad knee, and we'd violently butted heads. Reeling apart, clutching our foreheads in agony, Sam had stubbed his toe on the edge of the bed, and his howls of pain had disturbed a guest in the adjoining room. The man had phoned reception to report an 'altercation' and the manager had wanted to call the police, convinced I'd been attacked and was covering for Sam.

'I can just imagine them getting more suspicious the more Sam protested his innocence,' Tilly said, shaking her head with amusement. 'Especially when you turned up for breakfast the next morning with a giant lump on your forehead.'

'It's a good job Sam had one too.' Cassie – who had only recently heard the story – gave a tentative smile, and I guessed she was trying to gauge whether or not I wanted to bring Tilly in on my revelation.

'Have you thought any more about your *hen party*?' Tilly didn't disguise the ironic emphasis. She hated the idea of 'organised fun' and although Sam had suggested I book a long weekend somewhere with his sisters – also to be my bridesmaids – I wasn't keen. The eldest, Maura, was already planning to buy plastic willies, feather boas, and the obligatory 'L-plate', as if she didn't know me at all. 'One of my walkers was telling me her daughter's hen party involved naked butlers.' Tilly flicked up her eyebrows. 'One of the aunties got a bit frisky and tried to peek underneath their aprons.'

'I thought they were supposed to be naked.'

'They are, apart from the aprons,' said Cassie. 'We organised something similar when I worked at Five Star Events, and the bride ended up in bed with the naked chef.'

'Well, my hen party won't involve any bare bottoms.'

'Shame,' said Tilly. 'So, I take it the answer's no?'

'I haven't really thought about it.' In truth, I'd been hoping now that Cassie and Tilly were back in my life, they'd agree to a low-key meal at The Brook in Kingsbridge, and to resurrecting our karaoke act one last time at the Smugglers Inn, but I knew Sam's sisters would be upset if there wasn't a 'proper' hen do, and Beverley was keen to come too – she had already mooted the idea of us going glamping.

'That's if the wedding's still on.' As soon as the words shot out of her mouth Cassie pressed her knuckles to her lips. 'Sorry,' she mumbled.

'What do you mean?' Tilly jolted upright and looked from Cassie to me. 'What's she talking about?'

'She's been daydreaming about another man.'

'Cassie!'

'I'm sorry, but you know I can't keep secrets any more.' Cassie had initially kept quiet about being fired from her job in London, and when the truth came out had resolved to be more open in future. 'And, anyway, it's only Tilly.'

'When did this happen?' Tilly looked bemused. 'We were just talking about your hen party.'

'Oh, it's nothing,' I said, feeling silly. My daydream had lost some of its power since telling Cassie, and I began to wish I'd kept quiet. 'It's probably this heat.' I fanned my face with my hand. 'It's woken up my... you know.' I didn't want to say *libido* out loud, but couldn't think of an alternative.

'This isn't like you, though,' said Tilly, an ominous ring to her voice. She sat back, nudging her walking shoes off while Cassie poured tea for us all. 'You'd better tell me everything.'

'Really, it's nothing.' I fidgeted with the hem of my skirt. My knees were already starting to singe.

'You wouldn't have said anything in the first place, if it was nothing.'

Before I could speak, Cassie gave Tilly a rundown of the situation, and when she'd finished, Tilly smiled at me kindly. 'It's just a crush,' she said. 'Happens to the best of us.'

'A crush?' It sounded so childish. 'But... why now, when I'm getting married in a few months' time?'

Tilly shrugged. 'When you think about it, it's the perfect time,' she said. 'Maybe subconsciously you're panicking that Sam's the only man you've ever slept with.'

'He's not,' I protested. 'I told you about Bevan.'

'Ah yes, the weirdo with the curly red chest hair.' Tilly mimicked a look of horror that made Cassie giggle. 'But that was years ago, before you got back with Sam, and weren't you just proving a point because Sam was seeing someone else?'

I wished I hadn't told Tilly now, but when she'd come looking for me at the beginning of the year and dragged me out for a drink, she'd wangled out of me everything that had happened since she left – and clearly remembered every word.

'I wasn't proving a point, well maybe a bit, and it wasn't just the chest hair that put me off, his head was too big for his body. Plus, he used to say yummy whenever we kissed, and he laughed like this. "Heh, heh, heh, HEH HEEEEH."'

As Tilly and Cassie howled with laughter, I decided not to add that it hadn't felt right being with someone who wasn't Sam; that even though he'd avoided my calls for days, before finally phoning from halls to confess he'd met someone else, I'd still compared other men to him and found them lacking. Even the thought of kissing someone else had felt like a betrayal, which was why my reaction to Nathan felt doubly shocking.

Tilly dashed away tears of mirth with her fingertips. 'Maybe you should have a fling with this guy and get him out of your system,' she said. 'It sounds like the feeling's mutual.'

The laughter fled Cassie's face. 'That's terrible advice,' she scolded. 'You're not seriously advising Meg to sleep with another man a few months before her wedding?'

'Why not?' Tilly said again. 'Better to take the mystery away, don't you think?'

'If she's got real feelings for this guy, she should call off the wedding altogether.' Cassie picked up her pencil and twirled it between her fingers. 'Honestly, Meg, it wouldn't be fair to Sam if you cheated on him.'

'One night won't do any harm,' said Tilly. 'Sam need never know.'

'Er, that's still cheating.' Cassie frowned. 'And what if they fell in love?'

'Well, *then* she can call off the wedding.' Tilly made it sound obvious. 'But I'm telling you, it's just chemistry.'

'So, she'd be starting married life on a lie.'

I felt the prickly sting of perspiration breaking out. It was like listening to my conscience talking, except…

'Stop!' They froze, mouths half-open. 'No one's in love, or having a fling, or a one-night stand,' I said, though no one had even mentioned a one-night stand. 'For a start, Nathan's probably got a girlfriend already, and just because I had a daydream about him doesn't mean I don't want to marry Sam.'

'Of course it doesn't,' said Tilly, as if soothing a feral cat.

'Of course not,' agreed Cassie, but neither of them looked convinced, and I remembered how Tilly in particular had never been keen on Sam, and since she'd come back to Devon they hadn't even met. Because she was single, it had made more sense to meet up with her on my own, especially if Sam was out training, which had been most evenings this year – apart from Sundays – and afterwards he went for a drink with the other cycling club members to 'unwind'.

'I think I know what this is,' said Cassie.

'Pre-wedding nerves.' We spoke as one and I laughed, a little shakily.

'I suppose it's like taking a high dive,' said Tilly, a keen swimmer. 'There's a moment before you jump when your life flashes in front of you, and you think of all the things you haven't done. You know, in case you don't make it.'

Cassie and I stared at her. Tilly's relaxed attitude to life made it hard to imagine her having any regrets. As far as I knew, she wasn't given to bouts of introspection.

Then again, I wasn't given to bouts of daydreaming about strange men. (Joey from *Friends* didn't count.) 'Listen, you won't say anything to Sam about this, will you?'

They looked aghast that I'd had to ask. 'Of course not,' said Cassie.

'Isn't he going away next Monday?' Tilly gave a sly little smile.

'On his cycle challenge, yes.' I realised too late what she was getting at. 'I'm *not* having a fling while he's away, so please don't mention it again.'

'MEEEEG!'

My throat closed around a scream. 'I wish Gwen wouldn't yell like that.' I clutched my chest as I pushed my chair back and stood up. I must have overshot my break, which wasn't like me. 'I'd better get back inside.'

'It's so hot,' said Tilly, her eyes drifting to the cove and the inviting blues and greens of the glimmering water. 'I think I'll go for a swim.'

'I've another client in a minute, then I'm finished.' Cassie rose and stretched, the strap of her cotton dungarees slipping off her shoulder. 'Danny and I are taking Nan to the salvage yard later on.' Her grandmother's latest hobby was repurposing junk into something useful as part of a mission to be more environmentally aware.

'Good luck with that,' I said, grabbing her in a boob-squashing hug, then doing the same with Tilly who endured it more than enjoyed it. 'And thanks for, you know, not judging me.'

'Just think about what I said,' Tilly called after me.

I entered the café with her words ringing in my ears, to see Gwen point me out to a woman in tailored cream trousers and a floaty chiffon blouse, her beach-blonde hair scraped high in a topknot.

''Ere she is,' Gwen boomed as I approached, and I realised she was smiling. Or as close to smiling as she ever got, which meant she wasn't scowling and her eyes held an unaccustomed twinkle.

'Hello!' I fixed the woman with what I hoped was a sunny expression, praying she wasn't going to ask me for a recipe. Although flattering, I never knew what to say and Sam's suggestion of, 'I could tell you, but then I'd have to kill you!' hadn't gone down well in the past. I tended to leave it to Gwen these days. Her 'Mind your own bleedin' business,' seemed to work a treat without causing offence. 'How can I help?'

The woman, who looked to be in her late thirties and oddly familiar, pointed an elegant, pink-varnished fingernail at what was left of my chocolate and raspberry cake. 'I believe you're responsible for this beauty?'

'Already told you that,' said Gwen. 'She could do a baking book, if she put 'er mind to it.'

I looked at Gwen in astonishment. She'd never said that to my face.

'I'm Alice Denby, from *Britain's Hidden Gems*.' As the woman extended her hand, I felt a thrill of recognition. That's why she looked familiar. But why was a presenter from a popular Friday evening TV show shaking my clammy hand?

'Meg… Meg Larson,' I stuttered. 'Just one Meg, actually.'

Alice Denby's smile was wide, revealing flawless teeth. 'Seashell Cove is this week's *hidden gem*,' she explained, putting the words in italics. 'We've been filming around the area and someone recommended this adorable café, and your cakes in particular.'

'That was nice of them.' My face suffused with colour.

'I must say, I've never tasted anything quite as delicious.' She looked at the remaining slice of cake in much the same way my mum looked at newborn babies and patted her flat stomach with an exaggerated sigh of longing. 'I only came in to make some notes. I didn't expect to find our star of the week.'

'S-star?'

'You probably know that we run a segment at the end of the show, spotlighting local talent.' Alice's slightly posh, husky voice warmed up even further. 'We invite them to give a demonstration of their skill, and the chance to promote themselves or their business.' She looked at me with lively, intelligent eyes the colour of well-brewed tea. 'What do you say, Miss Larson? Would you like to be our guest this week?'

Chapter Five

'You want to be on television?' Sam said it as though I'd agreed to appear on a reality show, or have uninhibited sex on live TV.

'*Britain's Hidden Gems* is practically a documentary,' I said, handing him his plate of quinoa, kale and salmon as I dropped beside him on the grey, suede sofa he'd picked because it wasn't too 'girly'. 'It's a brilliant opportunity for me to plug the bakery.' I waved my fork around, excitement still humming through my veins. 'They're going to film me in the kitchen—'

'Won't you need permission?'

'Yes, but we'll sort that out,' I said. *I'd have to talk to Nathan.* 'I can mention how the bakery's been in Seashell Cove for over a hundred years, and that people still talk about Mr Moseley's loaves.' I could barely sit still as I poured out the words that had been building in my head ever since Alice Denby's invitation.

'Do they, though?' Sam paused his hungry chomp through his dinner. 'I thought people had stopped buying bread there ages before it closed.'

'Not everyone.' I gave my dinner a desultory prod. Even if I hadn't been too excited to eat, I hated kale. Obviously it was healthy, but I'd have preferred something with a crust. Or some chips. Anything carb-based really, but I liked to support Sam when he was eating healthily, and I could always eat the shortbread I'd brought home later on. 'Well, maybe I can talk about how good the bakery could be again, given a new lease of life.' I slid my plate onto the coffee table Sam's dad had made out of an old front door. 'If I mention it's for sale, someone might put in an offer,' I continued. 'The show has a pretty big audience.'

'Even if someone puts in an offer, it doesn't mean they'll keep you on, babe.' Having witnessed my heartbreak when the bakery closed, I knew Sam was only worried about my hopes being dashed.

'I was thinking I could treat it like an interview.' Leaning over, I poked my kale beneath a wedge of salmon with my fork. I couldn't even bear to look at it. 'It'll help that I've worked there already, and I'll bake such an amazing cake for the show that whoever buys the bakery is bound to keep me on.'

'You couldn't make a bad cake if you tried,' Sam said loyally, but it sounded half-hearted. He'd been supportive when my hours were cut because there wasn't enough money to pay me, and again after Mr Moseley died, but I knew he was having trouble under-standing my attachment to the place, or why I couldn't just find a job somewhere else, and I'd struggled to articulate the reason why myself. Maybe it was because the bakery had been like a child to Mr Moseley, who'd had no dependents of his own, or because I'd been so happy working there, developing my baking in the kitchen after hours, secretly dreaming that the bakery was mine. Or, maybe, I just couldn't bear the thought of it passing to someone who might not love it as much.

Whatever it was, I knew I wasn't ready to let it go without a fight.

'I'll need the perfect recipe,' I said as Sam finished his dinner, his attention drifting back to the television news. 'It needs to be something special.'

I'd thought of little else since accepting Alice's offer, thoughts of Nathan Walsh stashed at the back of my mind. OK, so the thought of appearing on television was weird and scary, especially as the programme had captured the public's imagination after one of their guests – a woman from a hamlet in Yorkshire – had won an award at the Edinburgh Fringe after doing a stand-up routine for the chickens on her farm, but I doubted I'd get another opportunity like this.

'It could be my big break, Sam.' I bounced back against one of the many flowery cushions lining the back of the sofa, all covered by Beverley, who sewed things for a living – the more garish the better, which was one of the reasons I'd been loath to let her make my wedding dress. 'It could change everything.'

'You know, I really thought you'd come to terms with the bakery closing.' Sam's eyes flipped round to mine, a trace of hurt in their depths; as if I was being unnecessarily stubborn. 'Why can't you let it go, Meg?'

I stared, the elation that had gripped me since Alice had left the café slowly fading. Even Gwen had been infected, clapping me hard on the back – the first physical contact we'd ever had – before making Dickens 'talk' to me in a terrifying cat-voice, ''Ain't she a clever girl, then, our Meggy-weggy?'

'You know it was always my dream to run a bakery, Sam. Of course I'm going to try my best to persuade someone to buy it.'

'But even if someone does, they'll want to run it themselves, and probably go all artisan.' He adopted a hippy voice. 'Yeah, we like, specialise in breads made of sourdough and beards.'

'Sam, don't.' Ending up without a role at the bakery was my worst-case scenario. 'And people *want* artisan breads. There's nothing wrong with that.'

'Babe, I'm sorry.' Sam put his empty plate down next to mine. 'I'm being an arse,' he said, dropping to his knees in front of me and taking hold of my hands. 'I just think whoever buys it won't make a profit because of its location, and they definitely won't be able to afford staff.'

'I know, you've said that before.' I noticed a sliver of kale between his teeth. 'I just thought you'd be proud of me for… you know. Giving it all I've got.'

'Oh, Meg, it's not that.' He lowered his eyes and I followed his gaze to my engagement ring: a rose-gold band, set with a flower-cut sapphire (to match my eyes) and surrounded by diamonds that twinkled in the light flowing between the chintzy, ruffled curtains that Beverley had made, and that we'd had to put up to avoid offending her. 'Of *course* I'm proud of you,' he said, with what sounded like forced conviction. 'And it's Mum's favourite show, she'll be made up…'

'But?'

He lifted his head, briefly meeting my eyes full on, and it struck me again that he rarely looked at me these days. 'No buts.' He squeezed my fingers. 'I'll have to watch the show on catch-up though. I'll be training on Friday evening.'

Disappointment flared, even though he trained pretty much every evening and weekends. 'I thought we could watch it together, maybe at Mum's.'

He got up, wincing as his knee protested. 'You know I can't let the team down.' He clenched a fist over his chest. 'I love those guys.' It was an attempt to make me smile that didn't work.

'You can see your *guys* any time.' I reached past him for my plate of uneaten food and got to my feet. The *guys* at the cycling club saw more of Sam than I did, and although I'd once suggested joining so that we'd have a hobby in common, he'd pointed out that the last time

I got on a bike, I fell off and bruised my coccyx. 'I'm going to be on *television*,' I said.

'Hey, you already sound like a diva.' His tone was teasing. 'What will your dressing room rider be?' He followed me through to the kitchen. 'How about a basket of puppies and a bowl of blue M&M's? Or some diced-up butternut squash, three white doves, and a pesticide-free apple?'

'Now you're being ridiculous. There won't be a dressing room.'

'Meg, I'm just joking.' He slid his arms around my waist as I tipped my dinner into the food-recycling bin. 'That's what catch-up TV's for,' he said, trying to nuzzle my neck.

'That's not the point.' I shrugged him off and started unloading the dishwasher. 'You should be supporting me.'

'Hang on, I *am* supporting you.' He leaned against the worktop and stroked the back of his neck. He'd changed into the grey joggers and white T-shirt he always pulled on after work, and had ruffled his helmet-flattened hair into clumps. 'I don't have to be there in person.'

'But it's nice to share experiences.'

He drew his chin back. 'You don't watch me training, but I don't accuse you of not supporting me.'

'I came to cheer you on when you did the Dartmoor cycle sprint last year and you said it put you off.' I crashed a pair of clean mugs onto the mug shelf, wishing we had proper cupboards with doors, instead of the open shelves that looked 'authentic' (weren't things only authentic because something better hadn't been invented?). Spinning round to face him, I said, 'And being on TV is different, Sam. It could be life-changing.'

'And I'm pleased for you, I really am.' He deftly plucked a dinner plate out of my hand and put it on the worktop. 'I'll be there with you in spirit, Meggle, I promise.'

'Don't call me Meggle.' I twisted away as he undid a couple of buttons on my shirt and tried to slide my skirt zip down. I hadn't even showered and changed. I'd been desperate to call Mum, or Cassie and Tilly to share my news, but had felt Sam should be the first to know, so had started preparing dinner as soon as I got in, while mentally running through my recipe database, trying to decide which cake to make on the show.

'I'm just trying to distract you.' Sam advanced towards me again with a sexy look in his eyes I hadn't seen for a while. 'Don't you want to get jiggy?'

'Oh, Sam, *please* don't say that, it's such a turn off,' I said, fumbling my shirt buttons closed like a housewife caught cheating with the window cleaner. 'And I don't want distracting, I want you to take me seriously.' I regretted my words as hurt spread over his face. We hadn't 'got jiggy' for weeks as he was so intent on training, and depriving himself of carbohydrates so as not to raise his body fat percentage made him a little bit grumpy. 'Sorry,' I said, softening my voice. 'I'm just a bit preoccupied.'

'It's fine.' His gaze slipped past me to the plate of shortbread on the worktop, lips tightening as if he was trying not to salivate. 'I haven't got much time, anyway.'

'I'm sure you could spare ten minutes,' I said, aiming for a playful tone. 'Five?'

He looked at his watch, and seemed to make a mental calculation. 'Go on then,' he said, as if squeezing in a last-minute work client. 'I'll have a shower and wait for you in the bedroom.'

As he bounded upstairs, my mind flipped back to the bakery, and I released an unsteady breath that had a lot less to do with sexual longing, and everything to do with the notion that maybe – just maybe – I could turn around its fortunes and resurrect my old job.

'Oh, and Meg,' Sam called from the landing. 'Mum was wondering which song we're going to have as our first dance.'

My mind went blank. Did we have a special song? We must have a special song; all couples had one. 'What did you tell her?' I called back.

'I said I'd ask you.'

Great. 'I'll have a think about it.' *Why didn't we have a special song?*

⸻

'Oh, Meg, shouldn't you be slowing down, not going on TV?'

'Mum, I'm thirty, not seventy, and why do I need to slow down?' As if I didn't know. She was in the corner of her sofa, cradling baby Milo, giving me pointed looks over his fuzzy-haired head.

'I was reading somewhere that stress can affect the reproductive system.'

Here we go. She'd been thumbing through *The Baby-Making Bible* again, partially hidden behind a jade figurine of a horse on her bookshelf. 'I've got plenty of time, Mum. I've told you, we're not even going to try until after the wedding.'

'Give her a break, Rose, she's going to be famous.' From beside her, Kath gave Mum's knee a gentle shove. 'About time she got proper recognition for those cakes of hers.'

'*This* is what's important, not being famous.' Mum glanced down at Milo, a mushy smile on her face, and I half-wished I hadn't popped round while Sam was out training, but I'd been too hyped up to stay at home – just as I'd been too excited to join Sam in the bedroom after his shower. Luckily, he'd taken it cold and hadn't seemed to mind.

'This is what it's all about.' Mum hunched over the snoozing baby as one of his tiny hands curled around her finger. 'Isn't he precious?'

Kath was looking after her grandson again – fortunately (depending how you looked at it) the discount clothing shop where she'd worked had recently closed down so she was out of a job – while Freya caught up on some 'beauty sleep', and they were clearly relishing every second; Mum, no doubt, wishing he was mine.

'Life's about a lot more than babies, as gorgeous as they are.' Kath waggled her hands and Mum handed Milo back with the reluctance of a child relinquishing a favourite toy.

Milo's face contorted suddenly, as though suppressing a sneeze.

'Don't you think he looks like Kim Jong whatsisname?' said Kath.

'Don't!' Mum's eyes widened. 'He'll take in everything you say.'

'Rubbish.' Kath flopped Milo onto her shoulder and rubbed gentle circles on his back until he let out a burp and a trickle of milk. 'And anyway, he knows I love him.'

'Maybe Meg would like to hold him, for practise?' Mum turned to where I was pacing in front of the television, which was tuned to *University Challenge.* Mum loved intellectual quiz shows, but was clearly too distracted by Milo to concentrate.

'Never mind the little one, we want to hear more about this television appearance,' said Kath, who lived next door but spent most of her spare time at Mum's.

I threw her a grateful smile as I dropped into the armchair, wondering how we'd have managed without her all these years.

'Thank god for another single parent,' she'd said, striding in with a steaming casserole, trailed by a grumpy looking Freya the day we moved to Salcombe, twenty-three years ago. 'You wouldn't believe the filthy looks I used to get when old Mr Fishburn lived here.'

It hadn't been hard to see why. Kath had favoured low-cut tops and short skirts with high heels, despite her ample figure, and still wore her dyed-black hair in a beehive, as if it was the sixties. She'd never minded the gossip at the school gates, flashing her gap-toothed smile at everyone, and was adored by customers at the library where she'd worked back then.

Mum – five years younger – had stood out at the school gates too, with her bell of golden hair and clear blue eyes, but even though she was nice to everyone, the mums had whispered about her behind her back. Kath had said it was because they were jealous, and worried their husbands would fall in love with Mum. Not that she'd have been interested. She'd had her heart broken when Mike, my father, was killed in a car accident before I was born, and wasn't interested in having a relationship.

'So, why do you need to go on television?' Mum was making an effort to be attentive now, sitting forward, smooth hands clasped together, as if to stop them making a grab for Milo.

'I don't *have* to, Mum. I was asked to give a baking demonstration, and I'm going to talk about the bakery.'

'I love Alice Denby, she makes her guests feel so relaxed,' said Kath, deftly lowering Milo into his Moses basket. 'They featured a young chap a while back, who does these amazing ice sculptures in a shed in Scotland. On the update the following week, they said he'd had more interest than he could cope with.'

'That's right, I remember.' Mum's face knotted with anxiety. 'I read that he's gone into hiding until the fuss dies down.'

I stifled a sigh. 'I'm not going to have a breakdown, Mum. You can come and watch me being filmed, if you like.'

Alarm flitted over her face. Despite a few fine lines around her eyes and silver threads in her hair – now worn in an easy-care bob – she was still an attractive woman, especially when she smiled. Apparently we looked alike, apart from the shape of my nose and a tiny mole by my right ear, which I'd inherited from my dad. I didn't know this for certain, as I'd never seen so much as a photo of him and had to rely on Mum's memories, which were more than a little rose-tinted, despite him having been engaged to another woman when I'd been conceived.

'Where is it happening?' Mum asked.

'In the kitchen, at the Old Bakery, so you wouldn't have to go far.' I was careful not to let my impatience show, used to the slow dance of getting her out of the house. After losing her job at the library just after I started college, she'd developed agoraphobia, and although she was much better now – mostly thanks to Kath – Mum still preferred being at home. 'I'm going to appeal for a buyer.'

'Oh, Meg.' From the slump of her shoulders it was as if I'd said I was planning to do some performance poetry. Mum had a dread of people showing themselves up in public, and wouldn't have watched me do karaoke with Cassie and Tilly at the Smugglers Inn, even if she hadn't been afraid of going out. 'I thought you'd accepted it was unlikely to still be a bakery once it's sold.'

'You sound like Sam.'

Mum's eyes brightened. 'Well, he knows what he's talking about.'

I wondered why it was always Sam who knew what he was talking about and not me. It wasn't that Mum wasn't proud of me; more that our ideas of achievement were radically different. For Mum, being successful meant marriage and children, and not having managed the first, or more than one of the second, she seemed determined to realise her ambitions through me. 'Neither of you are mind readers,' I said. 'Who knows what might happen?'

'Quite right.' Kath gave a wink that almost dislodged her false eyelashes. 'Who'd have thought I'd be a grandmother before the age of sixty?' she said, playing up her Devon accent, which was much stronger than Mum's.

'Or at all?' Mum's voice was envious. 'I still remember Freya saying she'd never have children because she didn't want a baggy tummy like yours.'

Kath snorted. 'While Meg was designing wedding dresses with her little fashion playset.' She smiled fondly as she reached for her glass of non-alcoholic wine, adding, 'No wonder they never got on.'

'Talking of babies.' Mum reached for her bag and dug out an opaque green bottle with a flowery label. She'd been ordering from Good Life again; the health food store whose accounts she did from home. 'Red Raspberry,' she said, rattling the bottle as though it was a magic elixir. 'Good for your uterus.'

I swallowed a groan. 'Thanks, Mum.' Unable to face another discussion about my internal workings, I shoved the bottle in my bag and got up to leave. 'I'd better go. Sam will be back shortly.'

'Don't forget to take them, will you?' said Mum, as I bent to kiss her cheek. She smelt of the rose-scented perfume I'd bought for her birthday. 'A woman on the website said she got pregnant within two months of starting the course, and she'd been trying for years.'

'She doesn't want to be thinking about that until after her wedding day,' Kath said, as I edged away, narrowly avoiding a side table holding a marble cherub plucking a mandolin. Mum's favourite pastime was bidding for 'collectibles' online. The small house was a treasure trove of curiosities she was convinced would be worth a fortune one day. 'Your dad was interested in antiques,' she'd said once – a rare snippet of information.

'She's more likely to be stressed if you keep going on about it, Rose.'

'Exactly,' I murmured. Kath always took my side, which I knew hadn't gone down well with Freya at times – because she'd told me once I was a massive, suck-up bitch, and that her mum just felt sorry for me because my dad was dead.

'You haven't got a dad either,' I'd retaliated, trying to hold back tears.

'No, but at least he's not dead,' she'd said proudly. 'I get to see my dad every weekend and he loves me.'

He'd spoilt her rotten, according to Mum, but Kath had stopped trying to do anything about it because she felt so guilty that she hadn't been able to hold on to her marriage, even though her husband was the one who'd left her for another woman when Freya was two.

And when he'd died of a heart attack just after Freya's fifteenth birthday and I'd tried to tell her how sorry I was, she'd said, 'Oh piss off, Meg, this isn't the dead dads' club.'

'But you *know* Meg always wanted a baby by the time she was thirty,' Mum was saying, and I left them discussing my younger self's wishes – I even had them written in a journal somewhere – knowing the time had passed to mention to Mum that the last thing on my mind these days was getting pregnant.

Chapter Six

'You're sure Lester's given permission for me to be filmed here?'

'One hundred per cent,' said Nathan, his eyes sweeping around the kitchen, taking in the ingredients I'd decanted into bowls and jars, as if I was Nigella. Perhaps I should have strung some fairy lights around, and worn my silky robe, instead of the green and white spotted tea dress I'd panic bought online that supposedly 'flattered a curvy figure'. Didn't TV add about twenty pounds? 'Basically, if it leads to the bakery being sold, Lester would be happy for you to do a bit of snake charming. Once you've finished baking, of course.'

I giggled nervously. I hadn't expected to be this nervous. Baking was when I felt most confident. I'd already trialled the whole cake, which was in the fridge, as Alice had warned the schedule wouldn't allow me to complete it to a high enough standard, as well as pre-baking the chocolate sponges. Barring the oven breaking down, things were unlikely to go wrong, but ever since she'd emailed a questionnaire, and explained we'd be talking as I baked, I'd been fighting an urge to run.

'It seems Lester's planning to open a beach bar with the money he's hoping to get for this place.' Nathan's voice stilled my teeming thoughts.

'Isn't he eighty?'

'Age is clearly no barrier to realising your dreams.' Nathan was leaning against the sink, watching me with open interest, and it struck me it was the first time he'd seen me without my hairnet and apron – both deemed 'too professional' by Alice (even though that was the point) and perhaps explained the exaggerated double take he'd given when I'd let him in.

'I can't imagine it,' I said, remembering Mr Moseley's description of his older brother as 'the most miserable bugger on the planet'. 'Apparently he hated the public, which is why he had no interest in the bakery.'

'Maybe living abroad all these years has softened him up.' Nathan loosened the knot of his paisley tie, which I had a feeling he'd worn especially, even though it was too hot for formal clothing. Though he'd quickly discarded his well-cut jacket and rolled up the sleeves of his shirt, as if they were too confining. 'Or maybe it's the woman he married. He was telling me she's thirty years younger than him, and a keen businesswoman.'

'Sounds like she might be a gold-digger.'

'Or, his true love.'

To break the little silence that followed, I checked again that I had everything I needed to make my chocolate brownie meringue cake with strawberry cream, unable to meet Nathan's eyes.

I'd called him on Tuesday morning to tell him about the show, and he'd dropped by the bakery an hour later for 'all the details'.

'Sounds like an amazing opportunity,' he'd said, accepting the coffee I'd made to dispel any potential awkwardness, and we'd sat on the back doorstep as the sun crept round the side of the building and warmed our faces. 'I bet the bakery will have sold by the end of the programme.'

I couldn't help being gratified by his response, especially as Sam hadn't mentioned it again; and then told myself that Nathan was just being nice because of the commission he'd make.

'And I'm not just saying that because I want my commission,' he'd said, nudging my shoulder, and whatever it was I'd sensed (imagined?) between us had shifted and settled into what felt like the beginnings of friendship.

Lester had been hard to get hold of initially – it turned out he'd been having a hip replaced – so Nathan had taken to calling, or dropping by, to update me, our theories as to Lester's whereabouts becoming ever more outlandish.

'He's probably on a space shuttle on his way to Mars,' had been Nathan's favourite, while I'd mooted the possibility of him being a spy, on a top-secret mission in Moscow. It had been so nice to talk with someone new, who hadn't known me as part of a couple, and to chat about more than babies or weddings – or cycling – that I'd found myself relaxing more and more in his company, happy to chat about films we liked, books we'd read, and what we thought of Donald Trump.

I didn't feel relaxed now. I felt like I might be sick.

'What are they doing?' I said, rearranging the bowls of ingredients. 'Alice said ten thirty and it's nearly eleven.'

Nathan ducked out and round the front of the bakery, where the small television crew had been filming exterior shots, and talking to the crowd that had gathered to see what was going on.

He returned seconds later. 'About ten minutes. Alice is still chatting to some locals about the area,' he said, raking a hand sideways through his hair. It looked constantly windswept, as if he'd been at the helm of a boat at sea.

'Meg?' He scanned my face. 'It's really hot in here.' He grabbed a tea towel, the muscles in his forearms clenching as he fanned me with it.

'The door's open.' I closed my eyes, enjoying the faint breeze on my face. The lingering smell of vanilla from the cake I'd made earlier mingled with something woody and spicy that must be coming from Nathan.

'There's only warm air coming in,' he said. 'It must be nearly twenty-eight degrees out there.'

I peered through my eyelashes and watched him cross to the sink and shove the window wide.

'There might be a bit of a sea breeze from this side, and I could open the front door to the shop to create a through breeze. Although people might be tempted to come inside if we open the front door.'

'Leave it, we don't want a crowd in here.' I picked up my apron to wipe my forehead with. How did TV chefs cope? Nigella never looked harassed. 'I'm not sure I want to expose myself on national television.'

'I thought you were going to make a cake,' Nathan said, prompting more giggles. I'd never been so giggly while at the same time so close to crying.

'I'm serious, Nathan. I don't think I can do it.'

'Or course you can.' He planted himself opposite the counter where I was fiddling with a whisk. 'Once you start, your nerves will go. Just imagine you're in your kitchen at home on your own.'

'But I have to *talk*.'

'Then imagine you're talking to your fiancé or a friend, or a family member.'

Did I imagine the faint emphasis on fiancé? 'I don't think that will work,' I said. Despite his 'Good luck, babe, you'll be great' this morning, I knew Sam had been hoping I wouldn't go through with it, and if I imagined talking to Cassie or Tilly I'd feel silly and clam up. Mum would be far too nervous on my behalf, and the thought of Sam's family listening – even at home – was too overwhelming. His eldest sister Maura could be a bit judgemental at the best of times. 'I'm supposed to talk about myself, but everyone I know knows everything about me already.'

'Then imagine you're talking to someone you've only just met.'

About to check that the carton of cream I'd poured into a jug hadn't gone past its sell-by date, I paused. *Did he mean himself?*

'Someone you're sitting on a train with,' he added, as if realising how it had sounded. 'Just you and one other person, a long journey ahead, and the chance to say whatever you like without judgement.'

'I probably wouldn't strike up a conversation with a stranger.' I tweaked a trailing strand into the twist of hair at the nape of my neck. 'What if they turned out to be unstable and ended up stalking me? Or fell asleep because I'm so boring?'

'Both outcomes highly unlikely.' He passed a hand over his mouth, as if wiping away a smile. 'You don't know Alice, so focus on her and forget about viewers at home.'

'Easier said than done.' The frantic fluttering in my stomach felt like batwings. 'What if I swear, or drop something, or get my words mixed up?'

'Hey, you won't, and if you do they'll edit it out. They're not here to make a fool of you, that's not what the programme's about.'

'It's just so important I get it right.'

'Well, even if nothing comes of it, remember there's a possible buyer in the wings.' Nathan's eyes grew big.

'Oh, don't remind me,' I said. When Nathan had told me the day before that a Don Williams had called the agency to say his wife was interested in turning the bakery into an ice-cream parlour, I'd known he was talking about Freya.

'No way!' I'd cried, to Nathan's evident surprise.

'It's not the American country singer,' he'd said. 'He's sadly passed away.'

'It's not that.' I'd quickly explained that the older man Freya had married had (according to Kath) promised her anything she wanted, and she'd decided she wanted to run a business now she'd got bored of being a mum. 'Why here?'

'It seems they've been looking for the prefect premises, and after hearing that *Britain's Hidden Gems* was filming in Seashell Cove decided it's the perfect location for an ice-cream parlour.'

'But the local shop sells ice cream, and old Giovanni pitches his van by the cove all summer,' I'd said, though in truth, if they'd been considering anywhere but the Old Bakery, I'd have welcomed an ice-cream parlour – though it was impossible to imagine work-shy Freya fronting it.

'That's why I need to get this right,' I said now, even as my bladder threatened to collapse. 'I have to give someone a reason to reopen the bakery.'

Nathan appeared to think for a second. 'Let's do some role-play,' he said.

'Beg pardon?'

He swiftly pulled my apron over his head and scooted behind the counter. Picking up my mixing bowl, he said, 'I'll pretend to be you, and you go over there and pretend to be Alice.'

'Nathan, this is silly.' I swallowed another giggle as he hugged the bowl to his chest, and started whisking imaginary ingredients. 'Be careful with that bowl, it was my grandmother's.'

'Don't worry I've got a good grip,' he said. 'I used to play baseball with my brother.'

'So, you have a brother?' I might as well play along. It was either that, or hyperventilating, which I'd seen happen to Mum a couple of times when she'd tried to leave the house and had to shallow-breathe into a paper bag. 'Younger or older than you?'

'Older by two years. His name's Hugo, he's much better looking than me, and is a brilliant dad to my four-year-old nephew, Charlie.' He swung round to the oven and pretended to peer inside, then nodded at me to carry on.

Trying not to picture a brother better looking than Nathan, I attempted to mimic Alice's warm but plummy voice. 'So, did you always want to work in real estate?'

'Absolutely not.' He exaggeratedly dusted his hands on my apron. It was too small for his frame, ending mid-thigh and straining across his chest. 'Walsh Property Agents belongs to my brother, actually. I'm just helping out while he recovers from a badly broken leg, as well as helping around the house while his wife's in Hong Kong on a business trip.'

'I did not know that,' I said. 'What do you normally do?' I was genuinely curious, having already decided he didn't fit my idea of a typical property agent, based on my previous experience of buying a house with Sam.

'Normally, I move around a lot, living off my inheritance.' He pretended to crack eggs into the bowl, and to shake some flour on top. 'Selling property's a lot harder than I thought, and a hell of a lot less interesting – apart from the historical element of the buildings.'

'You're joking.' I bit off a tiny laugh of surprise. 'About the inheritance?'

''Fraid not.' He gave me a steady look. 'My brother and I inherited a lot of money from our grandparents. They raised us, after our parents died when we were kids.'

I couldn't hide my shock. 'That's awful,' I said. 'How did they die, if you don't mind me asking?'

'Plane crash.' Nathan picked up a bowl of chopped hazelnuts and put it down again. 'Light aircraft, actually. My father had just got his pilot's licence and took the plane up, despite bad weather warnings.'

'God, I'm so sorry.'

Nathan twirled the whisk like a cowboy's gun and pretended to holster it. 'It was a long time ago,' he said evenly. 'I have good memories of them, and our grandparents were great. Plenty of aunts and uncles and cousins. Not saying we wouldn't rather have had our parents back, but there was plenty of love.'

The way he said it didn't invite sympathy, but I knew it couldn't have been that easy. And then to lose his grandparents…

'My dad was killed in a car accident,' I said, rushing on when his brow furrowed. 'I mean, it's not the same because I didn't know him, except that he was called Mike, he was Irish, and met my mum at a bar in London on his brother's stag night where they fell madly in love.'

'Romantic.'

'Not really,' I said. 'He was due to marry someone else, but he came back to see Mum a few times – she was living in London with friends and working at the British Library – and he was apparently going to call things off with his girlfriend, but never made it home.'

'That must have been really tough for your mum,' Nathan said quietly. 'Gone before they had a chance to be a proper couple.'

'He might not have stuck around,' I said, examining my nails. I kept them short and free of varnish, and wondered whether they looked too plain. 'He'd already cheated on his fiancée.'

'But he hadn't met your mum when he agreed to marry her,' said Nathan. 'He must not have known what true love was.'

I shot him a look. 'You're a romantic.' He smiled, but didn't comment. 'Anyway, Mum didn't know she was pregnant with me until a couple of months later. She was back home at my grandparents' in Plymouth by then.' I hadn't told this story for ages. Hadn't needed to, because everyone close to me knew, and it was an old story anyway and one I rarely thought about. 'Anyway, back to you, Mr Walsh. You were saying that you're filthy rich.'

'Not really.' He grinned, and resumed his pretend whisking while I settled on the wooden stool Mr Moseley had sat on every morning at ten o'clock to drink his cup of brick-coloured tea. 'Hugo used his money to invest in some property and set up the agency, and is doing really well. I… gave away a lot of mine.' I wanted to ask who to and why, but Nathan carried on talking, while pretending to chop an apple I'd brought in case I needed a snack. 'I kept enough cash to get myself to Asia, then moved around a lot from there. I don't normally stay in one place for very long.'

'No dependants, then?'

I wished I hadn't asked, but the words were out before I could stop them.

He pushed the apple aside. 'There was someone, but it turned out she had a partner back home, so that was that.'

There was something about the way he said it – a tightening around the mouth – that hinted at possible heartbreak. Deciding not to push it, I smoothed the skirt of my dress and, in my best Alice Denby voice, said, 'Did you work, while you were… moving around?'

'Of course.' His smile returned. 'Mostly bar work, and I wrote travel pieces for magazines and newspapers, which suited my lifestyle. I love finding new places off the beaten track. A bit like this programme, in fact.'

'Ever thought of moving into presenting?' The real Alice Denby stepped through the open door, followed by a burly cameraman with more beard than hair. She gave Nathan an appraising look. 'You'd be a hit with our female audience.'

'Sexist,' muttered the cameraman, smiling at me.

'Not my cup of tea.' Nathan came out from behind the counter, peeling my apron over his head. 'But, thanks for the compliment,' he added graciously.

Alice turned to me with a merry twinkle in her eyes. 'Hi, Meg. This must be your fiancé,' she said. 'You're one lucky lady.'

Briefly meeting Nathan's amused gaze, I said, 'I'm afraid not,' then, realising how it sounded, added, 'Not afraid, obviously. My fiancé – he's called Sam, I think I wrote that on the questionnaire – he couldn't make it today, so Nathan… he, er, he's—'

'—overseeing the sale of the bakery, and an interested spectator,' he broke in. 'Nathan Walsh.'

'And getting stuck into some baking by the look of things.' A flirty smile lifted Alice's sun-kissed cheeks. 'I like a man who's good in the kitchen, it's the reason I married my husband.'

'Oh, I'm terrible at baking.' Nathan moved easily past to pluck his jacket off the back of the door. 'I do a mean stir-fry though.'

'Too hot for that at the moment.' Pretending to swoon, Alice flapped the hem of the marshmallow-pink cotton top she was wearing with her white linen trousers and Roman-style sandals. Next to her, I felt overdone in my dress and open-toed wedges. I didn't usually wear make-up while baking, but Alice had advised I put some on to avoid looking washed out, and I hoped I didn't have lipstick on my teeth.

She came over and rested her hands on my shoulders. 'You're not nervous, are you?'

'A bit,' I admitted, wiping damp palms down my dress. 'Quite a lot, actually.'

'You'll be fine, don't worry.' After a final reassuring squeeze, Alice wriggled onto the stool I'd just vacated, indicating to the cameraman that she was ready to start. 'We've only ever had one person faint, but that was because of the heat blasting from the kiln where she fired her jugs.'

I bit my bottom lip and glanced at the heated oven, which had ramped up the temperature in the kitchen to Caribbean levels. I should have planned a no-bake cheesecake, or a summer pudding, not a complicated cake I'd only made once before. It didn't help that the cameraman had plugged in some lighting equipment, which would make things even hotter. What if I keeled over halfway through?

'Don't worry, it's just one light, and if any perspiration breaks through we'll pause to mop it up.' Alice had switched effortlessly into professional mode. After whipping an iPad from her outsize leather bag she started swiping. 'Just getting your details up.' She slid on a pair of cats-eye glasses, and raised neat eyebrows at Nathan lounging in the doorway, his jacket hooked over one shoulder. 'Can we have the room, please?'

'Of course.' He nodded politely. 'You'll be great,' he said to me, his face relaxing into a smile that made my pulse speed up. 'Remember what I said.'

The urge to beg him to stay – or take me away – was suddenly overwhelming, but before I could speak again, he'd vanished.

Chapter Seven

'If you just start baking like you normally would, we'll chat as you go,' said Alice.

'O-OK.' Gripping the edge of the table, I stared at my ingredients as if I'd never seen them before. *Egg whites, egg whites.* I was supposed to do something with them, but couldn't for the life of me remember what.

'And try not to look directly at the camera when you're talking, unless I ask you to.'

'S-sorry?' I seemed to have developed a stutter.

'If I say, "Could you tell the viewers at home what ingredients they'll need to make your…"' she glanced at her iPad, '"chocolate-meringue-brownie cake", which sounds delicious by the way, *then* look at the lens as if talking to the people at home.'

'Righty-ho.' I reached too quickly for a baking tin, and sent it crashing to the floor. The blush that had been hovering finally burst through to my cheeks. 'I'm so sorry.'

'Please don't worry, Meg, we'll edit out stuff like that.'

'I've already made the chocolate sponges.'

'That's fine,' said Alice. 'Go through the motions of making them anyway, and we'll cut to the pre-made ones, as if you've just brought them out of the oven.'

As I stooped to retrieve the tin, fighting the temptation to roll beneath the counter and curl up in a ball, I muttered to myself, 'Remember why you're doing this.'

Determined to hold onto the thought, and to not think of all the people who would be watching later at home, I straightened to see Alice turn her beaming face to the camera.

'So, here we are, in the kitchen of the Old Bakery at Seashell Cove, to meet our gifted guest of the week, Meg Larson.'

Gifted made it sound as if I had second sight, or could work out complicated sums in my head, not knock up a decent sponge. 'Hi.' I willed my smile not to wobble as knots of anxiety clustered in my stomach.

'The Old Bakery, a feature of the village for decades, sadly closed to the public earlier this year when the owner died, but star baker Meg is hoping a buyer will come forward and allow her to keep doing the job she loved so much, as well as keep this cherished building for the purpose it was intended.' I wanted to hug Alice for putting it so succinctly and sounding so compassionate. 'So, Meg, this is where you bake the fabulous cakes I've heard so much about?'

'Yes, that's right.' Why hadn't I rehearsed some snappy answers? 'In this very kitchen.' I imagined Sam saying, *Don't give up the day job, Meggle.*

'I've had the pleasure of trying one of your cakes, and have to say it was the most delicious thing I've eaten in ages. And I eat *a lot*.'

She made it sound feasible, despite her slender frame.

'That's so kind of you.' I pressed my hands flat on the table to still their trembling. I tried to remember Nathan's advice but my mind felt stuffed with fluff.

'Where *did* you learn to bake, Meg?'

I recognised this as her opening gambit, and froze.

'Meg?'

'Would it be OK to put my apron on?' I seized it from the end of the counter, where Nathan had draped it before he left. 'Only, I feel more like myself when I wear it. I've always worn one, right from when I used to help my granny in her kitchen. I suppose it reminds me of her, and puts me in the right frame of mind, and of course it'll protect my dress, which is hand-wash only. I didn't realise when I ordered it. It's from Topshop.' I was wittering, which I tended to do when nervous.

'Of course you can.' Alice had adopted a bedtime-story tone. 'Whatever makes you feel comfortable, Meg.' I yanked it over my head and fastened it securely. The red light on the camera was flashing, and I assumed that meant it was recording. 'Go on, whenever you're ready.'

I released a shaky breath, feeling as if dry leaves were stuck in my throat. 'I suppose it's like a comfort blanket, the apron, I mean.' Tugging the mixing bowl forward, I tipped in the sugar I'd measured out earlier and felt slightly more in control. 'My mum had a battle on her hands, trying to get it off me so she could wash it. The comfort blanket, I mean. It was pretty grubby most of the time, disgusting, actually, but – as my granny pointed out – it didn't do me any harm. At least, I don't think it did.'

Alice joined in when I laughed – probably out of pity. 'So… you and your mum lived with your grandmother until you were seven years old?'

'That's right.' I added the softened butter to the sugar, cracked in two eggs, and started beating the mixture. I preferred the bowl and spoon method to the food processor, finding the action soothing – as well as good for my upper arms. 'Granny was my mother's mum, I didn't know my father.' I sieved flour into the bowl and began gently folding it in. 'I might have a set of grandparents somewhere, for all I know, but I've never met them. My dad was from Ireland, so they're probably over there.' Aware I'd just told the story to Nathan, I quickly moved on. 'My grandmother made cakes for all her friends' birthdays, and I used to help and I suppose it took off from there, really. We were very close,' I concluded. 'All of us, I mean, my mum too.'

I picked up the bowl of broken chocolate, which was already melting in the heat, and carried it to the stove. 'It's not like I minded not having a dad,' I continued, as if I was still talking to Nathan. 'I mean, they say you don't miss what you've never had, and I had plenty of role models. Not my granddad, he died when I was two, but my friends had nice dads, so it didn't matter that my mum never married, or even had a boyfriend that I knew of.' I stirred the chocolate as it melted fully, looking awkwardly in Alice's direction over my shoulder. 'Not unless she sneaked them in when I was asleep. No, I'm kidding. She said my dad was The One, and was happy it just being the two of us after that. Not in a creepy way, she didn't smother me or anything, but she was focused on giving me a happy childhood like she'd had. Her best friend got her a job at the library when we moved to Salcombe, part-time so she could be at home with me as much as possible.'

My words were speeding up, along with my stirring. 'She worked there full-time later on and loved it, but I'd just started college when the library closed and she lost her job, and it was hard to find another one, so I had to leave and start working to help pay the bills at home, which was fine, it was in a bakery actually, not this one, but I loved it. Then Mum became agoraphobic and stopped going out.' *Shut up, Meg.* 'In fact, she's still not very good at going out, but she's working again, that's the great thing about the internet. She did some online courses and now looks after the accounts for Good Life, you know, the health food store in Kingsbridge?' Why the hell was I talking so much about Mum? They'd have to leave *all* of that out.

I scraped the melted chocolate into the batter, then shared the mixture between two cake tins and placed them in the oven for show. My face felt broiled, and my hair had come loose, but I daren't fiddle about with it in case it came tumbling down.

'You're getting married next January,' stated Alice, as I returned to the counter and tried to remember what I had to do next. 'Why a winter wedding?'

I smiled in her general direction, and my top lip stuck to my teeth. 'I always fancied getting married while it was snowing outside.' *Whisk the egg whites for the meringue.* 'That was when I was a teenager,' I said, switching on the food processor. It would take too long to whip the egg whites into peaks by hand. 'Obviously now I realise the chances of it snowing on the actual day are practically non-existent, but the venue's booked, so it's too late to change the date.'

There was a miniscule pause. 'Will it be a traditional white wedding?'

'I used to think that's what I wanted, but now I'm not sure.' *Oops.* Focusing on baking was giving my mouth free range to say what it liked. 'I definitely won't be wearing a white dress.'

'I doubt many of us want the same things now that we did as teenagers.' There was a reassuring trace of laughter in Alice's voice. 'At sixteen, I wanted to marry a footballer when I grew up, and have my own beauty salon.'

'Actually, the career part of my dream hasn't changed much.' Thank god, I was getting to the point. I added caster sugar to the glossy white mountain of egg whites in the bowl and added a handful of chopped hazelnuts. 'I always wanted to run a bakery, and have been lucky enough to work in this lovely old building for six years, but—'

'And you supply cakes to the local café?'

'That's right,' I said. 'They've been really successful, which is why I'd love the opportunity to—'

'Be your own boss, of *course*,' finished Alice, as if she was now trying to hurry me along. 'And I'm sure when our viewers see your super cake, the orders will come flooding in.'

The timer I'd set pinged and I removed my sponges from the oven, even though they weren't ready, then brought the ones I'd made earlier to the counter, awkwardly flopping them onto the cooling rack. Pretending to bake was much harder than the real thing.

'Don't worry,' said Alice. 'We'll edit it to look smooth.'

'About the cake orders flooding in.' I picked up a spatula and put it down again. 'That's not really the direction I'm hoping—'

'Can you do ones in the shape of a football pitch, or a guitar?' Alice chuckled. 'My husband had one that looked like a Tardis for his fortieth. He's a big *Dr Who* fan.'

'I don't do much creative cake decoration, I find it a bit fiddly.' I could feel the conversation veering in the wrong direction. 'I prefer to keep my cakes simple. For instance, this one will be filled with whipped cream and fresh strawberries, and the meringue topping sprinkled with pistachios.' I mimed a sprinkling action while cocking my head in a Nigella-ish fashion. 'Now, I need to get my meringue in the oven while the sponge is, er, cooling.'

'And does a family figure in your future, Meg?'

'Um, one day, yes, probably.' I didn't want a prospective buyer put off by the thought of me immediately going on maternity leave. 'It's not on the agenda for a few years yet.' I spread meringue on one half of the cake and raked the top into crests with a fork. 'But I hope I'd be able to carry on working when I do have children.'

'Would you say baking is a gift or a vocation?'

'I'd say nursing or teaching's a vocation.' I slid the half of the cake with the topping into the oven to brown, and set the timer again. 'Baking's more of a hobby. I'm just lucky I'm able to make a living at it. At least, I hope that's what I can carry on doing.'

'Well, I'd say you have a gift, Meg, one that brings a lot of pleasure to a lot of people, and I hope one day to come back and find you running the Old Bakery.'

'Thank you, Alice.' She really was excellent at her job. 'I'd love to buy it myself, but can't afford it.' Too honest? 'Not with a wedding to pay for.' Had I just smiled or grimaced?

'Ah yes, weddings can be *so* expensive,' Alice agreed. 'Although they don't have to be. Hubby and I went retro with a registry office do, and a fish and chip supper afterwards. Hardly cost a penny.'

Now I felt like a bridezilla, when Sam's mum was the one urging us to splash the cash on the 'most special day of our lives'.

'Sounds lovely,' I said wistfully.

'Where are you planning to honeymoon? We had a fun weekend in Blackpool, and found a marvellous "hidden gem" of a guesthouse. The landlady was a magician!'

'Oh, we haven't got that far yet.' It struck me that Sam might not like me airing our plans to the nation, and I turned to take the strawberries and whipped cream out of the fridge, welcoming the blast of cool air on my face. 'I'm totally focused on work at the moment.' Keen to get my 'interview' back on track, I went on, 'Baking means an early start every morning, and I love that quiet hour or two before most people's day really begins—'

'Meg, we're wrapping up now.'

I turned. 'Oh, right.' I reached back into the fridge and took out the cake I'd made earlier, pleased it looked so professional.

'If you could pop it on the counter and just run through the ingredients for the viewers, that would be great, Meg. Then we'll do a shot of me tucking in, if you have a spare fork.'

'Of course.' I grabbed one out of the drawer, and must have looked anxious because she smiled and added, 'Don't worry, this bit of our conversation won't make the final cut.' Most of it wouldn't, I hoped. 'Just take the cake across to the counter.'

I did as she asked and put it down carefully, then looked into the lens, as Alice had instructed, and reeled off the ingredients and cooking times, remembering to smile the whole time. Hopefully, my future boss was watching and would see me as the perfect face of the bakery.

'I'm sure when your book comes out we'll all be rushing to buy it,' said Alice, before forking a mouthful of cake between her tastefully pink-glossed lips.

'Oh, I don't want to do a cookbook, there are enough out there already.'

'Your own TV programme, then.' She dabbed some cream from the corner of her mouth with her little finger and dug into the cake again. 'Folks, I think we've found the next winner of *Bake Off*.'

'Oh no, I don't want to be on television, I mean, not in a competitive way.' The timer pinged again, and I rushed to the oven with a sense of anticlimax now that it didn't matter. 'Really, I want to be back in the bakery—'

'Cut!' shouted Alice, through a mouthful of nutty cake topping. Tearing off some kitchen roll, she delicately spat into it and tossed the crumpled sheet into the bin. 'That was amazing, Meg.' She squeezed my arm, looking as cool and composed as when she'd entered the kitchen – unlike the cameraman, whose already ruddy face had turned damson. I was certain I had sweat on my upper lip, but couldn't bear to check while Alice was studying me with such open admiration. 'I really admire your honesty, and wish you all the luck in the world.' She deftly scooped her bag over her shoulder. 'You signed the consent form?'

I nodded. It had been emailed to me, along with the questionnaire.

'Can we do a few shots of the shop itself, so potential buyers can imagine what it will look like, and maybe we can get the agency details too so anyone interested can get in touch.'

'That would be great,' I said, hope surging as I led them through, making sure they got a good view of the shelves and cabinets I hoped very soon would be bursting with loaves and cakes again.

'We'll give it all a good edit, don't worry,' Alice said when they'd finished, even though I hadn't been worried until she said it. 'Make sure you watch later, and brace yourself for lots of lovely publicity.' Her smile grew. 'I'd say you've been one of our best ever guests.'

She probably said that to them all, but I swelled up a little all the same. 'Thanks,' I said. 'You're just as lovely in real life.' It sounded too gushy but she smiled serenely, probably used to being gushed at.

'Hey, good luck with the wedding,' she said as we moved back to the kitchen, away from the curious stares we'd been attracting through the shop window. She gave an exaggerated wink. 'I hope he's as cute as that lovely estate agent guy.'

'Oh, he's *much* cuter,' I said, turning in time to see Nathan move away from the rear door.

'Well, thanks again, Meg, and good luck.' Unaware that my stomach had nosedived, Alice shook my sticky hand before leaving with a friendly wave, turning down my offer to take the cake with a rueful smile.

There followed a couple of awkward minutes while the cameraman fiddled with the lighting and cables, catching his bag on the edge of the counter as he left. The cake slid to the floor with a squelch, and I stared at the mess of strawberries and crumbs with the sinking conviction that, not only had I upset Nathan, I'd just given the worst interview of my life.

Chapter Eight

'Could you please pass the gravy, Meg?'

I reached for the china boat and passed it to Beverley. She took it without a word and sloshed brown liquid over her beef and Yorkshire puddings. Even during a heatwave, Sam's mum cooked a roast every Sunday lunchtime.

'How's the training going, Sam?' asked Neil.

'Good.' Sam stopped shovelling carrots in his mouth long enough to glance at his dad. 'I'll be in Paris this time tomorrow.'

'Will it be hot over there, love?' Still not looking at me, Beverley handed Sam the dish of roast potatoes. He relaxed his healthy eating a little on a Sunday, and after dinner would allow himself a child's sized portion of fruit crumble and a drizzle of custard.

'I expect so.' He took care not to graze my hand with his as he picked up his knife and began to cut up his meat. 'It might be even hotter.'

'I'd love to go to Paris,' said Sadie, propping her chin on her hand. 'It looks *soooo* romantic.' Aged eighteen, with a cloud of honey-blonde hair and puppy-brown eyes, Sam's youngest sister was training to be a make-up artist at South Devon College, and was normally full of recommendations about lipsticks to suit my skin tone, and what sort of mascara to wear, but even she hadn't looked at me properly since I'd arrived. I was surprised by how much it hurt.

I'd always enjoyed the Ryan Sunday lunches, enjoying the banter and laughter around the table, and being part of a family who'd welcomed me with open arms, but today, I'd rather have been anywhere else.

'Isn't anyone going to address the elephant in the room?' said Maura, refilling her mother's wine glass and topping up her own. 'No one's mentioned the *celebrity* in our midst.'

The word was said with unwarranted venom, considering a week ago Sam's oldest sister had been trying to persuade me to advertise my cake making to a wider audience, and offering her newly-fledged PR skills at a 'discount'.

'I just can't believe you spoke like that about the wedding, sweetheart.' Beverley bounced up from the table to open the French doors, then bounced back down on her chair. Everything about Beverley was bouncy, from her mass of curly blonde hair and generous bosom, to her dangly sliver and pearl earrings. 'You made it sound like you were being forced into it, love, when all we're trying to do is give you what you want.'

'It was a bit of a slap in the face,' agreed Maura. Their disapproval was like a blast of cold air, and my confidence started to crumple under the force of it. 'I'm wondering whether I should even be organising your hen party.' *I haven't asked you to,* I felt like saying, but Maura could be a bit scary when riled. 'Not that you've shown much interest.'

'Maura,' Sam said warningly, even though he'd been cool with me since watching the show on Friday evening after he got back from training. Recalling his thunderstruck silence as the credits rolled made my blood run cold, in spite of the steam rising from my dinner.

'I can't believe that was you, Meg,' he'd said, with the look of a man who'd narrowly avoided being hit by a bus. 'All the effort Mum went to, to help us find the right venue, and you're worried there might not be snow on our wedding day.'

'That's not exactly what I said.'

'It's what it sounded like to me, and probably to everyone who saw it.'

I hadn't even wanted him to watch it, in the end. Not after I'd sat through the show at Mum's, peering from behind a cushion when my face appeared. I'd already banned Cassie and Tilly from joining us, too nervous of their reactions, and Mum had turned away a protesting Kath at my request.

At first, I'd been pleasantly surprised that I'd looked so... *normal.* Attractive even – though it was true that the camera added pounds – not at all shiny-faced or crazy-haired, and the bakery kitchen had looked as quaint and appealing as I'd hoped.

Even Mum had stopped squirming with embarrassment and told me how beautiful I looked, and how proud of me she was. 'You look so *professional*,' she'd exclaimed, tears bulging in her eyes, and I'd snuggled against her on the sofa and allowed her to turn the sound on.

That had been my biggest mistake. After watching open-mouthed the segment where I was talking, Mum had shot up to her bedroom where she'd pretended to be tidying her already tidy room. 'Why did you say all those things about me?' She'd practically thumped her pillow. 'All that stuff about your smelly blanket, and me being a desperate, clingy Mum, mourning the dead love of her life.' Her eyes had bounced off mine, as though the sight of me hurt. 'It sounded so *dreadful.*'

'I'm so sorry, Mum.' I'd been on the verge of tears myself. 'I was really nervous and started babbling about the first thing that came to mind. I honestly didn't think they'd keep that in.' After all the years of good behaviour, making sure she never had reason to worry or feel bad, she was viciously fluffing her duvet and trying not to cry – because of me.

'*That* was the first thing that came into your head?' She'd dropped onto her flower-patterned duvet and studied her neatly trimmed nails. 'I didn't think you thought about your father, or whether I should have had another relationship.'

'Oh, Mum, I *don't*.'

'There was someone once, a customer at the library,' she'd blurted. 'He turned out to be married as well, so it didn't go very far.'

I hadn't mentioned that I'd suspected as much, because for a while she'd started wearing more make-up to work, and singing a lot in the bath.

'*Nobody* knows about your father, apart from you and Kath. I'm not proud that I fell in love with a man who was about to be married.' Her eyes had brimmed with tears again. 'You know I blame myself that he died.'

'I know, Mum, even though you shouldn't.' She'd let me take her hand. 'It was all so long ago, and…' I'd been about to say that it probably wouldn't matter that I'd talked about her private life, as she hardly ever went out so was unlikely to bump into anyone she knew. 'It's in the past,' I'd finished, weakly.

'What will Good Life think? They won't want me anywhere near their accounts after this.'

'It's not going to make any difference to them, Mum, what happened in the past.'

I'd placed an arm around her shaking shoulders. 'I'm so sorry.'

'And what was all that about a family not being on the agenda?' She'd twisted to look at me, her forehead creased. 'I thought you were going to get pregnant after the wedding.'

'I just said that in response to Alice's question, because I thought it might put off a potential buyer if I said I was planning to have a baby next year.'

'And you're planning to work full-time afterwards?'

'I never said I wasn't, Mum. People do these days.' I'd squeezed her hand, desperate to put a smile back on her face. 'I'll have you to help out, won't I?'

'That's true.'

'Anyway, I doubt anyone will have watched the programme. It's such lovely weather, they'll all have been outdoors.'

'Local people will watch it, Meg.' Mum's frown had reappeared. 'Everyone who lives in Seashell Cove will have seen it.'

'We live in Salcombe.'

'But you *work* over there.' She'd pulled a tissue from the box on her nightstand. 'God knows what Sam will say when he hears you don't want a winter wedding.'

'I didn't *say* that.'

But he'd clearly taken it the same way, leaving the room in the middle of my fumbled apology and refusing to discuss it further, and things had been frosty since. He hadn't commented on the rest of my interview, or my cake, which had looked good if I said so myself. He'd clearly zoned in on the wedding stuff, and blocked out everything else.

On Saturday, he'd risen early and announced with a pained expression that he was fitting in an early training session with Chris and that I 'should have a think'. Words that had prompted me to invite Cassie and Tilly over.

'It's not like you said anything *terrible*,' Cassie had said, once we were settled in the garden with cold drinks. 'You looked amazing, and sounded really natural. I thought it was cute the way you talked about your mum, and Twitter loved it. There were some lovely comments about your dress, and you looking like a young, blonde Nigella, and people were saying you were a credit to your mum, and to Seashell Cove.'

'Really?' It hadn't even occurred to me to look online. I was a bit of a dinosaur when it came to social media, and although I had a Facebook account, I rarely posted anything. 'I thought, if anything, I'd get trollied.'

'You mean, trolled. And, honestly, you came across really well, we were so proud of you.'

Tilly had nodded her agreement. 'It was a bit Jeremy Kyle, but in a good way.'

'Tilly! You don't think the personal stuff distracted from the bit about the bakery being for sale?'

'There'll be a follow-up piece in the local paper, I'm sure they'll give it a mention.'

'They did a piece when the bakery closed down, but that didn't do any good.'

'It's early days yet,' she'd said. 'Have you heard from Nathan?'

His name had prompted a panicky, 'No of course not, not yet. I haven't spoken to him, it's the weekend. I expect he'll call on Monday. Or I'll give him a ring. Or not. I expect he'll call me if there's been any interest.'

Tilly's mouth had twitched, and she'd made wide-eyes at Cassie.

'As long as you-know-who doesn't get her claws into the place.' Cassie had inclined her head next door, even though we were at my house and not my mum's and Freya now lived in Totnes, in a gated house with a swimming pool that Kath had only seen once. 'Can you really see her running an ice-cream parlour?'

Before I could reply, Tilly had leant forward, her sunglasses dropping from her head to the tip of her nose. 'Have you really changed your mind about a winter wedding?'

I'd managed to convince her and Cassie that I hadn't; I'd simply meant that, with hindsight, it was unlikely to snow on my actual wedding day, and I'd been naive to think otherwise.

I'd said much the same to Sam – for at least the tenth time – on the drive to his parents' house in Kingsbridge, desperate to break the brooding silence that had reigned since his cycling session, but he'd only tightened his lips in response.

And now his family was giving me the silent treatment, too. At least, they had been.

'You saw the show then?' I said. It was a poor attempt at a joke, because nothing involving the Ryan family went unnoticed. Beverley had invited us to watch it at their house and had sounded miffed when I turned her down, explaining I was going to Mum's. She got on with Mum, when they'd met in the past, but didn't understand her reluctance to leave the house. 'Can't think of anything worse than staring at the same four walls,' she'd once said, on her way to a Zumba class, as if Mum was just being difficult.

'You looked like you were showing off a bit for the camera,' Maura was saying, doing an exaggerated wiggle of her shoulders. 'Sashaying about all sexily, like Nigella.' I wondered whether she'd been drinking before we arrived. There was a lot of socialising in her new PR job, which she'd taken to rather well.

'Hey, how come when Nigella pretends to sneak into the kitchen in the middle of the night in her dressing gown to eat some fudge cake out of the fridge, she doesn't notice there's a cameraman in her kitchen?'

To my relief, everyone laughed, including Sam.

'Good point,' said Neil, stabbing a parsnip with his fork. Square-jawed and jug-eared, with an affable smile, his only resemblance to Sam was the colour of his close-cut blond hair. Personality-wise, Sam was more like his mum. 'Enough to give anyone a heart attack.'

'So, was that little outburst your not-so-subtle way of calling the whole thing off?' Maura had clearly got her claws in, and wasn't about to let go.

'Of *course* not,' I said, into the expectant silence, giving up all pretence at eating my dinner. I knew I'd choke if I took as much as a mouthful. 'Everything I said has been taken out of context.'

'Has it?' Elbowing her half-empty plate aside, Maura looked at me coolly. Although she shared the same colouring as the rest of her family, she'd recently bleached her hair peroxide, and had it cut in a crop that made her jaw seem wider, and her eyes too close together. She looked older than twenty-six, with none of Sadie's dreamy softness, or her Mum's more obvious charms. 'Sounded to us like marriage and kids are the last things on your mind.' Another slurp of wine. 'All you seem to care about is that bakery.'

'I *do* care about it, you know that.' I carefully put down my knife and fork. 'But not more than I care about Sam.' I glanced at him, but he was staring at his plate, jaws moving as he chewed. 'I'm sorry if that didn't come across.'

'Don't worry about it, love. You sounded fine to me,' said Neil, reaching for the dish of rapidly cooling potatoes and spearing two with his fork. 'I hope someone does put in an offer. We used to pop in there, if we were ever in Seashell Cove, don't you remember, Bev?'

Bev clearly didn't want to be reminded, and narrowed her slightly bulbous eyes at her husband. 'That's hardly the point, Neil.'

''S'cuse me,' he said, giving a comical grimace that elicited a giggle from Sadie and a loud tut from Maura.

'Whose side are you on, Dad?' she said.

'I didn't realise we were taking sides.' He spoke mildly. 'We're not at war, are we?'

I could have hugged him, but despite the Ryans' code of loyalty, and oft-repeated declarations that 'family was everything' they didn't go in for physical displays of emotion, which had come as a shock to me, brought up as a hugger.

Grabbing the bottle of wine, I sloshed the remaining quarter into my glass, at last drawing a look from Sam. Unfortunately, it was disapproving. Alcohol wasn't allowed on his training diet, and he expected me to support him by not drinking either.

Suddenly, I didn't care, and drank the wine in one long swig. 'What did you think of the rest of the show?' I banged my glass down, and gave Beverley a belligerent stare. 'The bit where I wasn't *subtly* calling off my wedding?'

'Meg!' She looked shocked, clutching her cleavage as though I was pointing a gun. 'There's no need to talk like that.'

'Isn't there?' I stared around the table, as though seeing them all for the first time.

Only Neil had improved with age, despite the accident that had ended his career as a tree surgeon. He'd taken up as a carpenter, and had the air of a man grateful to have been given a second chance. If I'd had a dad, I'd have liked him to be like Neil, but Beverley had become more judgemental over the years, dressing up her opinions with endearments, as if to render them harmless, and Maura was going the same way – though she'd always had a bitchy side. Sadie was still forming, dreaming of falling in love with an actor while working as a make-up artist on a film set. Hopefully, she'd turn out more like her dad than Beverley.

'I don't know why you're having a go at us, my lovely.' Beverley made a big deal of pushing her plate away, her glittery nail varnish sparkling. 'We're concerned, that's all, pet. You didn't sound like the Meg we know and love.'

The Meg they were used to, she might as well have said. The Meg who did what was expected, right down to letting Beverley make her wedding dress, even though Mum had wanted us to choose one together.

'You do still want us to be bridesmaids, don't you?' Sadie stopped moving her food around her plate, and gave me a sideways look. 'I know you've got your two friends back now and that, maybe… you know.'

My anger evaporated. 'Oh, Sadie, of course I do.' She'd been like this since Tilly and Cassie had come back. 'I don't need any more bridesmaids.' I didn't add that Tilly thought traditional weddings old-fashioned, and Cassie had said she'd prefer a civil partnership. 'And I still need you to do my make-up, remember?'

Her smile vanished when Maura glowered at her across the table. 'Don't you think it looks a bit desperate, you still hanging around the bakery every morning?'

'I'm not hanging around there, I'm *baking*. It's my job.' I waited for Sam to say something, and when he didn't experienced a drop of disappointment. 'I don't see you complaining when I bring a cake round.'

'Oh, we love your cakes, peanut, you know we do.' Beverley reached across to pat my fingers, one hand still pressed to her cleavage. 'But there are more important things in life, and it seems like you're a *teeny* bit obsessed with that place.'

Now she sounded like Mum.

'And when you were talking about role models, you didn't even mention Dad, even though you've known him for years, and he's offered to walk you down the aisle.' This was a sticking point with Maura. As the eldest daughter she felt that right was hers alone, which I completely understood. It was why I'd turned down Neil's offer.

'You know I think the world of Neil.' I glanced at him and caught a wink. 'But I've already explained that if anyone's going to walk me down the aisle, it'll be my mum.' She'd already looked into which herbal supplements would help her relax on the day.

'Let's hope she can get out of the house then, sweetie.' Beverley's laugh was more like a snort.

'Let's hope the wedding's still on,' muttered Maura.

Tears rising, I gazed at the table I'd sat at so many times over the years, its polished surface as familiar as the house itself. 'Look, I had a bad case of nerves on the show, and I'm sorry if I said things you didn't like—'

'You're not sorry you said them though.'

'Maura,' Sam said, finally stepping in, but I'd had enough.

'Thanks for dinner, Beverley, but I'm not feeling very well.'

I scraped my chair back, picked up my bag and rushed outside, not caring that I was only giving them more ammunition.

Sam caught up with me at the car. 'You can't drive, you've been drinking,' he said. 'And we haven't even had pudding.'

I wheeled round. 'Are you joking?'

'I was, actually, but seriously, Meg, don't let them get to you.' He grabbed my hand. 'They're looking out for me, that's all.'

'I wasn't trying to hurt anyone,' I said, frustration sharpening my response.

'Weren't you?' Letting go of my hand, he dropped his gaze to his navy canvas shoes. In his summer-Sunday outfit of combat shorts and T-shirt, he looked more like the Sam I used to know; when cycling was something he did to and from school, and didn't absorb most of his time.

'Why are you giving me a hard time?' I blinked away hot tears. 'You know I only agreed to be on that show to try and sell the bakery.'

He rubbed the back of his neck. Bending over handlebars made it ache and normally I'd offer a massage, but today felt far from normal. 'So you said.'

'You didn't even stick up for me in there.'

'Well, you have to admit they have a point.'

'What?'

'You *do* seem to care more about that bakery.'

'Like you care more about your bike.'

'What's *that* supposed to mean?'

I tipped my head to the basin of blue sky above. 'I just think we should be supporting each other, that's all.'

'Cycling's different,' he said.

'How?' Lowering my head, I glanced at the cream-fronted house, where a plant with flowers shaped like stars cascaded down the walls. Catching a flash of Maura's bright hair at an upstairs window, I guessed she was spying on us.

'It's not my job,' he said. 'I haven't been on television, talking about it.' His logic was flawed, but it was hard to argue with the firm certainty in his voice, and before I could begin to assemble a defence, he was glancing at his watch.

'Anyway, if we're done here, I might squeeze in a quick training session before tomorrow.'

Chapter Nine

'Do you think he was giving you an ultimatum?' Cassie's voice was cautious. 'That doesn't sound right.'

I wiped away a tear with my finger. 'I don't think so,' I said. 'I just wish he understood why the bakery matters to me, and that he'd stuck up for me in front of his family.'

'He should have,' Cassie agreed. 'But I suppose old habits die hard. Didn't you say, he doesn't like upsetting his mum?'

'Oh, but it's OK to upset me?'

'No, of course it's not.' Cassie put down her bag. 'I'm surprised he's still gone to France, if things are a bit up in the air between you.'

'He had to,' I said. 'He's been training for months. I wouldn't expect him to cancel, just because we had a bit of a falling out.' I didn't add that he'd started packing as soon he got back from his training session, as though nothing had happened – except he'd barely spoken to me, apart from to ask if I'd seen the sachets of energy gel he'd bought to keep in his backpack (they were already in his backpack). 'He probably won't give it another thought, once he's over there.'

'I still don't get why he's behaving as if loving your job is a crime.'

'Because on TV I came across as being too passionate about baking, or something, I don't know.' Exhausted from a bout of weeping, after watching Sam leave for Paris with the air of a man who couldn't wait to get there, I lay on the sofa and covered my face with a cushion to hide my burning eyes. I was supposed to be working after lunch, but hadn't been able to face the café, so I'd called in sick, leading Gwen to speculate that I was 'up the duff'. When I'd disputed this, she suggested I was scared to face the public because of my 'rabbiting' on television, and had assured me everyone was being supportive and I'd done the old bakery proud. 'What abart your cakes, we're running short?'

I told her I'd made a couple earlier and that Cassie would bring them over as she had customers booked in for her cartoon sketches this afternoon.

'Why are you baking if you're ill?' Gwen had barked, contrarily. 'We don't wanna catch whatever you've got.'

I'd told her it wasn't anything infectious, just something I'd eaten (not cake), which she'd grudgingly accepted. 'Good job Tamsin needs some extra shifts. And that I don't mind working me bleedin' fingers to the bleedin' bone while everyone else does whatever the 'ell they bleedin' well like.'

I'd called Cassie afterwards, guilty at disturbing her, but she'd insisted she needed a break from a tricky commission she was working on; a series of paintings of someone's back garden during different seasons.

'I'm working from photographs, but they're virtually identical,' she'd said, after turning up in Sir Lancelot, the ancient green Morris Minor that used to belong to her nan. 'When I mentioned it to the owner, she said there hadn't been much variation in the seasons last year and to "use my imagination". Add flowers to the summery one, and snow for the winter version, and when I asked what sort of flowers and where – there weren't any flowerbeds or anything – she said, "Maybe some pink ones. Or red. In flowerpots. Or maybe round the edges of the lawn." So, basically, no help whatsoever.'

Then she'd clocked my face and shepherded me to the sofa as if I was an invalid, before bringing me a glass of water and instructing me to 'tell her everything' – the same words we'd used as teenagers, when anything out of the ordinary happened.

It struck me now, as she whipped the cushion off my face, and opened the window above the sofa to let some air into the stuffy room, that I hadn't appreciated her and Tilly enough towards the end of our time at Kingsbridge Academy where we'd met. I'd started seeing Sam in the fourth year – overjoyed that he'd asked me out – and had practically dropped them, barely noticing when Tilly left for Vancouver a couple of years later, and Cassie moved to London.

'I'm sorry I didn't stay in touch,' I said weepily, not for the first time. 'I was too wrapped up in Sam and his family, and when he went to uni I was lost. I mean, I made new friends once I started working, but not like you and Tilly. I was always too tired when I got home to go out, and I didn't like leaving Mum on her own...' I stopped. I'd told her all this before, but Cassie's smile was gentle as she stroked my hair off my face.

'You don't need to apologise, Meg. None of us kept in touch. We all had our own things going on, but we're here now, and that's the main thing.' She sat on the floor in a pool of sunlight and gave me a considering look. 'What are you going to do now?'

'Eat my own bodyweight in biscuits and watch back-to-back episodes of *Friends*.'

'Oh my god, Meg, you and Sam are *actually* on a break.' Her eyes brightened. 'Like Ross and Rachel!'

I managed a weak smile. 'That's not really helpful, Cass. Remember what happened with Ross.'

'But they got together in the end.'

'Still not helpful.'

'Sorry.'

I rubbed my aching forehead, trying to erase an image of Sam, strapping his bike to the back of Chris's car before climbing inside and giving me a solemn look through the open window. *No contact,* he'd said. *I need to stay focused. We'll talk when I get back.*

Watching them drive off had reminded me horribly of twelve years earlier when he'd left for Edinburgh, despite me having begged him to choose somewhere closer to home to study, so we could still see each other.

I want to spread my wings a bit, Meg, but it doesn't mean we're going to break up. I love you as much as I always have, and you can visit whenever you like. It'll be good for us. We'll miss each other, and our time together will be precious.

Only, I never did get to visit because a few weeks later, he'd met Andrea.

'You have to let him go,' Mum had said sadly, as I soaked her shoulders with tears, night after night. 'If it's meant to be, he'll come back.'

His parents had been shocked by our breakup, but naturally their loyalties lay with Sam, and their pride that their son was at university – the first on either side of the family to do so – had quickly outweighed their dismay. I'd been welcome to drop by and I had, for a while, keen to hear what Sam was up to – and because I'd missed Sadie – but it had been agonising to hear about his partying, and the whispers about Andrea, and the pitying looks from Beverley became too much. I'd stopped going round after that – until the day Neil fell out of a tree and nearly died.

It wasn't that I expected Sam to meet someone else on his cycling trip – apart from anything else, he'd have no energy leftover – but seeing him joshing with Chris as they drove away had fanned a flame of uncertainty. It was as if he'd already forgotten I existed.

Out of sight, out of mind.

'If you could wave a magic wand, what would you like to happen next?' Cassie said, wrapping her arms around her lightly tanned knees, her gaze encouraging. She was wearing paint-patterned blue shorts and a loose white vest top, and the tips of her fingers were green.

'I'd like to get a call saying someone has bought the bakery and they want me to run it for them.'

She cast me a long and significant look. 'I meant with Sam.'

'Oh no.' I pressed my hands over my eyes. 'It's true, isn't it? I'm putting work before my fiancé. I should be deciding whether I want a scoop-neck or sweetheart neckline for my wedding dress, and freesias or lilliputs in my bouquet, not worrying about what happens to the bloody bakery.'

I peeped through my fingers to see a smile lifting Cassie's mouth. 'Lilliputs,' she said. 'I had no idea there was such a flower.'

'You can put them in your painting.' I half-heartedly lobbed a cushion at her, and it shot over her head and hit the shelf above the fireplace, sending a framed photo tumbling to the floor. It was of me in Trafalgar Square with a pigeon on my head, which Sam had taken on our trip to London, not long after we'd got back together.

'That feels like a sign,' I said, as Cassie picked up the photo and studied it.

'I thought you were scared of birds.'

'I am, but I suppose it was pretty funny when it landed on my head, even though I weed myself a little bit, and Sam shooed it away once he'd taken the photo.'

'Remember when Kath let her budgie out of its cage, and it flew through your living-room window while we were doing our homework?'

I winced at the flashback. 'I didn't think I'd sound like that when I screamed.'

Cassie hooted. 'It was more of a prolonged wail,' she said, doing an impression that made me shake with laughter, in spite of myself. 'Your mum thought you'd been possessed, you looked so spacey.'

'And then she saw Wilma – who calls a budgie Wilma? – on the mirror frame, and she started screaming as well.'

'Oh god, those ear-piercing shrieks.'

'And Kath came rushing round and said she'd called the police, not realising Wilma had escaped.'

We were both breathless from laughing and I sat up feeling better – until Cassie said, 'No calls from Nathan?'

My smile faded. I'd expected him to drop by the bakery that morning, or at least to phone. I hadn't even wanted to go in after Sam had left with Chris, but knew if I didn't I'd end up crying in bed all morning, going over everything in my head. And I'd had to admit that a tiny part of me – in spite of everything – had been curious to know whether my TV appearance had prompted any queries about the bakery.

But although I'd checked twice that my phone was working, and had made sure to leave the back door propped open, Nathan hadn't called, or put in an appearance.

I'd wondered whether it had anything to do with him overhearing me tell Alice that Sam was much cuter than him – I still winced, thinking about it – but he hadn't struck me as someone who'd let a silly comment get in the way of business. Or friendship.

'Nothing yet,' I said, breathing deeply to blot out self-pity. 'It looks like being on the telly has done nothing but get me into trouble.'

'Oh, Meg.' Getting to her feet, Cassie glanced at her outsized watch. 'Can I do anything before I head to the café? Make some coffee, or rub your feet?'

'You've done enough already.' I stood to give her a hug, conscious that I hadn't had a shower since returning from the bakery, and I still had traces of scone mixture beneath my nails.

'Why do you always smell like candyfloss?'

I laughed. 'Thanks for coming, Cassie. I'm dreading Mum calling, because I can't face telling her Sam's annoyed with me, but I needed to talk to someone.'

'There's nothing much to tell her.' Pulling back, Cassie gave my upper arms a squeeze. 'I'm sure it'll all blow over, and once Sam's back you'll carry on as you were.' Her eyes swept over my face. 'I mean, it's you and *Sam* we're talking about. You guys are made for each other.'

Once Cassie had left for Seashell Cove, my cake boxes stowed safely in Sir Lancelot's boot, my spirits sagged again, and a long cool shower did nothing to restore my mood.

Wrapped in a towel, I stood in the bedroom, which was decorated in cream and blue with built-in wardrobes, and a giant oak bed that took up most of the floor. I considered climbing under the duvet, but knew it would smell like Sam, and I'd just lie there staring at the photo on my bedside table of us at Sadie's eighteenth birthday party in February, holding up moustaches on sticks. He hadn't wanted to go, I remembered, because he'd just started training and was trying to avoid food temptation, and left early because he'd been up since five thirty and was tired.

Sighing, I pulled a red, strappy sundress from the wardrobe and, leaving my hair damp, got dressed and wandered downstairs and into the back garden. It was a dazzling display of freshly-mown grass with lavender and geraniums jostling for space in the borders. Neil and Beverley had worked their magic when Sam and I had moved in three years ago. They'd transformed the front garden too, where a row of rose bushes lined the path to the door. I'd have preferred something wilder – maybe lupins, hollyhocks and foxgloves – but had bowed to Beverley's superior knowledge, and they did look pretty.

We'd started saving for our own place as soon as Sam landed a job at Randall Surveyors in Kingsbridge, and I'd secured a small pay rise at the bakery. He'd refused to allow his parents or my mum to help out, but agreed to use a windfall his grandfather left him as a deposit on the grey-stone, end-of-terrace we'd fallen in love with. Although the rooms were small and had needed updating – and I'd have preferred a bigger kitchen for baking – there'd been a glimpse of the twinkling estuary from the landing window, and the tiny light-filled room at the back of the house would make a perfect nursery.

Sighing again, I pulled a garden chair into the shade of the apple tree at the bottom of the garden, remembering for some reason the argument we'd had after our housewarming party, when Sam had been a bit prissy about people removing their shoes so they didn't trample dirt on our newly-varnished floorboards.

'Isn't the point of floorboards that they're easier to clean than carpets?' I'd said later, embarrassed for Mum, who'd blushingly asked if she could keep hers on because there was a hole in the toe of her tights, only for Sam to insist, in front of his family and some of his cycling friends, that she take them off.

'We know what toes look like, Rose,' he'd said jokily, but the sight of Mum's crimson cheeks as she'd slipped off her 'going-out' kitten heels, apologising for not having painted her toenails, then chatting too brightly to distract attention, had made me want to cry. I knew it had taken her all day to pluck up courage to come in the first place, and that she wouldn't be able to stay long.

'If I'd let your mum keep hers on, it wouldn't have been fair for everyone else to remove theirs,' Sam had said when we were getting ready for bed, seeming baffled that I was 'making a fuss over nothing'. 'She was fine with it, Meg.'

'Well, I bloody well wasn't.' I only ever swore when I was angry, or tipsy – neither of which happened often – and Sam had gone all serious, and reminded me that we'd paid a lot for the flooring, and there was nothing wrong with wanting to protect it.

I'd let it drop because I was still so happy that, not only were we back together, but we finally had our own home, and I didn't want anything to spoil it.

Snapping back to the moment, I wondered who would get the house if Sam and I were to break up. My throat balled with tears at the thought of it. Admittedly, Sam had had more input into the décor, but that was because he had better taste than I did. My creativity was limited to baking, and the rooms would have been decked out in shades of brown and custard if I'd been let loose. Tilly, a natural at interiors, and responsible for redesigning Maitland's Café, had been appalled that during a brainstorming session I'd suggested painting the wood-panelling magnolia to 'brighten it up a bit'.

'Wow,' she'd said with a grin. 'That's like me suggesting you ring the changes by making a nice plain sponge cake.'

'Nothing wrong with a sponge cake, as long as it's the lightest, spongiest, tastiest sponge cake ever,' I'd argued, to no avail.

A manic shriek next door brought me to my feet. Our neighbours were back from their week in the Cotswolds, and it was only a matter of time before a football or Frisbee sailed into the garden, or one of the seven-year-old twins directed the hosepipe over the hedge at me. The boys suffered from a severe lack of discipline, from parents who believed that children should be allowed to 'express themselves'.

It was a shame the old lady who'd lived next door for years had gone to live with her sister, and the Hippy Henshaws, as Sam called them, had moved in. Still, at least he had a week away from everything.

I jumped horribly with shock when a flop of straw coloured hair and walnut-tanned face popped above the hedge. The boys were on their trampoline again. 'You look like a tomato!' yelled Finn – or maybe it was Fenton, they were identical so it was hard to tell – before disappearing, then reappearing with his tongue out.

Eyes burning with tears (it was surprisingly hurtful being insulted by a child), I returned to the house, in time to hear my phone ringing. I guessed it was Mum, surprised she hadn't called yet, but instead saw Nathan's number.

My heart gave a lurch as I answered. 'Hello?'

'Hi, Meg, I'm at the bakery.' His voice was friendly but neutral, and I had the immediate sense he wasn't alone. 'Can you come over?'

Chapter Ten

I drove to Seashell Cove in record time, and parked my Clio round the back of the bakery, behind the kind of shiny, curvy car that bikini-clad models used to pose with. It wasn't Nathan's – he drove an agency BMW – so it must belong to whoever was sizing up the property. Someone with plenty of money, if the personalised number plate was anything to go by. It looked somehow familiar, but I couldn't imagine where I would have seen it.

As I opened the car door, I caught sight of myself in the wing mirror and let out a gasp. I'd rushed straight out in my 'tomato' red sundress, not realising it looked both creased and limp, or that my hair was clinging to my neck like tentacles. Combined with a shiny face and bloodshot eyes, I looked to be in the throes of a terrible hangover.

I delved into my bag to look for my lipstick, or at least a band to tie my hair back, but before I'd found either, Nathan appeared in the doorway and beckoned me over with a pantomime wave.

Regretting my T-bar sandals, which looked a bit primary school, I hurried over and followed him into the kitchen, detecting smells that didn't belong in a bakery. The scent of spicy perfume was overwhelming – or maybe it was aftershave. Not Nathan's, which was far more subtle.

A horrible suspicion took root, as I remembered the only people interested in the bakery so far were Freya and her husband. 'Where are they?'

Nathan pressed a finger to his lips. 'Out the front,' he stage-whispered, eyes conducting a survey of my appearance. He managed not to look revolted. 'Having a look around.'

I detected the low murmur of voices. 'Is it the Williams'?' When Nathan nodded, my heart dropped. I'd hoped it might be another couple – even a hipster pair, intent on running the bakery on their own, would have been preferable – but I realised why I'd recognised the car. I'd seen it outside Kath's house, since Freya had taken to dropping Milo off there nearly every day.

'Meg?' Nathan had picked a sheaf of paperwork off the counter, and was giving me a concerned look. 'I'm really sorry,' he said. 'I was hoping to get rid of them quickly and call you later, but they specifically wanted to speak to you.'

'Why are you sorry?' I threw my bag down with a thud, and turned to the sink to wash my hands, trying to calm my thoughts. 'I asked if I could be here if anyone wanted to look around. You should have called me earlier.' I dried my hands and pulled my apron on. Not that I was going to start baking, but it would hide my crumpled dress, and add a professional air.

'Shall I go and give them the low-down, or have you gone through everything already? Do they know there's accommodation upstairs?' I'd almost forgotten about Mr Moseley's rooms, filled with years of accumulated junk that Lester had said he would pay somebody to get rid of once the sale had gone through. I'd occasionally sat in the living room on my lunch break – the only one allowed to go up there – on Mr Moseley's lumpy and faded green velvet sofa. I'd liked the way the light slanted through the sash window, and hearing the sounds that floated up from the bakery, and to imagine what it had been like in Mr Moseley senior's day, when he'd lived there with his sons. 'Maybe the state of it will put them off,' I said. 'Nathan?' He looked peculiarly intense, his lips clamped together as if he didn't want to say whatever it was. 'What is it?'

'They're offering over the asking price, and I promised Lester we'd accept the highest bid.'

'We could say there's been lots of interest since the TV show, and we're waiting for a better offer.'

He took a deep breath through his nose. 'The thing is, even though it's very early days since you were, ah, on television,' his eyes dropped, and a flood of heat rushed through me as I wondered if he'd watched, and what he must have thought, 'there haven't been any calls so far, and we don't know that there will be, so... I don't think we're in a position to put them off.' It was kind of him to say 'we', considering the decision wasn't mine to make. 'Like I said, I'm sorry, Meg.'

The heat in my body evaporated. Was there such a thing as a cold flush? 'Can't you invent a condition of sale?' I angry-whispered. 'Tell them Lester will only sell to people who want to resume trading as a bakery?'

He widened his eyes in mock horror. 'Lie, you mean?'

'Isn't that what estate agents do?'

'Ouch.' He winced. 'Firstly, I'm not an estate agent and secondly, my brother runs a clean and honest ship. Believe it or not, it's not in his makeup to manipulate potential clients, even if it loses the company a sale.'

'Sorry,' I mumbled. 'I just can't believe they're our only option.'

'Actually, I did tell them that the client was hoping to keep the bakery going in his brother's memory, but she's adamant about the ice-cream parlour.'

'Bloody hell.' Freya always got her own way. I remembered when our mums were still set on us becoming friends, and I'd suggested we bake some fairy cakes and sell them to our neighbours, and Freya said baking was for babies (how was that even possible?) and demanded we play on her skateboard instead, only to wet herself laughing when I fell off.

'I think the husband might have been interested, because he asked a lot of questions and wanted to see the paperwork from when the bakery was doing well, but she kept on interrupting—'

'That sounds like Freya.' I pulled a face. 'Sorry, I just interrupted.'

A smile touched his lips, and I noticed distractedly he was wearing jeans and a round-necked white T-shirt in place of his usual suit, as if he'd been doing something altogether different when Don Williams had called.

'I was supposed to be taking Charlie, my nephew, to the zoo this afternoon,' he said, seeing me looking. 'I didn't have time to get changed. He's been a bit full-on over the weekend.'

'I'm sorry.' I wondered whether that was why he hadn't been in touch. 'This is probably the last thing you want to be doing.'

He shook his head. 'It's fine, we can go to the zoo another day. I just wish the call had been from anyone but…' He paused, and I turned to see Freya flashing an insincere smile as she sashayed through in a silky off-the-shoulder dress with a blue and white zigzag print, looking boot camp fit, despite giving birth less than two months ago.

'Meg, hiiii,' she said, stretching her vowels so she sounded like someone from Chelsea, rather than South Devon. 'S'been *aaaaa*ges.' We were the same height, but her high, block-heeled sandals gave her a couple of extra inches, and she had to stoop to pretend to kiss my cheek, her perfume enveloping me like toxic smog. 'I haven't visited Seashell Cove in *yeeee*ars.'

That didn't surprise me. She'd barely returned to Salcombe since leaving home at eighteen to work as an au pair for a wealthy couple in Exeter. She'd ended up having an affair with the husband and, although it hadn't lasted, she'd discovered a taste for the finer things in life. After joining a dating website charmingly called SugarDaddy.com she'd dated a couple of millionaires, and eventually met Don at a charity auction where prizes had included dinner at home, cooked by a celebrity chef, and tickets to the BAFTAs. According to Kath, he'd rescued her from the clutches of an octogenarian, intent on discovering whether Freya was wearing knickers under her side-split gown.

Kath – who'd naively championed her daughter's attempts to 'better herself' – hadn't seen much of Freya since her wedding a year ago, but was obviously coming in useful now Freya had a baby she couldn't be bothered to look after.

'No Milo?' I said, to make a point, noting she still had a habit of swishing her long hair and running her fingers through it. With her flawless skin and tiny waist, it was hard to believe she'd once been overweight, with a monobrow and crooked teeth.

'The housekeeper's got him for a couple of hours.' She swished her hair again. 'Mum had a dentist's appointment, and your mum's apparently quarantined herself. I must say they've been maaaaarvellous with Milo, but the sooner I get a nanny sorted out—'

'Quarantined?'

Freya's high-arched brows nipped together. 'She's apparently got a summer flu thing that's been going round, and didn't want to infect the baby.' She wrinkled her upturned nose. 'Perhaps she should be taking those vitamins Mum says she's always going on about.' Her laugh grated on my nerves. She'd always tried to make out that Kath gossiped about Mum behind her back, but I knew it wasn't true.

'You know your mum would love to visit you more often,' I said, remembering Kath's mortification that the first and last time she'd been invited to the Williams's mansion, she'd been mistaken for the cleaner.

Freya's face reddened. 'Mum's welcome to visit any time,' she said haughtily. 'I can't help it if I live an hour's drive away.'

'Your mum doesn't drive, and it's over two hours by train, plus tickets are really expensive.'

'It's not my fault she doesn't drive, and I don't see why I should pay her train fare.'

Nathan cleared his throat. 'So what do you think? Of the building, I mean.'

'Yeah, it's really cute, but definitely needs gutting.' As Freya started talking about installing new, refrigerated display cabinets, I zoned out, a niggle of worry diffusing my irritation.

Mum had seemed fine on Friday evening, and although I hadn't spoken to her directly since, we'd exchanged a few texts about Sam's reaction to my interview (I'd been a bit creative with the truth) and she hadn't mentioned feeling unwell. Thinking back, it was odd that she hadn't called; she usually liked to hear my voice every day.

'You must be the neighbour Freya's told me about.'

A man had materialised, tall and trim with silver hair, and politeness dictated that I let him shake my hand. 'We thought you were wonderful on *Hidden Gems*.' He had a rich voice, deep tan, and a strong, handsome face – like a Roman centaur or old-fashioned Rat Pack crooner, and his eyes were dark and kind. I'd expected him to look old and rich, and while it was obvious his gold watch, and well-cut shirt and trousers hadn't been bought on the high street, he wore them lightly. My immediate thought was that he was too good for Freya.

'Freya thought you'd be perfect to run Two Scoops.'

'Two Scoops?'

'Isn't it a cute name?' Our previous exchange apparently forgotten, Freya nestled against her husband, one hand stroking the front of his shirt, and he smiled indulgently. 'I know it's not baking cakes, but it's sort of similar,' she said. 'In fact, it'll be much easier, because it's just… well, cream and sugar from what I've read.' She gave a dramatic little shudder. 'Unhealthy as all hell, of course, but people love it.'

Glancing at Nathan, I saw a pained expression cross his face.

'You won't be running it yourself then?' I said. To my knowledge, apart from her stint as an au pair, which had involved more seduction than childcare, she'd never had a proper job.

'God no, I'm a full-time mum, now.' She gave Don a coy smile. 'And I've a gorgeous husband to attend to.'

Attend to? Yuk. Catching Nathan's horrified look, I had to swallow a giggle because this surely couldn't be happening. It was a game to Freya, who'd always been easily bored. 'If you're not going to be working here, why not let it be a bakery?' Obviously, I'd loathe having Freya as a boss, but as she'd be unlikely to ever set foot in the place, I'd probably never see her.

'Freya's done her sums,' said Don, though I doubted this was true. She'd mostly skipped maths lessons at school. 'She thinks ice cream makes more sense.'

'Oh, and I'll be here as the *face* of Two Scoops.' Freya turned her wide blue eyes on me, supposedly to convey sincerity. 'I just won't be doing, you know,' *any work,* 'any of the ice-cream making stuff. And Don's people will take care of the boring admin, so really, it'll be a walk in the park.' Freya cocked her head, her smile patronising. 'It was really moving, the way you talked on telly about not knowing your dad.' She moved her hand to her throat. 'I felt really sad at you having to give up your job here, you were so lovely to me when we were children.' I'd tried, it just hadn't been reciprocated. 'And then you had to leave college to help your mum. It's awful she still can't go out much and relies on you to…' She let the words drift off, a look of sugary sympathy all over her smug face.

The tap dripped and the fridge gave a shudder, as if it had heard enough. Sounds of laughter drifted through, and I wished I hadn't answered Nathan's call.

On cue, he cleared his throat. 'You know the local shop sells ice cream and there's a van down by the cove all summer?' I could have hugged him for remembering. 'There'd be a lot of competition with an ice-cream parlour.'

'I thought you were here to sell the place?' Freya gave him the contemptuous look she probably reserved for anyone earning less than a million a year. 'Why do you care whether we're selling bread, ice cream, or sex toys?' The look she gave Don made my stomach roll. He didn't seem to have noticed, as he was watching me with an inscrutable expression.

'What my wife is trying to say is, she'd love you to run it, which is surely a good thing.' I couldn't think of a way to argue with that, even though every cell in my body was rejecting his words.

'And it's not just about making money, Mr Walsh,' Freya said. 'I have enough of that already. Obviously we're very lucky,' she added, in an over-earnest way, perhaps not wanting to reveal her true colours to Don. It wasn't hard to see that she'd needed a father figure to replace her own dad, and I would have felt sorry for her if she didn't make it so hard. 'Though Don has worked very hard for his money, and does a lot of good work with it,' she added, hooking her arm through his. He'd owned a chain of travel agencies, selling them before the bubble burst and people started booking holidays online, and had made some clever investments, which had put him on the super-rich list. We'd looked him up after Kath told us Freya was marrying a billionaire.

'So, what do you say?' Don gave me a pleasant, white-toothed smile. 'You'll get a generous salary, and as much time off as you need – once the ice cream's been made, of course. Freya tells me you're getting married yourself, in the not too distant future.'

The Salcombe grapevine was clearly in full working order. I was just surprised that Freya was remotely interested in what I was doing. Probably checking I was still worse off than she was.

'Well, she *was* getting married.' Freya had adopted a tone of bouncy intrigue that didn't suit her. 'After what you said on that show, I wouldn't be surprised if your chap has got the right hump with you.'

'I should think her chap is very proud of her.' Nathan's voice was ripe with disgust. 'Miss Larson's passionate about the bakery, and that really came across.'

So, he *had* watched it.

'Oh, of course,' Freya, back-pedalled. 'I just meant not everyone would be so understanding if their fiancée was having second thoughts about getting married on national television.'

'I was *not* having second thoughts,' I said and, in the ensuing silence, I had a clear vision of what it would be like to work with Freya. There'd be constant sniping and undermining, because she always felt threatened by other women, and even if she got bored and stopped turning up – which I had no doubt she would – the thought of making ice cream wasn't really appealing. Would it be better to wait for Tamsin to go off to university in September and ask the Maitlands if I could work her hours at the café? At least I'd be working for people I actually liked.

Then again… I wasn't sure I could bear to leave the building entirely in Freya's hands. It was as if something was urging me to stay – to at least keep an eye on the place; keep it safe. *Mr Moseley?* Nonsense. I didn't believe in spirits, and yet…

Aware of Nathan at my side, I gave him a little smile to show I was grateful for his support. Don and Freya were looking at me, Don's expression impenetrable, Freya's edging towards cocky.

'Thanks for the offer.' I forced the shakiness from my voice. 'I'll think about it.'

Chapter Eleven

I woke the following morning from a tangled dream, and mooched around the kitchen feeling lost. I couldn't face going to the bakery, knowing it would soon belong to Freya, and had made a fruit cake and a batch of ginger cookies for the café the night before, glad of something to do.

It had felt odd being at home alone, but not unpleasant. No Sam dashing in from work and bolting his dinner, before whizzing off to the cycling club or gym, returning to join me on the sofa in front of Netflix (if he wasn't too tired). His recent fixation had been a series set in the eighties, featuring a dark, alternate world called the Upside Down, which I'd watched through my fingers, as I was easily spooked.

Once I'd finished baking, I watered the garden – Sam would hate to come back to find everything wilting – then changed into a pair of baggy pyjamas Sam referred to as my passion-killers. I'd curled up in the granddad chair – so called because it had belonged to Sam's grandfather – where I'd tried to phone Mum, worried that I hadn't heard from her since I'd left the bakery the day before, when she'd texted to say she was fine.

She didn't answer my call.

In the end, I'd tried to watch as many episodes of *Friends* as it would take to make me sleepy, but even their antics couldn't distract me. Neither did an email from Alice Denby, thanking me again for being on the show, which had drawn great viewing figures. If I hadn't agreed to appear on the stupid show, I'd have been in touch with Sam, hearing all about his first day in Paris. *Or would I?* He'd more likely be out celebrating with the group, not giving me a second thought. I'd begun to wonder whether he had a point, and the fallout from being on TV was a sign that I should be concentrating on what was really important: our relationship and our wedding.

Or maybe it was a sign that Sam and I weren't meant to be. The treacherous thought had worked its way in as I stared at the television, where Joey was promising not to tell anyone that Chandler and Monica were sleeping together. It wasn't the first time I'd had doubts. A couple of years earlier, I'd come home early and caught Sam staring at a photo on Facebook, and when I'd asked who the people in it were, he'd said too casually, 'Oh, I just wondered what some of the gang from uni were up to these days,' and I'd known, deep in my bones, he'd been looking for Andrea. And when I'd failed to get pregnant after our first few tries, I'd seen it as a sign – though of what, I wasn't sure. Both times the feelings had been swiftly banished, put down to a lingering jealousy (the photo) and raging hormones (my period starting).

This time though, the thought had wormed its way into my dreams, and however much I'd tried to shake it off, I couldn't dislodge the queasy feeling that instead of planning a wedding, we should be considering couple counselling.

Ugh. My mind rejected the idea. Sam would never agree and anyway, all relationships had blips, and Sam's and mine weren't *that* bad. It wasn't as if we even argued very often, which was probably why I'd taken the scene at his parents' to heart. He'd merely expressed his opinion, which he was perfectly entitled to do without me getting all 'female' about it, as his friend Chris would have said.

Sighing away the heaviness around my heart, I decided it was time to stop mooching and eating toast, and pay Mum a visit. I wanted to see for myself how she was, and to check that she didn't need a doctor. I wasn't due at the café until after lunch, but could drop off my cakes there after seeing her, and maybe head to the beach for a while; have a think about some of Beverley's wedding suggestions, to show I was taking them seriously. She'd texted me a link to a website that offered 'quirky' wedding favours such as adult colouring books of Benedict Cumberbatch's face, and bottles of 'Happy Ever After' fairy dust, with the question *Wouldn't these be fun?!*

Maybe there was something wrong with me that my instinctive response was *no.*

Drying my hair after a quick shower, wishing I'd done the same yesterday before rushing out, my gaze fell on the well-thumbed itinerary at Sam's side of the bed. Switching off the hairdryer, I picked up the typed printout and read,

Day 2. Early start to negotiate Paris before rush hour, heading from the hotel towards the Eiffel Tower, where we'll have the obligatory group photo! Our route will take us along the boulevards of the capital's Left Bank as we ride south-east, following the course of the River Seine...

Group photo. Surely it would be up on the Facebook page by now, as Sam had planned to post pictures along the route to chart their progress.

Unplugging my phone from its charger, I sat on the bed and logged on, which took a few goes as I'd forgotten my password and had to request a reminder, then make up a new one which I promptly forgot, and had to request another.

The first thing to appear on my timeline was a filtered photo of Freya, reclining on a lounger by her dazzling swimming pool, her long, tanned legs drawn up to support baby Milo, and to show off the heart-shaped tattoo just visible on her ankle. Milo was well covered in a matching white onesie and sunhat, but Freya's plunging swimsuit revealed more bronzed flesh than it covered. She was peeking at the camera over outsized sunglasses, under the words *Summer babies are happy babies! Just loving being a mom!*

Someone called Babs had written underneath *Oh my god, hun, he's adorable, and how gorgeous do you look? Can't believe you've got your beach-bod back already. Took me two years to shift the baby weight *sad face**

I was tempted to post that Freya's 'mom' and her 'mom's' best friend looked after the baby every day, so Freya had plenty time to spend her husband's hard-earned money on looking 'gorgeous'. Instead, I unfriended her. I shouldn't have accepted her request in the first place. She'd only wanted to show off. I was surprised she hadn't mentioned Two Scoops, and wondered whether Lester had accepted Don Williams's offer yet. He'd probably snatched his hand off.

Switching my mind away, I found the Pedal Pushers page and, sure enough, at 8.30 a.m. Sam had linked to the photo of the twenty-strong group, posed in front of a sun-drenched Eiffel Tower, each of them standing beside a shiny bicycle, wearing adrenaline spiked grins. They looked like alien-bugs in their helmets, sun-goggles, and bright colours, and I recognised Sam right away from his royal-blue top and super-tight shorts. He'd removed his goggles and his head was inclined towards the only woman, as though he'd been in the middle of saying something to her.

I hadn't realised there were any women in the group, and scanned the names underneath. He'd never mentioned a female member, and none of the names gave a clue. *Chris, Jack, Iain, Dom, George…* I ran through all twenty, twice. I'd met several of them at some point, and knew Chris well because he'd been Sam's best friend since school, but there'd been no mention of a woman. George was the newest member. I remembered he'd joined in February, and there'd been some debate about whether there was enough time for him to train for the challenge. *George.* It could be short for Georgina. Hadn't Sam once mentioned that Chris was impressed with George's thighs because they were stronger than his? I hadn't taken much notice at the time, and knew instinctively he'd have assumed I would think George was male.

Heart thumping, I scrolled down all the pictures I'd missed, because I rarely ventured on Facebook, and saw that 'George' featured in several of them. In one, she was holding up a gold trophy, her arm looped around Sam's neck, her face radiant with laughter. She was ruddy-cheeked with wild, auburn hair and sparkly blue eyes, and Sam was giving her an openly appreciative look.

I studied the picture for a full minute, waiting for the jealousy to kick in, like it had when I'd seen him looking at the picture of his uni friends, knowing he was thinking of Andrea, but the feeling I now had wasn't jealousy, it was closer to… resignation? Déjà vu, even. *I've been here before.*

Sam and I needed to talk. Properly. But now wasn't the time.

I flung my phone in my bag, got dressed, and left the house.

Mum didn't answer my knock, and when I tried my key in the door it wouldn't budge. The safety catch inside must be on.

Shielding my eyes, I stepped out of the porch and peered up at her bedroom window. The curtains were drawn, which meant she must still be in bed. I felt a creep of unease. She must be really unwell. Despite working from home, Mum was usually in front of her computer by nine, dressed as if for the office, with a cup of tea and morning television or the radio playing quietly in the background.

Should I phone, to check she was still alive?

Moving round the back of the house, I looked through the living-room window. It was hard to see properly through the slatted blinds, but I could just make out a champagne flute on the dining table, and tried to see if there was another. Mum didn't drink alone, but Kath had given up the 'lady petrol' so why the champagne flute? And why would Mum be drinking if she was ill?

Maybe she hadn't been drinking champagne, but had merely used the glass for a drink of water. I dug my phone out of my bag and rang her number.

'Hello?'

Oh god, she did sound rough. All throaty and sleepy, or as if she'd just had a coughing fit. 'Sorry to disturb you, Mum. I'm outside.'

'Meg, is that you?' She sounded so alarmed, I pulled my phone from my ear and stared at it.

'Of course it's me. I'm worried, Mum. Can I come in?'

'NO!' she yelled, then coughed. 'I told you, Meg, I'm not feeling very well.'

'I know you did, but I'm not worried about catching whatever it is you've got, I'd probably have got it by now, anyway. Let me in, and I'll do a bit of tidying up and make you something to eat before I go to work.'

She'd always looked after me when I was unwell, it would be nice to do the same for her, and would hopefully stop Sam, the wedding, the bakery, Nathan, and Freya from churning around in my mind on a loop. Not that thinking about Nathan was tricky. In a way, he was the one bright spot in the last few days; the way he'd leapt to my defence in front of Freya, and followed me out of the bakery to check that I was OK before I'd driven off, watching until I'd rounded the corner. 'Mum?'

'Meg, I'm fine, I just need to sleep it off, please don't worry.'

Still husky-voiced, there was something else in her tone I couldn't decipher.

'Mum, this hasn't got anything to do with me being on that show, has it?'

The little silence at the other end, made my heart plunge. 'It has, hasn't it? Mum, I can't tell you how sorry—'

'Meg, sweetheart, you've got it all wrong.' There was a rustling sound, as though she was sitting up in bed. 'There's nothing to worry about, I promise, just… give me some time.' The huskiness had left her voice, though she still sounded a bit off – not like her usual self.

'How much time?' I pressed my forehead to the window again. Something wasn't right about the room, but I couldn't think what – something out of place, but it was hard to tell with Mum's collectibles on every surface.

A thought hit me sideways. What if someone had broken in and tried to steal her valuables, and she'd interrupted them and now they were holding her hostage? Lowering my voice, I said, 'Mum, you're not being held against your will, are you?'

'Against my will?' Mum's laugh was a touch hysterical. 'I'm definitely not being held against my will, love.'

'And you definitely don't feel like getting out of bed and letting me in?'

'Oh, Meg, you're so sweet, but really… I'm going to be fine. Everything's going to be OK.'

Wow, she sounded really emotional now, but flu could muddle your emotions. I'd had it in my teens, and in-between bouts of painful coughing had been a sobbing mess. 'And you're sure it's got nothing to do with me?'

'Nothing at all.' Her voice was starting to sound strained. 'It's just something I have to deal with alone.'

Odd way to put it. 'What about work?'

'Hmm? Oh, I'm up to date with this month's accounts, so nothing to worry about there.'

I frowned. For a second, she'd sounded as though she didn't know what I was talking about, but again that was probably the flu.

'You seemed OK, I mean health-wise, last Friday.'

'Have you heard from Sam?'

Neat change of subject. 'He's on the road, having a great time.' Now I sounded overly bright, but where normally she'd demand to know what was wrong, she merely said, 'That's lovely, Meg. I'll see you very, very soon.'

'Oh, OK. Love you.'

'Love you, too. So much.'

I hung up, feeling like I'd been fobbed off, and jumped when I heard Kath's muffled voice from her garden next door. 'She all right, your mum? I haven't seen her around for a couple of days.'

I turned to see Kath hanging out baby clothes, a plastic peg in her mouth. 'No, she's been hit with this flu virus.'

Kath nodded, clipping the peg to a tiny, lemon bootee on the washing line. 'Poor love. Maybe she caught it from that visitor of hers on Saturday afternoon.'

My head jerked. 'Visitor?' Mum rarely had visitors, and normally told me when she did. 'Who was it?'

Kath shook her head, her beehive wobbling. 'Didn't recognise the car, but the only vehicle I've ever seen parked outside your mum's is her boss from the health food store. What's his name? Gavin. Comes to discuss the accounts every month.'

I remembered now, Mum saying that Gavin was 'quite dishy'. He'd been there once when I'd called in, supposedly going through some paperwork, but drinking coffee and eating a batch of my shortbread biscuits, his jacket flung on the sofa. I'd briefly wondered whether there was more to it, because Mum's skirt had ridden up over her knees and her cheeks were a rosy red, but she'd not said anything since and neither had I.

'Maybe he's got a new car,' Kath said, 'and him and your mum are doing the biz.' She laughed with her whole body. 'I keep telling her, get yourself a man, Rose, or you're going to rust over downstairs.' Her eyes bobbed downwards, and I mentally recoiled from the image, though I'd occasionally thought it a bit unhealthy that Mum had only ever slept with my father.

'I'm sure she'd have said if she was seeing Gavin like *that*.' *Wouldn't she?* Maybe she was keeping it quiet, in case things didn't work out, but Mum was an open book where emotions were concerned, and we saw each other so often it was impossible to imagine her hiding a whole relationship. 'You'd surely have seen a car out there more often.'

'True.' Kath hoisted the empty laundry basket onto her hip. 'Any news about the bakery, love? I thought you were great on the telly, by the way, nothing to be embarrassed about.'

'Did you know Freya's husband's going to buy it for her?'

'WHAT?' The word shot out so loudly, a magpie flew out of the hedge with a startled squawk and I ducked as it flew over my head. *One for sorrow. Another sign?* 'But she's got a new baby to look after.' Kath's face was screwed up with shock. 'What the hell's she doing buying a *bakery*?'

'Apparently, she wants it to be an ice-cream parlour.'

'Ice-*cream* parlour?' Kath's face straightened out. 'I don't know where I went wrong with that girl, I really don't. Marrying a man old enough to be her father, even though he's lovely, and her constantly wanting this and that.' She gave me a sad little smile. 'Shame she didn't turn out like you, Meg. You didn't even have a dad, but you're a credit to your mum.'

'Oh, Kath, don't say that.' Now I felt even worse. 'I'm really sorry, I shouldn't have said anything.'

'If only she'd met someone a bit younger, who would stand up to her a bit more,' Kath said on a sigh. 'Don gives in to her far too much.'

Guilt twisted my insides. 'He does seem to really love her.'

Kath's mouth turned down. 'He's far too soft, giving her whatever she asks for. It's not healthy. She's never going to grow up at this rate. She's tried to replace her dad, and that's not healthy either.'

As I tried to think of something consoling, I caught a movement out of the corner of my eye and looked up. Had the curtain just twitched? Mum's bedroom was at the front, so we couldn't be disturbing her – unless she'd moved into the back bedroom where it was usually quieter.

'I'd better go,' I said to Kath, remembering my cakes were in the car, probably overheating. 'I'll call Mum later. And please, don't feel bad about Freya, she actually offered me a job, and I might end up taking it.'

'Oh, Meg, *I'm* sorry.' Kath's face hardened. 'I'll be having a word with the little madam.'

Back in my car, driving to Seashell Cove, I thought again about working for Freya. As much as I detested the idea, Don had promised a good salary, and he seemed like a man of his word. If I could keep a few shifts at the café, who knew? Maybe one day, when Freya was desperate to move on, I'd have enough money to buy the place myself.

Buoyed up by the thought, I pulled the car over at the top of the narrow road that led to Maitland's Café, and sat for a moment, looking over the cove where the sun-silvered sea was gently lapping the sand. The beach was strewn with bodies, sunbathing on towels, or paddling at the water's edge, without a worry in the world to a casual observer.

Sighing again – I'd never sighed so much in my life as I had in the past week – I took out my phone to call Nathan, and almost dropped it when it rang and his number came up.

'Nathan, hi, I was about to call.' I had to say it quickly before I changed my mind. 'I've been having a think about staying on at the bakery when it's an… ice-cream parlour.' It was so hard to say those two words. 'I wondered whether you could pass on a message to the Williams's to say I'd like to accept.'

There was a momentary pause, as if Nathan needed a moment to absorb this information, and I pictured his face in detail, as if he was sitting beside me. 'Actually, I was calling to say they've just this minute pulled out.'

'*What?*' I slumped back in my seat. That was that then. Back to square one. I didn't know whether to feel relieved or cry. 'I can't believe it,' I said, pushing my hair off my cheek. 'I didn't even want to work for Freya, but I'd just got my head around it.'

'Are you working at the moment?'

Barely able to summon the energy, I said, 'Not until two o'clock. I was just heading to the beach at Seashell Cove for an hour. Why?'

'Would you mind if I joined you?'

Chapter Twelve

'Charlie didn't fancy the zoo today, then?'

Nathan shook his head. 'He got it into his head this morning that he wanted to build the biggest sandcastle in the world. I thought the beach here might be less busy than the one near us.'

I slid him a look, sensing he was making excuses, secretly pleased that he might have wanted a reason to see me. After fleeing the bakery yesterday, and the way I'd reacted to his phone call, he was probably concerned about my state of mind, and it was nice that he cared enough to check up on me.

I hadn't expected him to arrive with his nephew, but the sight of them in the car park behind the café had boosted my mood. Charlie was a sturdy little boy, with dark eyes and brown curls peeking through his back-to-front baseball hat. He'd gurgled with laughter as he rode down to the beach on Nathan's shoulders, and said shyly, 'Hello, Meg,' when Nathan introduced us.

'Did Don say why they'd changed their minds?' I said, as Charlie got busy with his bucket and spade and Nathan pulled a blue beach towel from his rucksack. He flapped it onto the sand in the shade of the grassy headland beneath the café, and indicated for me to sit down.

'Just that they'd had a chat and decided it wasn't the right time with a baby to take care of.' He dropped beside me and leaned back on his elbows, his legs stretched out in front of him. In navy swim shorts and a plain white short-sleeved shirt, he looked like he'd stepped off a yacht – all tanned skin and wild hair – and a couple of passing females in bright bikinis looked at him and nudged each other before running into the sea.

'I was under the impression that Freya was looking for a nanny.' I smoothed my daisy-patterned skirt over my knees, conscious of my vampire-pale skin compared to Nathan's.

'She was obviously put out that you didn't jump at her offer,' he said, through a yawn. 'She went all sulky after you'd gone, and flounced off.'

'So now she's changed her mind and it's all my fault.' I wriggled my back against a rock and primly crossed my ankles, wishing I'd thought to touch up the varnish on my toenails. 'Lester won't be happy, and the agency won't get any commission.'

'Lester doesn't know,' said Nathan, batting away a persistent wasp. 'I was waiting until they'd made a firm offer before I called him.'

Charlie, squatting beside a heap of sand, looked over. 'Is Uncle Nafan gone to sleep?'

'I don't think so.' I smiled. 'He's just resting his eyes.'

'I can still see you.' Nathan peered at his nephew through half-open lids. 'Do you want some help with your sandcastle?'

'No fanks, you won't be very good like me, 'cos you're not as strong for digging, see?' Charlie demonstrated by jabbing his orange spade in the sand and waggling it about.

'I see what you mean.' Nathan sat up and hooked his elbows over his knees. There was a pair of sunglasses nestling in his hair that he seemed to have forgotten about. 'But where's this sandcastle you were telling me about?'

'I've not started yet, silly.' Charlie pushed his baseball hat off and scratched his forehead. 'I've got to fill up my bucket to the top.'

'Of course you have.' Nathan petted Charlie's curls as though cosseting a poodle, before squashing his hat back on. His affection for his nephew was clear, and obviously returned in full. 'We might need to get some water though to make it stick together.'

Charlie looked at the sea. 'It's very full today.'

Nathan and I exchanged smiles. 'That's because the tide's in,' he said.

'What does that mean?'

'It's when the water comes right up the beach because of the moon, then later it goes out again.'

Charlie tipped his head and looked at the sky. 'But it's not night, Uncle Nafan.'

I gave Nathan a look that said *get out of that*.

He grinned. 'No, but the moon's still there. You just can't see it during the day.'

'Nicely done,' I murmured.

Seeming satisfied with Nathan's explanation, Charlie hunkered down and returned to shovelling sand into his bucket.

'You'll make a good dad one day,' I said, and immediately wished I hadn't. 'Sorry, I hate it when people say that sort of thing to me. You never know what someone's circumstances are. I mean, you might not want children of your own, or even be able to have them, so I shouldn't have said anything. I'm sorry.'

'Hey, it's OK, I don't mind.' He looked at me with a mixture of puzzlement and amusement on his face. 'I didn't used to think I wanted kids, too much responsibility et cetera. But I must admit, being around Charlie has changed my mind.' He hesitated. 'Is the topic a sore point with you?'

My face felt on fire. 'No, not really, it's just… I always thought I wanted a big family, being an only child, and planned to have my first child by the time I was thirty. I wanted to be a young mum, like mine was, but now…' I hesitated, a knot of discomfort tightening my insides. 'Now, I'm not sure.'

'You're only, what?' Nathan turned and scrutinised my face, which felt as if it was glowing like a beacon. 'Late twenties?'

'I turned thirty in March.' I pushed my fingers into the sand. 'Did you know that the optimum age for fertility is eighteen? Technically, my eggs are already past it.' I couldn't believe I'd just said that.

'That doesn't mean they're no good.' Nathan knelt forward to help Charlie lift the bucket off his mound of sand. 'If you're not ready for a family yet, you're not ready.'

'Try telling that to my mum.'

'Have *you* tried?'

'Well… no.'

'Why not?'

'It's hard, because she desperately wants to be a grandmother and she's still trying to persuade me that having children's the most important thing I'll ever do.'

'But, it's your life too.'

'I know, but it makes her happy to think about it.'

'And if you decide you *don't* want children?'

'I'm sure I do, I mean, I just don't…' *want them with Sam?* A chill swept over me, as if the sun had gone in. 'I just don't want them yet,' I finished, quickly.

'How did you and Sam get together, if you don't mind me asking?' Nathan was helping Charlie put sand back in his bucket, compacting it down with his fist.

'Oh, it's quite a boring story, really.' I watched a woman holding a child by the hand as she jumped through the waves, laughing and squealing. 'We were high school sweethearts,' I said, preparing to tell the tale that Beverley had wanted us to incorporate into our wedding invitations, and which most people already knew. 'He smiled at me in the corridor one day, even though I had a really bad cold and my nose was bright red, and I just fell for him.' I didn't say that most boys hadn't been interested in me, because I was shy and overweight, and that no one had ever smiled at me like Sam had. 'One day, he asked me to go fishing with him, and I think it was a test because most of the girls weren't into fishing. In fact, my friend Tilly thought he was totally lame, but I said yes, and actually quite enjoyed it. I even caught a tiddler.' I clasped my hands, and made a face meant to convey teenage joy. 'Our fate was sealed. I was welcomed into his family, we snogged in his dad's shed, I made him a cake for his sixteenth birthday and the rest, as they say, is history.'

'Wow.' Nathan sat back, and looked at me with renewed interest. 'So, you've been together, what, nearly fifteen years? That's longer than a lot of marriages last, and you're not even married, yet.'

I felt myself blush even harder under his scrutiny. 'Actually, we broke up for a couple of years. Sam went to university in Edinburgh and met someone else while he was there.'

As if sensing something in my voice, Nathan turned to me and narrowed his gaze. 'That must have hurt.'

'You could say that.' I curled my legs beneath me and picked at the pile on the towel with my fingernails. 'I always hoped we'd end up back together, though.'

I sensed Nathan trying to read my face and kept it averted. Charlie was oblivious, quietly chanting 'Bam, bam,' as he rhythmically slapped the sand in the bucket with his spade.

'And you did,' said Nathan. 'End up back together, I mean.'

I nodded, and pushed a lock of hair behind my ear. 'His dad fell out of a tree and nearly died, and Sam came home for good. His dad's accident had made him realise what was important, and he still cared about me.' That's what he'd said, now I thought about it properly. Not, *loved*. *Cared* about.

'What about her?'

It was as if my thoughts were flashing in a bubble above my head. I puffed out a long breath of air before I spoke. 'They'd broken up by then.' I was still plucking at the towel. My engagement ring had swivelled round, so it looked like any old ring. We hadn't picked our wedding bands yet. Sam's mum had suggested a matching pair in rose-gold with our initials engraved inside, but at over six hundred pounds each, we hadn't yet made up our minds. 'He doesn't like to talk about it.'

I'd tried just once, asking lightly to disguise my thudding heart, 'What was she like? She wanted to be a model, didn't she?' I'd overheard Beverley and Maura talking about her. 'She must have been pretty.'

He'd paused in the act of pulling his T-shirt over his head. We'd been getting ready for bed, after an evening out with Chris and his then girlfriend. 'It's over, Meg,' he'd said, folding his T-shirt with his back to me, his muscles tensed. 'It doesn't really matter what she was like.'

The tinkle of Giovanni's ice-cream van trickled into the pause as Nathan surveyed my face. 'Do you think he would have stayed in Edinburgh, if they hadn't broken up? Or if his dad hadn't fallen out of a tree, which, by the way, has got me curious.'

'He was a tree surgeon,' I said, ignoring the first bit. 'His rope snapped, and he fell a long way. The doctors thought he'd never walk again.' I kept my face impassive, reliving Sam's ghostly pallor when I'd met him that night at the hospital, where I'd been attempting to console eleven-year-old Sadie who'd made herself sick from crying and had called me. 'I guess I'll never really know whether he'd have come back, or whether he would have stayed.'

'You might have moved on and met someone else if he hadn't.'

We looked at each other for a long, slow motion second. 'But he did and I didn't.' My heart was pummelling my ribcage as Nathan gave a slow nod.

'I hope he knows how lucky he is.'

The chill I'd felt was replaced by a hot wave of panic. The way he said it sounded so… *accepting.* Yet, why wouldn't it? I'd made such a big show of telling him I was getting married – I'd even told Alice that Sam was cuter than Nathan – and could hardly turn round now and say I was having second thoughts – not before I'd spoken to Sam.

Second thoughts. Oh god, it was really happening. I was having second thoughts about marrying Sam. And it wasn't just because I'd met Nathan, and imagined us passionately kissing. After seeing that photo of Sam with George, and the way he'd been looking at her with such warmth in his gaze (when had he last looked at me like that?) I'd been thinking about him searching online for Andrea after we'd got back together – how many other times had he looked for her? – and I knew that I didn't trust him properly; that I didn't feel the love for him I once had.

'Meg?' Nathan was looking at me strangely. 'Are you OK?'

Breathe deeply, I told myself. *Don't say anything rash.*

'I'm fine.' My voice had shot up the scale with dismay. 'I just… I'm fine.'

In a fit of agitation, I kicked my legs out in front on me, and accidentally crumbled the turret Charlie had just built.

'Oh, you've killed it, Meg.' He dropped to his knees and poked at it with his finger.

Tears threatened. 'I'm sorry, Charlie.'

Nathan began scooping the sand back into the bucket with his hands. 'Meg didn't mean to knock it over.'

Charlie tilted his head. 'It's OK,' he said kindly. 'There's lots more, but I fink I'd like to have a paddle now, and get some water from the sea.'

'That sounds like a very good idea.' Nathan pushed himself to his feet and dusted his hands on his shorts. 'Fancy coming with us?' The sun's brightness caught his smile and turned his eyes sea-green, and I wanted to say yes, almost as much as I wanted to run away and be alone with my thoughts.

'Actually, I'd better get to work.' I cupped my hand over my eyes as I looked in the direction of the café. 'You should pop in for a cold drink and some cake.'

'Ooh, cake!' Charlie clapped his hands. 'Or maybe ice cream?' He'd noticed the van on the path leading up from the cove.

Nathan grinned. 'It'll be one or the other, I expect.'

'It was nice to see you both.' I got inelegantly to my feet as my phone began to buzz. 'I'd better get this.'

Nathan's eyes rested on me a moment longer. 'Sure you're OK?'

'Perfect!' I lied, tears welling in my throat. 'Just a bit warm, that's all.'

'We'll leave you to it,' he said. He took Charlie's hand and they walked to the water's edge, where sparkling waves foamed on the damp sand, and I turned to the path leading up to the café, my phone pressed to my ear.

'Hi, Beverley.' My voice sounded thick, but she didn't seem to notice.

'Poppet!' she said, as loud as if she was with me. 'Listen, I'm sorry about Sunday lunch, I think us girlies had a little bit too much vino. Let's put it behind us shall we, sweetie?'

'Sure,' I said, because there didn't seem to be any other answer that would do. 'Have you heard from Sam?'

'Oh, you know what he's like when he's in the zone, he won't be thinking about home, but we're cheering him on in spirit!' *In the zone.* That seemed to sum Sam up. As long as being in the zone meant doing exactly what he wanted. 'Why don't you pop round later on, and we'll talk wedding dresses? I've found a lovely pattern I think you'll like. I think a scoop neck would show off your lovely cleavage and the design will nip your waist in, and I know you said you didn't want white, which is probably as well with your skin tone, my lovely, you'd look very washed out, but maybe cream, or even champagne...'

I let her chatter on until I reached the top of the path where I stopped and turned, searching the sea for Nathan and Charlie, but there were too many heads bobbing in the water and I couldn't pick them out.

'OK, Bev, I'll see you later,' I said flatly and rang off. I would have to go along with things until Sam got back – or at least until I'd talked to him.

I took a few more deep breaths, and entered the café terrace through the white picket fence outside, where I spotted a familiar blonde-haired figure draped over a chair at one of the tables, scanning her phone.

Hurrying over, I threw Gwen a wave through the window to let her know I'd arrived, and she semaphored back with two dishcloths.

'Sadie, what are you doing here?' The Ryans rarely ventured over to Seashell Cove, but once Sadie had passed her driving test, she'd taken to occasionally dropping into the café if she had a spare hour. 'I'm afraid I have to work,' I said, noting her faultless complexion and expertly outlined eyes. 'Shall I fetch you a drink?'

She shook her head, her cloud of hair floating around her face. 'I saw you,' she said, putting her phone down and resting her chin on her palm as she gazed up at me.

My heart bumped. 'What do you mean?'

Her smile was guarded. 'I was in the car park when you got here,' she said. 'I was going to suggest we get an ice cream. I wanted to apologise for Mum and Maura on Sunday, but then you met that guy with the little boy.' She twisted her head to look at the cove. 'You were down there for ages.'

My breath was coming in shallow leaps that had nothing to do with the walk up from the beach, or my shredded thoughts. 'He's the agent in charge of selling the bakery,' I said, hitching my bag up on my shoulder. 'The little boy is his nephew, Charlie.'

'Oh, right.' She coiled a strand of hair around her finger. 'So, it was a business thing?'

My face and neck became fiery hot. 'He wanted to update me on a possible buyer.'

'And he couldn't have just called you?'

'MEEEEEEEEG!'

I almost leapt out of my clothes at the sound of Gwen's caterwaul, but didn't turn. I was transfixed by Sadie's expression, which was a curdled mix of pity and curiosity.

'He was looking after his nephew today and wanted to bring him to the beach, so we arranged to meet here.'

'And you talked *business*?'

My gaze travelled to the white, ruched-front crop top she was wearing, which showed her delicate collarbones. I couldn't remember ever seeing my collarbones. Perhaps I didn't have any. 'What are you getting at, Sadie?'

'I followed you,' she said, unwinding the strand of hair and examining it closely. 'It didn't look like a business meeting to me.'

Chapter Thirteen

'What was that all about?' Gwen met me at the doorway, looking past my shoulder to see who'd been keeping me from work.

'Oh, it was Sam's sister,' I said. 'She… wanted a word about something.' I turned and watched her leave, not sure I'd managed to convince her I hadn't done anything wrong. I supposed me chatting to a good-looking man on the beach while Sam was away might look suspicious, coming so soon after my TV disaster, but I didn't like the fact that she'd followed me. I wondered whether she planned to tell her family and felt a tug of apprehension.

'Skinny little thing,' said Gwen. ''Ow is Just Sam?'

Following her inside, I said tiredly, 'Cycling his way across Paris.'

'Oh yeah, I forgot 'e likes to get on 'is bike. Surprised it don't mess with 'is nutsack, all that chafing against the saddle, if you know what I mean.'

I did. He'd even mentioned it to the doctor, but tests had showed Sam's 'swimmers' as he called them had 'full motility'.

'It's a myth that cycling affects fertility,' I said. 'Exercise boosts it.'

'I was only kiddin'.' Gwen gave me a beady look as she let me behind the counter. 'You've trampled sand in.' She glanced at the floorboards. 'And your 'air could do wiv a brush.'

'I had an hour on the beach,' I said, defensively. 'I needed some fresh air.' I smoothed my hair, which felt as ruffled as if I'd been rolling around on the towel. With Nathan.

'Missing 'im, are you?'

I jumped. 'Sorry?'

'Just Sam?'

'Of course.' It came out without conviction. 'I mean, yes, I suppose so.'

'Pity you 'ain't got a pussy to stroke, it would do wonders for your blood pressure.' It was very hard to tell when Gwen was joking.

'I'm allergic,' I reminded her, as I had nearly every shift since Dickens had appeared on the scene. 'And, anyway, cats don't like being stroked as much as dogs.'

'Dickens does, 'e lives for the feel of me 'ands.'

We both knew the conversation was a diversion, but Gwen didn't push it as I went to hang up my bag. I quickly checked my phone, but there were no messages from Mum. Could she still be sleeping off her virus? I needed to check after work.

I pulled a comb through my hair feeling oddly lightheaded, as if my brain had been replaced with feathers, and had to run cold water over my wrists before I felt able to go through to the café.

'I fink Tamsin's agreed to go out wiv Dom tonight, for 'er sins,' said Gwen, as I sidled behind the counter and checked my cakes had been put out and neatly sliced. Gwen wasn't delicate with a knife, and tended to hack out uneven portions that didn't always favour the customer. 'Gawd knows what she sees in 'im. I reckon she only said yes to put 'im out of 'is misery.'

I looked to where Tamsin was chatting to Dom as they cleared a table together, their faces flushed and smiling.

'Maybe they've fallen in love,' I said, but in a desultory way. It was too hot in the café, despite the open doors, and I kept thinking of Nathan and Charlie paddling in the sea and eating ice creams.

'Love?' Gwen's bark startled a sleeping baby on its mother's lap, its hands flying out to the sides. 'What do they know abart love at their age?'

I flashed her an incredulous look. 'Some people do, Gwen.'

She held up her palms. 'Sor*ree*,' she said, unapologetically. 'Forgot abart you and Just Sam.'

'I wasn't talking about us.' I grabbed a cloth and began wiping the already clean counter.

'I thought you were the expert on love's young dream.' Gwen's voice was sly.

'I never said that.' I wiped more vigorously, my face burning with the effort. 'I just don't think you should give Tamsin a hard time for falling in love.'

I looked up to see Gwen was wearing her 'bad-smell' expression. 'Yeah, well,' she said with a sniff. 'I don't believe you can truly love someone until you know everyfink abart them.' Guessing she was referring to her own doomed marriage, I didn't bother responding. 'Although,' she added, ruminatively, 'I did fall for my Dickens at first sight, and I can't imagine not loving that furry little bleeder for the rest of 'is life.'

To my relief, one of our regular customers, Valerie Jones, was approaching the counter with a tentative smile on her tanned and friendly face. 'I thought you were great on *Hidden Gems* the other evening,' she said to me, eyeing what was left of the cake I'd dropped off earlier. 'I hope a buyer comes forward for the bakery, it would be nice not to have to buy our bread at the supermarket. It's not the same.

Not that we eat as much of it now the kids have left home, but my husband and I are partial to a decent loaf.'

'Thanks,' I said, feeling shy. I'd almost forgotten that people might recognise me, but it was good at least one person had picked up the point of why I had been on the show in the first place. 'I hope so too, and you're right, Mr Moseley's loaves were the best.'

'Oh, I saw the programme as well,' said the woman with the baby on her lap, giving me a broad smile. 'That cake you made looked amazing! Is Alice Denby as nice in real life?'

'Oh, she's lovely,' I said, happy to talk about something besides my personal life for a change. 'She was really supportive.'

'I think under new ownership, the bakery could do really well,' the woman went on. 'I know a few people who've said since seeing the programme they'd love it to reopen, and would definitely shop there.'

'That's good to know.' I returned her smile. 'Fingers crossed,' I said, crossing mine to demonstrate.

'My husband was looking to invest in a new business earlier this year, but thought the location wasn't quite right,' she added, extinguishing the faint flicker of hope that had begun to burn. Clearly no one with any business sense was going to see the bakery as a profitable proposition, and no amount of appealing, televised or otherwise, was going to change that.

'Well, if it does reopen, I'd love a job there,' said Valerie, her eyes suggesting I ignore the other woman's comments. 'I've always fancied working in a bakery and I've a lot more time on my hands, now the kids have left home.'

I served the next few customers on autopilot, accepting compliments about the show with as much grace as I could, keeping half an eye on the door in case Nathan and Charlie showed up, and tried not to think about Sadie following us to the beach – spying on me – or about what I would say to Sam the next time we spoke.

Tilly appeared at one point, to meet her walking group outside the café, but only managed a wave, as one of the ladies was loudly protesting that Tilly was running late (she wasn't the best time-keeper).

I was about to take my coffee break outside and give Mum a call – something still felt off about this morning – when I glanced through the window to see Nathan coming off the path in a lurching half-run, Charlie under his arm waving his baseball hat like a flag.

'We've runned all the way!' he cried, as Nathan burst into the café and came straight to the counter, panting and red-faced. 'Uncle Nafan said my legs was too small, so I had to be a parcel.' He grinned at Nathan, but Nathan was looking at me like a man who'd won the lottery.

'What's going on?'

'Can we get Charlie a drink?' he said, putting his nephew down and wiping a hand across his brow. 'He's heavier than he looks, especially when you're running uphill,' he added, in a manner I could only interpret as jolly. Despite his breeze-tangled hair and heightened colour, his eyes were as shiny as glass and his smile wider than I'd ever seen it.

'I know our drinks are the bleedin' best, but I 'ain't never known anyone run all the way to get one,' Gwen observed, her eyes darting between us. 'What gives?'

'I just need a quick word with Meg.' His tone had an air of urgency that made my stomach squeeze and, seeming to grasp that whatever he had to say was important, Gwen tutted.

'I'll keep an eye on the young 'un,' she said. 'What do you want to drink, little fella?'

Charlie's rosy face bunched into a frown. 'Please may I have a stwawberry one?'

'He means a milkshake.' Nathan rested a hand on his nephew's curly head and scanned the menu. 'That's if you…'

'We do,' said Gwen. 'The best milkshakes in Sarf Devon.'

Charlie did a jump of excitement and looked at his uncle for permission.

'Sounds good to me,' Nathan said, with a smile.

''S'e all right wiv cats?'

'I LOVE cats *and* dogs, and *anyfing*, really,' said Charlie, earnestly. 'Don't I, Uncle Nafan?' He was amazingly cute. Nearby customers were smiling mushily and making 'isn't he adorable?' faces.

'You certainly do,' agreed Nathan.

'TAMSIN!' Gwen bellowed. 'Make this young man a strawberry milkshake, while I take 'im out the back to see Dickens.'

Looking as if he might explode with happiness, Charlie followed Gwen without a backwards glance.

'Will he be OK?' Nathan scratched his head when they'd disappeared. 'She seems nice, but kind of terrifying.'

I suddenly wanted to laugh. 'He'll be fine,' I promised. 'She's a teddy bear, really.'

'The sort you imagine coming to life when you're asleep and wreaking havoc.'

I smiled, but my mouth had dried up. 'What did you want to talk to me about?'

'Can we go somewhere more private?'

My heart started racing. 'Round the back?'

I led the way outside and round to the car park, trying to imagine what could have warranted a dash from the beach in a heatwave, carrying a four-year-old.

In a spot of shade at the rear of the café, Nathan let his rucksack slide to the ground.

'So, I got a call just after you left.' He held up his phone, and his voice dropped low in his throat. 'It's about the bakery.'

The world seemed to slide to one side. 'Go on.'

'It's been bought by an anonymous buyer.' His eyes danced over my face. 'He must have seen the show and was apparently impressed by your passion.'

I pressed my hands to my cheeks. 'You're kidding?' A grin stretched across my face. 'I can't believe it!'

'It gets better.' Nathan's smile grew even wider. 'He wants you to run it.'

'WHAT?'

'I know.' He widened his eyes. 'He doesn't want to knock it down, or work there, or open an ice-cream parlour. He wants you to reopen the bakery.'

I clutched my hair. 'I've just done a triple cartwheel in my head.'

Nathan let out a deep, uncensored laugh. 'It's being done through a solicitor, and he's keen for it all to go through right away. Lester's over the moon, as you can imagine.'

'So am I!' Through a whirl of joy, a horrible thought struck. 'Oh, Nathan, I'm not sure about him being anonymous. Is it definitely a man?'

'That's the impression I got, at least, the solicitor referred to the buyer as "he".'

'What if he's a money launderer, or, you know, a bit dodgy?'

'He isn't. I called the office back, and had it all checked out. Everything is completely above board. It's quite uncommon to do business like this, but not unheard of.'

'Oh my days.' I was half-laughing, half-crying. It was exactly like the daydream I'd had, where Nathan had said more or less those exact words, and I'd leapt into his arms. Any minute now, we'd be kissing madly. 'It seems almost too good to be true,' I said shakily. 'Are you sure it's not a prank?'

'It definitely isn't.' Nathan's eyes were full of feeling. 'I've passed on your details and the solicitor will be in touch.'

'But…' My contrary mind was still looking for pitfalls. 'How will it work? I mean, how will I pay for things like staff and overheads, and… flour?' I wouldn't be getting paid at the café any more and I could hardly ask Sam to help out.

'I expect there'll be a business account.' Nathan pocketed his phone. 'There'll be money for all that sort of thing.'

'Oh my *god*. How does that even work?'

'I don't know.' He laughed. 'It'll all be explained in the paperwork.'

'But… why would anyone do this?'

He hunched his shoulders. 'Why not?' he said. 'Maybe he's a rich, bored businessman looking for a new investment, or just wanted to do something nice.'

I shook my head, feeling stunned. 'It's too much to take in.'

'I'm so pleased for you, Meg.' Nathan's voice grew serious. 'I know this is what you wanted, so just make the most of it.'

I was taking deep breaths again, hoping this time the extra oxygen would help it all sink in. 'It's literally a dream come true.'

'I know.'

The air between us fizzed.

My heart thundered in my chest and my body flooded with adrenaline, and before I could work out who'd made the first move I was in Nathan's arms and we were exploring each other's mouths, his hands pressing me close while my fingers raked through his hair. Heat drenched my body as I pushed against him, our breathing erratic as the kiss grew deeper, and Nathan's arms tightened around me.

The sound of a revving engine jumped us back to reality. Nathan let go and stepped back unsteadily, a clash of emotions on his face. His hair was more tangled than ever, where I'd run my hands through it, and his lips were as swollen as mine felt.

'I don't…'

'I'm sorry…'

We spoke at the same time in hoarse, bewildered voices.

'I'm sorry, Meg.' Nathan lifted his arm then let it drop. 'I shouldn't have done that.'

'It's OK. It's fine, I…' I was panting, and couldn't speak properly. 'I was overexcited about the bakery and got carried away. It was my fault. I'm the one who's sorry.'

Except… I wasn't. *Oh god, why wasn't I sorry?* Because I'd just had the best kiss of my entire life that was why. I'd read about fireworks going off, and bodies 'flooding with desire', but I'd never felt it before. *Ever.* My first kiss with Sam had been chaste, the physical side of our relationship gradual. It had been nice – *really* nice – after the awkwardness of our first time, but even after we got back together, I'd never experienced anything close to the feelings my kiss with Nathan had just unleashed. Something in me felt different, as if a stone had been lifted and light was flowing in. Except… it couldn't be real. I was confused, my emotions in disarray. The photo of Sam and George was still fresh in my mind, jostling with the realisation that I didn't trust him. My feelings were all over the place, straining for release, and Nathan's good news had been a catalyst. OK, so a victory dance, or a celebratory coffee would have been more appropriate, but Nathan was so attractive and thoughtful, and he'd been so pleased for me and… *oh SHIT!* This could *not* be happening.

'I liked it,' I blurted out.

'Me too.' Nathan's smile was sad as he gently touched my arm. 'But, we both know it can't happen again.'

'Of *course* it can't.' Every nerve-ending was alive to the feel of his fingers. 'I honestly don't know what just happened, it must be this hot weather. Maybe I've got heatstroke.' I gave an odd cackle that was so unlike me, I nearly burst into tears. 'So, what's next?' I blinked and thrust my hair back with both hands. 'On the property front, I mean? Can I reopen right away?' With difficulty, my mind returned to the bakery. 'I can't wait to tell Big Steve. He's a baker I know. I'm going to offer him a job.'

Nathan pushed his hair sideways, only adding to its dishevelment. 'I don't see why you can't reopen as soon as the paperwork's signed.' He paused. 'I'll be in touch if any problems arise, but I can't see that they will.'

He was clearly making a big effort to be professional.

'Great!' I gave him my brightest smile. 'That's that then. Thanks again for letting me know.' *And for the magical, heart-stopping, world-shattering kiss.*

He gave a small shrug, and I could see he was struggling to keep his own smile in place. 'Happy to have been the messenger.'

'I guess you'd better go and drag Charlie away from his new furry friend.'

Nathan nodded, and looked as if he wanted say something else. I held my breath, but he seemed to change his mind at the last second. 'I'll get him,' he said, picking up his rucksack and hoisting it onto his shoulder. 'You stay here, and take everything in properly.' He meant, compose myself, and I knew I must look unbalanced. 'Good luck, Meg.'

He lifted his hand in a farewell gesture, before turning and hurrying back the way we'd come, as if worried he might change his mind.

A sound broke free from my throat when he'd gone, and I looked around the car park as if I'd never seen it before. It was always full during the summer, as people visiting the cove tended to leave their cars there, but I immediately recognised a candy-pink Mini in a bay at the opposite end.

My heart gave a crazy thud.

It was Sadie, and she was staring right at me with a look in her eyes that could have burned through rock – and not the seaside variety.

Chapter Fourteen

'Here's to the reopening of the Old Bakery!' Tilly and I chinked glasses with Cassie, and I tried my best to smile.

'I can't believe you'll soon be in charge, selling your lovely cakes.' Cassie took a big swallow of champagne and topped up her glass. 'And I can't believe Bill actually had some champagne in this dive.' It was just after six, and we were celebrating my news in the garden of the Smugglers Inn. 'I knew going on that show would pay off in the end.'

Tilly opened her packet of crisps and flicked a fly off the table. 'Is that why Gwen looked angrier than usual when I got my walkers back to the café?'

'Believe it or not, she was happy for me,' I said. 'Even when I told her I'd be leaving at the end of the week.' By the time I'd gathered my wits after watching Sadie drive off, Nathan and Charlie had gone, and I'd explained my agitation to Gwen as being the result of Nathan's good news.

'Halle-bleedin-lujah,' she'd said, when I'd explained about the anonymous buyer, giving me a great whack on the back. 'Good on yer, girl. As long as you promise to still make us a cake of the day.' I'd promised I would, mustering a smile when she'd added, 'Ain't that little boy nice, for a kid? His uncle seems like a decent sort as well.'

I started when Tilly spoke. 'So, you've no idea who this mystery buyer is?'

'Apparently, it's common to remain anonymous if you don't want your name in the public domain.' I was parroting what I'd read, after looking it up on my phone when Gwen had asked the same question. 'He could be a philanthropist who doesn't want the limelight, or own a string of lap-dance clubs he doesn't want people to know about, or be doing it secretly for tax reasons.' I fervently hoped he was a philanthropist.

'He could be a weirdo millionaire who'll turn up at the bakery one day and demand you repay him in kind,' said Tilly, her eyes flashing with mischief. 'He'll lock you in the kitchen and demand you cover him in whipped cream and raspberries.'

'Gross,' said Cassie. Her brow furrowed. 'Tilly's got a point, though.'

'It's fine,' I said. 'Nathan's checked it out, and it's all above board. Solicitors won't deal with anyone dodgy in case it backfires on them.' I felt my face go hot as I said Nathan's name, but they didn't seem to notice.

'It could be someone you know.' Tilly straightened. 'It might be my dad,' she said. Her dad was an award-winning architect and had never been short of money, even before he started winning awards. 'It's the sort of thing he'd do, and not shout about it.' She wriggled her phone out of her jeans pocket. 'I'll message him.'

As she typed, I tried to banish an image of Sadie, flinging her car out of the car park before I could even attempt to explain what she'd seen. Not that there was an acceptable explanation.

Did Sam already know?

I briefly considered telling Cassie and Tilly what had happened, but couldn't face it. I desperately needed to order my thoughts, but they kept springing about like a basket of unruly puppies, and I wasn't ready to announce something life-changing like calling off my wedding.

Tilly's phone pinged. 'It's not Dad,' she said, scanning the message. 'He says he wishes he'd thought of it, though.'

'It wouldn't be my dad,' said Cassie. 'Now they're paying Gwen to manage the café for them, they wouldn't be able to afford it.' She helped herself to one of Tilly's crisps. 'It's hard work, you know. Running a business.'

'But I know I can handle it,' I said. 'It's not like I'll be doing anything very different to when I worked there before.'

'You'll need an assistant.' Tilly jammed a crisp in her mouth. 'You can't be in the kitchen baking, *and* in the shop.'

'I was thinking of asking Kath. Discount Clothing closed last month, so she's out of a job.'

'Discount Clothing's a terrible name,' said Cassie. 'No wonder they closed down.'

'What about bread?' Tilly pulled a face. 'You're rubbish at baking bread, but the bakery's always sold bread. People expect to buy bread from a bakery.'

'Stop saying bread,' I said, fixing my mind on the bakery. 'I'm going to ask Big Steve.'

Cassie's eyebrows lifted. 'Big Steve, the butcher's son?'

I nodded. 'He hates working at that Tesco's in Newton Abbot and he'll be right next door, so the early starts won't be a problem.' I smiled, imagining his reaction. 'I won't even need to go in too early, so Sam can't quibble about that.'

I'd said it automatically, as though everything was normal between us, and Tilly pounced on the words.

'Do you think he will? Quibble, I mean.'

I doubt it, I nearly said. *He probably wouldn't even notice I'm gone.*

Luckily, Cassie was speaking now. 'Are you going to have your name above the door? Danny could paint a sign for you.' Signwriting was one of Danny's many skills.

'I'm not sure I'm allowed to, but I'll check,' I said, then realised I was thinking of an excuse to call Nathan and mentally kicked myself. I'd managed not to think about the kiss for seconds at a time, but it kept on creeping in.

I trained my gaze on a couple at the next table, holding hands and scrolling through photos on their phones. They were clearly in love, and I tried to remember whether Sam and I had ever sat close together like that, heads touching, even in the early days.

'Do you feel like fireworks are going off when you and Danny kiss?' I said to Cassie, before I could stop myself.

She dropped the crisp she'd been about to put in her mouth. 'Meg!' She laughed, her cheeks turning pink. 'Where did that come from?'

'Just wondered,' I said, feeling silly.

'Answer her,' ordered Tilly. 'Do you go all tingly and hear a chorus of bluebirds when your lips meet?'

'Ew!' Cassie threw the crisp at her. 'As it happens, it does feel a bit like that, yes.' Her colour deepened. 'It's early days though,' she said. 'I'm sure we won't feel as strongly in fifteen years' time, if that's what you're worried about.'

'I'm not.' I twisted my engagement ring round. 'It's just…' *It wasn't ever like that with Sam.*

'Are you OK?' She looked at me more closely. 'Has something happened?'

Everything. 'No, no, it's just…' I couldn't meet her eyes. 'Sam's away and I haven't told him my news yet.' It struck me as another bad sign that I hadn't even thought about his reaction, and it hadn't occurred to me to discuss it with him.

'He'll be at a hotel tonight though, surely you can call him then,' said Tilly, and I realised Cassie must not have told her about my little meltdown the morning Sam had left. 'Or is he like De Niro and has to stay in character, even when he's not cycling to Timbuctoo?'

'He'll have dinner with the group when they get to Burgundy,' I said, not rising to Tilly's bait. I'd already checked Sam's itinerary to see where he was going to be. 'I'll tell him then.'

'He'll be so excited for you,' said Cassie. 'I bet your mum is too.'

Tilly ran a finger around the rim of her glass. 'I think your mum would prefer you to be barefoot and pregnant.'

'Of course she wouldn't.' Cassie aimed a slap at Tilly's shoulder. 'Rose knows how much Meg's always wanted this.'

Cassie didn't get that not all parents – or boyfriends – were as supportive as hers.

'Actually, Mum was quite pleased when the bakery closed, because it meant I got to spend more time at home.' I noticed a faint lipstick smudge on my glass that wasn't mine, and pushed it away. 'I think she wants me to have the family she always dreamed of having.'

'That's not fair of her.' Tilly rested her elbows on the table. 'She could have had that life, if she'd wanted. She could have remarried and had more kids.'

'I think she could be seeing someone.' I told them what Kath said that morning, omitting the bit about Mum's 'area' rusting over.

'Well, it's about time.' Tilly gave an approving nod. 'I know she's had her problems, from what you've said, but she's still an attractive woman. She could end up being a stepmother. Or, he might have grandkids already.' She raised her glass in a toast. 'That would take some of the pressure off you.'

I couldn't picture Mum with stepchildren. I might have longed for siblings when I was younger, and it might have been easier sometimes with a brother or sister to help when she became agoraphobic, but

I'd got used to having her to myself. I couldn't even imagine her with a man.

'I'll pop round and see her in the morning.'

'Maybe text her first,' said Cassie. 'Give her a chance to get used to the idea.'

'What, of Meg popping round to see her?'

'Idiot.' Cassie grinned at Tilly. 'To Meg reopening the bakery.'

Her words sent a little thrill of excitement running through me. I got my phone out of my bag and texted:

Guess what Mum? The bakery's mine! Anonymous buyer. Hope you're feeling better, see you in the morning xx

Cassie was right, it was better to give her a heads-up.

To my surprise, a reply came through straight away.

Oh Meg, that's wonderful! I'm so proud of you, you deserve this! You'll do an amazing job, well done! XX PS don't come round tomorrow, still got a chesty cough, and you're going to need all your strength for your new job xx

'Weird,' I said.

'What's that?' Cassie strained to look at the screen.

'She sounds really pleased for me.'

'Told you!' She flourished her glass. 'Mums can't help being proud, it's in their nature.'

'Even if you murder someone?' said Tilly.

Cassie giggled. 'OK, maybe not that.'

'It just doesn't sound like Mum.' I reread the message. 'It's a bit flowery.'

'Either she's fallen in love, or she's been at the Night Nurse,' said Tilly. 'Didn't you say she's got the flu?'

'She's had Night Nurse before; it tends to knock her out. She wouldn't be looking at her phone never mind typing messages.'

'Must be love then,' said Tilly. 'Not that I'd know about that.' She indicated her empty glass. 'Shall we get more drinks and make an evening of it, if you've no Sam to go home to? It's board games night. We could thrash each other at Monopoly.'

'I'm in,' said Cassie. 'I've finished my latest commission, and Danny's round at Rob and Emma's, painting a mural in the nursery.' Rob was Cassie's brother and about to become a dad. 'I've done enough painting for one day, so left him to it.'

I was about to agree, when I glanced at my phone and saw that I'd had a missed call. *Beverley.* 'Oh, dammit.'

'What's up?' said Tilly.

'I'd completely forgotten.' I got up and grabbed my bag, almost wishing I'd drunk all my champagne so I'd have an excuse not to drive. 'I'm supposed to be talking wedding dresses tonight, with my future mother-in-law.'

Chapter Fifteen

As I pulled up outside the Ryans' it struck me that Beverley might have been calling because Sadie had told her about Nathan, and I wondered if I could justify it by telling them that Sam and I were on a *Friends*-style break. But, with the wedding approaching, Beverley wouldn't buy it. She'd be livid, and I couldn't risk her calling Sam to find out what was going on before I'd had a chance to speak to him.

I switched off the engine, feeling sick. I hadn't eaten since my toast at breakfast, which seemed forever ago. So much had happened since then, I felt like a whole new person. One who could survive hours without carbs, and kissed other men. *Argh!* How was I supposed to explain to Beverley why I'd been kissing a man who wasn't her son? Could I get away with blaming it on being excited about the bakery and play the whole thing down? How much had Sadie actually seen from where she'd been sitting? The kiss hadn't lasted long. But there'd been tugging, and pressing, and hair mussing and… The point was, it clearly hadn't been a peck on the cheek in a moment of gratitude.

I sat for a moment, trying to think. Outside, evening sunshine glimmered through the leaves of the tree outside the house, and birdsong floated through the window. I'd sat outside Sam's family home so many times before. After I passed my driving test, I'd turned up in my new car as a surprise and could still remember Sam's look of astonishment when he saw me from his bedroom window, before he ran out to leap in the passenger seat. I'd driven us to Seashell Cove, while he pretended to be terrified and carsick. At least, I'd thought he'd been pretending. And the night we'd babysat three-year old Sadie, and I'd sat in the back of the police car shaking with fear while the police had searched the house, and a white-faced Sam had held my hand, and promised they'd find her soon.

I dropped my face into my hands. *How had it come to this?* Sam a million miles away, enjoying another woman's company, and me throwing myself at Nathan.

A rap on the car door made me screech with fear, and I looked up to see Beverley's heavily made up face looming at me in the open window.

'What are you doing out here?' She reeked of wine, and her lips were stained a reddish purple. 'Thought you were crying for a sec.'

She'd been drinking. *She definitely knew.* I might as well face up to her wrath, and get it over with, and then call Sam. Clearly, this couldn't wait until he got home.

I attempted to open the door, but Beverley was in the way. 'C'mon, sweetie.' She pawed my shoulder with chubby fingers. 'Got some material I think you'll like. It's pink, but not a horrid pink, it's very, very pale, almost not pink at all, and I think it'll look perfect with your hair, if you tie it up so it's not all hanging around your lovely face. Your hair, not the fabric, hahahahaha.'

She didn't know. She couldn't, or she wouldn't be babbling about dress fabric, and fingering my hair. Pink dress fabric. Pink, but not pink. *Who got married in 'not pink'?*

'Is Sadie here?' I forced the words over my tongue, which felt Sahara dry.

'Sadie?' Beverley stopped pawing my hair and pulled in her double chins. 'She's out with her college mates, I 'spect. Don't see as much of her now she's in her second year of that course. She's loving it, you know.' Her lips pulled back in a smile that made her teeth look yellow. 'She wants to work on *Casualty*, doing the wounds. I didn't know that was part of being a make-up artist, but I s'pose someone's got to do it.'

Finally, she bounced back from the door. 'C'mon in, I'll pour us a little drinkie.'

'Not for me, Bev, I'm driving.'

Sadie hadn't said anything. Why? She'd looked like she hated me before driving off. Like the first thing she planned to do was tell someone.

'Have you heard from Sam?'

'Sam?' Beverley paused her bouncy stride up the garden path and looked at me over her shoulder. She was wearing a floaty, strapless dress that needed hoisting up, and chunky, wooden bangles on both arms. 'I told you, sweetie, he won't get in touch when he's away, unless there's an emergency. If he breaks his leg or something.' She sounded jaunty, as if she couldn't care less whether Sam broke his leg, or even his neck. 'He's a big boy, not tied to the apron strings. He can do whatever he likes, and I'm sure he does.' She tapped the side of her nose, nostrils flaring. 'What happens in Vegas and all that.' Her laughter lacked a ring of humour, and I wondered what she was talking about.

Was she not-so-subtly saying she *did* know about the kiss, but wasn't letting on? Maybe she didn't want to rock the boat with the wedding looming, but I couldn't imagine Beverley letting something as potentially explosive slide by without comment – especially after her outburst over my TV appearance.

She shoved open the front door with so much force it hit the wall and bounced back. 'Oops,' she said, lifting her hands and aiming a karate chop at the wood, as though it was fighting her. As she disappeared inside the house, my phone vibrated, and I paused on the threshold to quickly read a message.

Just so you know, I'm not going to tell anyone. Whether you do or not is up to you. Sadie X

Tears pricked my eyes. It felt so sordid having a secret. Especially with Sadie, who'd always looked up to me.

'Now where've you gone?' Beverley's voice was plaintive, verging on argumentative.

'Coming!' I called, quickly thumbing a text back.

Thank you, but we should talk soon X

I thrust my phone in my bag as Beverley's curly head poked round the living-room door. 'Come and look at this.' She was dangling a swatch of fabric, presumably meant for my wedding dress. 'See what you think.'

'Where's Neil?' I said, entering the room, which was full of plumped upholstery, framed family photos, and vases of vibrant flowers from the garden.

'In his shed, where else, my love?' Beverley thudded on a chair at the table by the window, in front of her sewing machine. The curtains were half-drawn, and a dust-laden beam of sunlight squeezed through the gap. 'He's making a cradle for when you... you know.' She leaned back, shaping a dome over her stomach with her hands. 'I've told him he's tempting fate, but he won't have it.' She shook her head, earrings wobbling. 'He's a soppy bugger.'

'That's so kind of him.' Now I felt even worse. How could I even begin the complicated process of unravelling myself from Sam's family? 'I'm not planning to be pregnant for quite some time,' I said, feeling sick. At least that much was true.

'Ah, don't worry, sweetheart.' Beverley plucked an almost empty wine bottle off the floor and I thought for a moment she was going to drink straight from it. Instead, she peered at the label then kissed the rim to an empty glass on the table, refilling it to the top. 'It's more a means of escape, being in that shed.' She turned her gaze to the window, as if she had X-ray vision and could see Neil, sawing away. 'He's sick to death of us, you know.'

'Beverley!' I dropped on the arm of the sofa. 'Neil thinks the world of you all.'

'He used to.' She swivelled her head, and gave me a smile so wide it looked almost painful, before bursting into tears. 'I'm losing everyone,' she sobbed, face crumpled in misery. 'Sam's marrying you; Sadie's doing a house share with her friends from next month; Maura's never here; and Neil's always fiddling with his wood in the shed.' She pressed the fabric she'd been holding to her face. 'I liked it better when the kids were little and I knew where they were and what they were doing. Or when Neil had his accident, and we all pulled together. Now everyone's doing their own thing, and I can't bear it.'

'But that's how it should be, Beverley.' I went to kneel by her chair and rested a hand on her knee. It felt hot through the fabric of her dress, which had slipped even lower down her breasts, but I knew better than to try and hitch it up. I'd had no idea she felt like this, but then I'd never spent much time alone with her. She'd always just been Sam's mum; capable and jolly, who loved her family and her garden, and liked keeping busy and having sly digs at people.

'I think I've got empty nest syndrome,' she said, blowing her nose then swiping the fabric over her eyes, trailing snot and mascara across her cheeks. 'Listen to me, going on.' She gave a gargly laugh. 'You'll soon be married to Sam, and there'll be grandchildren to look forward to.' She drained her wine in noisy gulps, still clutching the slimy fabric. 'You know, I can't wait to be a grandma, my darling.'

Alarm fluttered in my chest. It sounded as if she was relying on Sam and me to keep her fulfilled for the rest of her life.

Just like Mum.

I returned to the sofa, running my hands down my skirt, wishing I'd stayed at the pub. 'I found out today that the bakery's sold and I'm going to be the new manager.' My upbeat tone sounded forced. 'I can reopen once the paperwork's been signed. Isn't that amazing?'

Beverley was staring at the ruined fabric in her hand with a glazed expression. 'Look what I've done,' she said, as if I hadn't spoken. Throwing it down, she bounded out of her chair and weaved to the magazine rack by the fireplace. 'I'll show you a pattern I found in this month's *Beautiful Bride*.' She leaned down to find it, revealing a glimpse of pink thong through a small tear in the stitching of her dress. Swaying slightly, she flipped through the pages, straining to see in the half-light. 'Ah, yes, here we are.'

Bringing the magazine over, she thrust it under my nose, and I stared at a picture of a model in a rose-pink wedding dress that gripped her enormous bosoms and flared to the ground from a heart-shaped V at the waist. She looked like Porno Barbie.

'I don't think it's really me,' I said, smarting that she hadn't mentioned the bakery, and wondering whether she'd picked the wrong page in her inebriated state. 'A bit too…' *slutty?* I settled for, '… fussy.'

'Are you *mad*?' Beverley yanked the magazine back, then trained her eyes on my chest, as though picturing me in the dress. With her ruined mascara, shiny nose, and wine-stained lips, she looked like a psychotic clown. 'It's *exactly* you.' She flapped the magazine at me. 'Maybe not that exact shade, my darling, but the style is *perfect* for your shape.'

Absurdly, I felt like crying. After biting my lip to stop it trembling, I picked up my bag and tucked it under my arm. 'If I get married, I want to choose a wedding dress with my mum.'

Beverley staggered back, and I realised I'd said 'if', but it clearly hadn't registered. 'But your mum hardly ever goes out,' she said.

'She'd make the effort, for me.' I hated having to explain Mum to her yet again. 'Or, we could order something online for me to try on at home.'

Her mouth opened and closed. 'But… Sam said you were happy for *me* to make it.'

'I hadn't thought it through properly. I suppose I was trying to please you both, but I'd really like my mum to be more involved.' I got up to leave. 'I'm sorry, Beverley.'

Her face hardened. 'You're not good enough for him, you know.' She rolled up the magazine, as if planning to hit me with it. 'He should have stayed with that girl he met at university. She was a model, you know.'

'*Aspiring* model, you said.' It was childish, but her words felt like darts, pricking my skin.

'Don't get me wrong, Meg.' She stretched out a wavering arm. 'You're a *lovely* girl, and we adore you being part of our family, but Sam could have had anyone he wanted.'

'And yet he chose me.' I wasn't even sure I believed that any more, or why I was bothering to argue, but it suddenly felt as if Andrea was standing in the room with us.

'And I'm very happy for you both.' Beverley was over-enunciating now. 'I just wish you were a *little* bit more…' She waggled her hand, as if trying to conjure the right word.

'A little bit more what, Beverley?' My voice shook. I felt as if I'd entered a stranger's house. A horrible stranger, with bad make-up.

'*Devoted*,' she said, and smacked her lips with apparent satisfaction.

'Devoted?'

'Do you love him, Meg?'

I stared at her. 'This is getting silly.' I began to back away. 'You've been drinking. I shouldn't have come.'

'Just answer the question.'

'We're supposed to be getting married, aren't we?'

'And yet you haven't got round to organising anything.'

I stopped moving. 'I haven't had time, that's all,' I said. 'And you *wanted* to help.'

'You don't like any of my suggestions.'

'That's… not true,' I said weakly. 'I like Studley Grange.'

'You pooh-poohed that display I liked at the Chelsea Flower Show, when I suggested something similar for the tables at the reception.' She pronounced it *reshepshun*.

'Only because I don't like lilies.' There'd been lilies on my granny's coffin, and ever since, I'd associated them with funerals. 'They remind me of death.'

'Charming,' huffed Beverley, as though she'd invented lilies. 'I had them at *my* wedding.'

'I've nothing against anyone having lilies at their wedding. I just don't want them at mine.' I wondered how long she'd been waiting to get all this off her chest – whether she'd said any of it to Sam. 'And I don't want to learn a wedding dance to Ed Sheeran, and I really don't want a harpist. I know I said I did, when I was sixteen, but I really don't any more.'

Beverley was squinting at me, as if I'd sprouted a beard. 'What's wrong with that harpist I tracked down? She won *Italy's Got Talent*, for heaven's sake. Or was it Germany?' She tapped her forehead with the rolled-up magazine. 'She's definitely got talent, love. You could do a lot worse.'

You've just told me I'm not good enough for Sam.

'What's going on in here then?' Neil strode in, carrying the scent of sawdust and linseed oil. 'Hello, Meg, love,' he said. 'You girls talking weddings?' His gaze slid from me to Beverley and back. 'It's a bit dark in here.' He crossed to the window and rasped the curtains open. 'Shall I get us something to eat?' He seemed totally oblivious to the tension swilling about. 'Bev's stopped cooking, except on Sundays, but I could rustle up some ham sandwiches.'

He smiled amiably, as Beverley studied the hastily unrolled magazine, seeming unbothered by the empty wine bottle and glass, and screwed up fabric on the floor. Maybe he was used to his wife's drinking. Maybe she often had outbursts. I realised I had no idea about the true state of their marriage, and suddenly didn't want to.

'Actually, I was just going,' I said.

'But you've only just got here.' Neil's smile faltered, and I wondered how he knew I'd only just got there if he'd been busy in his shed. Maybe Beverley had a point, and he'd been in there watching the house, waiting for her to go to bed before he came out.

'I've… got plans,' I said, and before either of them could respond, I hurried out, slamming the front door behind me, feeling as if I'd had a lucky escape – though from what, I couldn't have said.

Chapter Sixteen

As soon as I got home, I sent Sam a message, asking him to call me, still reeling from my encounter with Beverley. He didn't reply, even though I could see he'd read it.

I sent another. *We need to talk. NOW.*

While I waited for him to reply, I turned the television on and off again, sat on the sofa, then got up and paced round the living room. Should I tell Sam about the kiss first? I'd never been good at keeping secrets, even blurting to Mum once what I'd got her for Christmas, when she'd teasingly asked.

I remembered Cassie saying 'She'd be starting married life on a lie' when Tilly had jokingly suggested I have a fling with Nathan, and pressed my knuckles into my eyes until stars danced behind my lids.

Calling the wedding off over the phone seemed too drastic, but telling him I'd kissed another man was no better. Either way, his cycle challenge would be ruined, and he'd be less likely to forgive me for that than anything else.

Maybe I should wait until he got home.

Flopping back on the sofa, I picked up my phone and clicked into Facebook. A couple of new photos had been posted – one of Sam cycling past a field of sunflowers that morning, with the caption *Bligny-sur-Ouche here we come! Our most challenging ride so far*, and another, a couple of hours ago, sitting at a restaurant table surrounded by smiling faces. He was probably in his hotel room now, having an early night, and on impulse I called his number, a tide of sickness rising inside me at the thought of what I might say. My gaze filmed with tears as I listened to the phone ring and ring, and I'd just convinced myself he must be asleep, and I was being selfish by calling to unburden myself, when he finally picked up.

'Hello?'

His voice was filled with laughter, as though he'd been in the middle of a joke, and I heard the sounds of a restaurant or bar in the background. *So much for being in bed.*

'Sorry for calling, Sam, but I needed to talk to you.' I didn't sound like myself, but he apparently didn't notice.

'You wouldn't believe the climb we did today, Meggle!' He sounded drunk. 'It's a good job I trained hard. Some of the guys can't feel their thighs tonight.'

Ribald shouts and laughter greeted his comment, and I recognised Chris's voice. 'Someone wants to feel your thighs tonight, mate.' Followed by female laughter: flirtatious laughter. *George.*

'You didn't tell me there was a woman in the group.' *Not what I'd meant to say.* 'I saw her in the photo.'

'Georgie-Porgy, pudding and pie, kissed a boy and made him cry,' Sam sang, in a high, girly voice. More laughter erupted.

'The bakery's sold and I'm going to be running it,' I said baldly. I'd never liked drunk Sam. He became belligerent, and I was suddenly reminded of Beverley and her hateful comments. 'And your mum doesn't think I'm good enough for you.'

Silence swelled at the other end – at least, from Sam. The rest of the group were now singing, 'One man went to mow, went to mow a meadow.' I doubted they could find their hotel rooms right now, let alone ride a bike, and it was barely ten o'clock in France.

'What has she said?'

'That you should have stayed with your model girlfriend in Edinburgh.'

'For fuck's sake.' Sam only swore when he'd had too much beer. 'I can't deal with this right now, Meg. I need to get to bed.'

More laughter, and Chris's voice again. 'Whose bed though?'

I suddenly hated Chris. He'd pushed for Sam to do the challenge in the first place, but Chris was single and could do whatever he liked.

'The man's giving you the wedding of your dreams, so you can't begrudge him a few days pedalling through France,' he'd said at the start of their training, even though I hadn't said a word in protest.

Was that why Sam had proposed?

'Would you have stayed in Edinburgh if Andrea hadn't broken up with you?'

'Why are you raking that up now?' he said. 'I've no idea what would have happened if Andrea hadn't broken up with me, but she did.' My breath caught. It was the first time he'd admitted their break up wasn't mutual. 'Meg?'

I eased out a shaky breath. 'Did you come back to me on the rebound?'

'OK, I'm not doing this.' His voice was low now, and sounded clenched. 'We'll talk when I get back.'

Except, he'd have forgotten our conversation by morning – he never remembered anything he'd said while drunk. 'Sam, wait…'

He rang off before I could say anything else, and I wept frustrated tears as I went outside and watered the garden. He hadn't even commented about the bakery – probably hadn't heard me – and I had to resist an urge to call Cassie or Tilly and ask them what I should do.

This was something I had to work out for myself, and my mind swung back and forth over everything that had happened that day until finally, the noise from next door as the twins wielded lightsabres and yelled, 'May the force be with poo!' drove me back inside.

Emotionally exhausted, I put together a salad, which I ate with a toasted cheese sandwich in the kitchen and, slightly restored, I sat in the granddad chair and checked my emails, a flicker of excitement igniting when I saw that the solicitor had sent over the documents for me to read, and an invitation to drop by the office to sign off the following afternoon. I read through them twice, barely taking it all in the first time, beyond the sight of my name as the manager of the Old Bakery in Seashell Cove – but it all looked fine. It was just a shame there was no clue as to who the buyer was. I'd have loved to be able to thank him personally, but presumably, whoever he was, he knew how much it meant to me, and that was enough.

On impulse, I emailed Alice Denby with an update and asked if she could thank the buyer on my behalf, perhaps on her next show. Then – in spite of my intention to go to bed – I googled Nathan Walsh, and found some links to a couple of features in the *Telegraph*, about little known travel destinations. There was a tiny photo of him in profile, and my heart gave a flutter as I studied the angle of his face, wishing he'd turn so I could see what was in his eyes, or – better still – that I could dive into the photo and see what he was seeing.

One of the places he'd written about was a mysterious 'Crooked Forest' in Western Poland, with four hundred pine trees all growing with a ninety-degree bend at the base, and another was about the indigenous people of Pakistan's Rumbur Valley, who lived without electricity, phones, and newspapers, and were known for throwing harvest celebrations. Another link took me to a series he'd written for a construction magazine, featuring unusual homes around the world, such as a soccer-ball shaped house in Japan that had been built to withstand an earthquake. It was fascinating reading. Nathan had a way with words that drew the reader in.

Finally, my eyelids grew heavy, and the room darkened as the sky outside deepened to indigo. After locking up the house, I stood for a moment in the stillness of the hallway, letting the silence settle. It was nice not having to watch Sam do a hundred press-ups or squat lunges before getting into bed, or listen to him talk about work, which he often did before falling asleep. It wasn't that I hadn't been sympathetic to the problems of costing a job, and difficulties with documents submitted by designers, but he tended to use 'quantity surveyor'-type phrases like 'The QS compiled the BoQ' and 'Evaluated as a variation, in terms of the contract condition', which I didn't understand, however much I'd tried.

I didn't bother turning any lights on, feeling my way to the bathroom to brush my teeth, and after I'd undressed, I turned the photo of Sam and me to the wall, got into bed, and fell into a deep and dreamless sleep.

I rose just after six and drove to the bakery, nourishing the spark of excitement that had ignited the minute I opened my eyes. I was determined to hold on to it, and to not think about Sam for at least a few hours.

Light from the morning's sunrise poked fingers of gold into the water at Seashell Cove, and streaks of orange and apricot flared across the sky. I opened the car window, and breathed in the warm, salty air, a surprising feeling of well-being washing over me.

Big Steve was standing by his rust-coloured Fiat when I drew up, as if struggling to motivate himself to get in the car and drive to work.

His face brightened when he saw me. 'Someone looks like the cat that got the proverbial,' he observed, as I tried to get out without unfastening my seat belt, lolling towards the ground. He chuckled, and came over to help. 'Has the mouse been playing while the cat's away?' He waggled his eyebrows. 'Seen your gorgeous estate agent, by any chance?'

'Don't you start,' I said, my voice perkier than his comment warranted as I stepped out of the car.

'Ooh, so there is something going on?'

'Steve!' I retrieved my bag, trying to hide a blush.

Steve's barrel-like tummy wobbled with laughter under his Tesco's shirt. 'Touchy subject, hmm?'

'I won't tell you my good news, if you don't stop.'

He gave a theatrical gasp and pressed his fingertips to his mouth. 'A showbiz agent's been in touch and wants you to present your own show.' He flung his arm out. 'Meg's Kitchen,' he said, in an announcer's voice. 'Meg Larson chats to a member of the public, while baking their favourite cake. This week…' He made a sweeping motion with his hand. 'Nathan Walsh, agent extraordinaire. His favourite cake…' He thought for a second. 'Something dark and sinful, with cherries.'

I giggled, anticipating Steve's reaction when he heard the real news. 'He's not James Bond,' I said, fishing my keys out of my bag. 'He's not even an estate agent, he's just helping his brother out.' I smiled. 'I do like the name Meg's Kitchen though. And the sound of the show.'

'You'd ace it,' he said, following me to the bakery door, instead of back to his car. 'So, what's your amazing news?'

I let myself into the kitchen, heart racing with anticipation. 'Come in,' I said, twirling round to face him, like a hostess welcoming a dinner guest.

He gingerly stepped over the threshold, eyes darting from side to side as if suspecting an ambush. 'What gives, Larson?'

I flung my bag down and went to stand behind the wooden table, smoothing my hands across its worn surface. 'How would you like to work here?'

Steve's face gave a little quiver. 'You mean…?' He pressed a hand to his cheek. 'Are you saying what I think you're saying?'

A smile spread over my face. This must have been how Nathan had felt telling me the day before. Except there wouldn't be any kissing with Big Steve. 'What do you think I'm saying?'

'I… don't know.' His gaze flicked round in wonderment, now, as though finding himself in Narnia. 'That you've talked Mr Moseley's brother into letting you continue running the place at a loss, and you need my bread-making skills to help you win over the public?'

I could see he was trying not to get his hopes up, even as he was starting to believe it. 'Half right.' I was enjoying myself. 'The bit about me needing your bread-making skills.'

This time his gasp was genuine. 'Tell me you're not joking?'

'I'm not joking.' I filled him in, including that he'd be paid a proper salary thanks to my bakery angel – as I'd whimsically started to think of him – and while it wouldn't be more than he got at the supermarket, he'd save money on travel costs.

'I love this guy, whoever he is.' Steve was moist-eyed by the time I'd finished explaining. 'I didn't think this sort of thing happened in real life.'

'Me neither.' We were silent for a second, contemplating my good fortune. 'How soon can you start?'

He moved to the oven, arms outstretched like a zombie. 'How about now?'

'Really?' I said.

'Sadly, no.' He pirouetted around. 'I'll have to give notice at the big T, but I've loads of holiday due, so they might let me go right away. There'll be plenty of applicants queuing to take my place there,' he said, as if he thought I might be about to protest. 'And, if you reopen before I've worked my notice, I could always bake a batch before I go in to work.'

I grinned. 'I'd like that very much, if it wouldn't be too much for you.'

Grabbing his proffered elbow, we did a dignified Highland fling, picking up pace until we were slumped over the table, breathless and panting, and complaining of having a stitch.

'Going on that programme was the best thing you ever did, Meg,' Steve said, hand pressed to his chest, as if to steady his heart. 'I won't let you down. Or Mr Moseley, god rest his soul.'

'I know you won't.'

He gave me a tight hug that smelt of sleep and yeast. 'Thank you, thank you.'

'Your family won't mind you working right next door?'

'They know I'm wasted at Tesco's.' He released me from his clasp, and swiped the back of his hand across his forehead. 'And they'll have free loaves on tap, so what's not to like?'

'They can make sausage sandwiches,' I said, a touch hysterically, and we performed another jig, before he realised what time it was and let out a yelp.

'Better go, or I'll be sacked before I can hand in my notice.' He rushed to the door, and I was glad he wanted to do the right thing, and not leave his boss at the supermarket in the lurch.

'I'll talk to you soon,' I called after him.

When he'd gone, tooting his horn as he drove off, I went through to the shop and looked around. Sunshine pushed through the window and spilt across the counter, and I imagined the shelves brimming with golden loaves, and the display cabinet full of cakes, and a queue of customers trailing to the door. I couldn't wait to get started, and hoped that, wherever he was, Mr Moseley approved.

Chapter Seventeen

After ringing the local wholesalers and placing an order to be delivered later that morning, I closed and locked the back door, to minimise the temptation to look out for Nathan, and opened the window instead to let in some air.

Still buzzing from Big Steve's reaction, I cleaned down the surfaces and set to work, baking a lime and pistachio cake for the café, and a date and walnut loaf to take to Mum's. If she was feeling better, I wanted to ask if she'd take on the accounts for the bakery, and if Kath was around I was hoping she'd agree to come and work with me. The date and walnut cake was a bribe for Kath, as it was her favourite. Not that I thought she'd need any persuading.

As I worked, I sang along to an Abba playlist, and whenever a negative thought threatened to interrupt the flow, I sang louder. It was hard to be miserable while singing 'Dancing Queen'. Providing Nathan stayed away (had his 'Good luck, Meg' been a farewell?) and I didn't think about Sam (how much time had he spent alone with George?) or Beverley (did she actually hate me?) or Sadie (why had she decided not to say anything, when she thought the world of Sam?), I'd be fine.

When I'd finished and cleared everything away, and signed for the delivery of fresh ingredients, the cakes had cooled. I boxed them up, still humming 'Does Your Mother Know', and drove to the café to drop off the lime and pistachio cake.

''Ow the bleedin' 'ell do you spell pisstatcheeo?' Gwen said, acting as if Dickens wasn't rolling about in the middle of the sun-warmed floor, being fussed over by twin girls with waist-length plaits. 'You'd better write it on the board, before you bugger orf.'

After complying with her sweetly worded request, pretending I hadn't noticed Dickens slip back behind the counter, I drove to Bray's Property and Commercial Solicitors in Kingsbridge, trying not to think about what Sam would say if he knew I was doing it without him. Words like 'reckless' and 'haven't thought it through' came to mind, but I'd given him an opportunity to say something the night before, and he hadn't taken it. Anyway, I didn't need Sam's permission, *or* his approval. He hadn't asked for mine when he took on his cycling challenge. And, anyway, we had bigger things to talk about when he got back than me signing some documents without him knowing.

I eyed myself firmly in the rear-view mirror and noticed I had a dusting of flour on my forehead. Once I'd parked, I brushed it off, and nervously tidied my hair with my hands, hoping my fifties-style rockabilly dress, patterned with lemons, didn't make me look frivolous.

In Mr Bray's light-filled office, we went through the documents together, and after he'd checked I had no further questions (no, he couldn't reveal the buyer, even if I said pretty please, but would certainly pass on my heartfelt gratitude), I signed the employment contract, and once he'd taken my hand in an iron clamp, and wished me all the best, I emerged on the sunlit pavement, feeling as if I really had won the lottery.

Wanting to mark the occasion in some way, I treated myself to an ice cream, which made me think of Freya, and how furious she must be with Don for withdrawing his offer (I almost felt sorry for him, having to deal with the fallout). After browsing a homeware shop, and treating myself to some heart-shaped cookie cutters, I drove back to Salcombe with the radio at full volume to blast any thoughts of Nathan from my head.

Arriving at Mum's twenty minutes later, the first thing that struck me was that her bedroom curtains were still drawn. I'd have thought she'd have recovered enough by now to be out of bed – her text had been so chirpy – and a slight disquiet rose, but before I could approach the front door, Kath came up the road, pushing the sort of all-terrain pram I knew cost an absolute fortune. When Mum had gone into her frenzied phase of pre-baby excitement she'd started emailing me links to the Mothercare website, with comments such as, *Prams didn't have detachable baby seats when you were little!* and *What's the difference between a pram, a pushchair, a buggy and a stroller, they all look the same?!*

'He's here again,' Kath said, and for a second I thought she meant Milo and peeped obligingly into the pram where he was sleeping, long lashes kissing his cheeks.

'He's lovely,' I said, then realised Kath was angling her beehive at a car, parked a little way down from Mum's house: a grey hatchback I didn't recognise.

'Obviously trying to be discreet,' Kath said, leaning over to adjust the hood to shield Milo, her pillowy bosom almost escaping her baggy vest top. 'It's only because I'm a nosy mare, or I wouldn't have noticed it,' she said, straightening. 'That and the fact that it's been there all night, and your mum's not answering the door.'

'All night?' Startled, I looked from the car to the house, with its closed curtains like shut eyes. 'Have you seen him?'

Kath shook her head, her mouth turned down. 'I popped round last night for a chat, and to see how she was but there was no answer, even though I could hear music coming from upstairs.'

Upstairs? Music? A man? I didn't know where to start. 'You heard music?'

Kath's flush deepened to crimson. 'I might have had a peep through the letterbox, but only because I had visions of Rose lying at the foot of the stairs in a pool of blood. And because I really needed a chat.'

I looked at Kath properly and noticed the whites of her eyes were red, and she wasn't wearing her false eyelashes, and her baggy trousers and vest top looked more like pyjamas. 'What's happened?' Even her beehive wasn't secured properly. I could see pins poking out. 'Kath?'

Her chin wobbled, and she bent over the pram again, but when she straightened, tears had pooled in her eyes. 'Freya's gone.'

I stared. 'Gone?'

'She's left Don. And Milo.' She glanced at the baby again, a tear spilling down her cheek. 'Can you believe that girl?'

Actually, I could. 'But why?'

'She was bloody furious with me, because I had a word with Don about buying her the bakery. I said it wasn't on, that it should be yours, and that Freya's got a son to take care of, and that she'd lose interest after five minutes, like she does with everything, and she doesn't even like bloody ice cream.'

Another glance at Milo, the tears falling faster than she could brush them away. 'Apparently Don withdrew his offer and told her she should wait a while before making any decisions about her future. I didn't think he had it in him, but Freya went bloody ape. Came storming round first thing with Milo, and said she's going to live in Marbella, she's got a friend out there, and divorce Don and take him to the cleaner's, and she's never coming back.'

I swallowed. Even for Freya, this seemed extreme. 'Do you think she means it?'

Kath nodded. 'I think she does. She said I can bring up Milo, if I bloody love him so much. She actually said that, Meg, as if she didn't love him at all.' A sob erupted and she pressed a hand to her mouth. 'How can she not love her own baby?'

'Oh, Kath.' Shifting the cake box I was holding, I gave her a one-armed hug. 'I should never have said anything to you about Don putting in an offer.'

'Don't be daft.' She sniffed and squeezed my hand, not taking her eyes off Milo. 'I'd have found out at some point,' she said. 'I just don't know what's wrong with that girl. I've done my best, but I think there's something missing, you know? Inside her. Maybe she's like her dad, or it's to do with losing him at such a young age, I don't know, but I've obviously failed her terribly.'

'No you *haven't.*' I was almost crying myself. 'Maybe you're right, and Freya's looking for something she hasn't found yet, but it's not your fault, Kath, you've been a brilliant parent.' I peppered her hair with kisses. 'You'll always be my second mum.'

'Oh, you.' She gave a watery smile as she fished a tissue out of her trouser (pyjama?) pocket and passed it over her face. 'You're a credit to yours.'

We looked at baby Milo, sleeping on, blissfully unaware of the unfolding drama that looked set to shape his life.

'What are you going to do?' I asked her.

Her shoulders lifted. 'Help take care of him, as if he was my own. He's got my blood in him, somewhere. I've got to hope that means something, and Don's a good man,' she said. 'He called me after Freya walked out, to tell me what had happened. He's coming round later, to talk, but he's already said I can have as much access to Milo as I want. Apparently, his younger sister's never had kids and wants to be involved, so he's already asked her to stay.'

'He doesn't think Freya will be back?' I remembered the way he'd looked at her at the bakery. 'He must be devastated.'

'He is, but more for Milo,' said Kath. 'He actually sounded more angry with her than anything.' She sniffed and dabbed at her nose. 'Whatever was said, I think he's finally seen her in a different light.'

'I can't help thinking it's partly my fault.'

Kath shook her head. 'I'm just sorry the offer for the bakery's fallen through.' Her voice was thick with tears. 'That's my fault, for sticking my oar in.'

I realised she couldn't have spoken to Mum since I'd texted her my news. 'Actually, Kath, another buyer came forward.' I pressed her close. 'I'm going to be running the bakery, and I was going to ask if you'd like to come and work there.'

She twisted to look at me, a smile bursting over her face. 'I'm so pleased for you, Meg, that's the best news I've had all week.' Her watering eyes flicked to Milo. 'I've a feeling I'm going to be needed a lot more here, so I might have to work around that.'

'That's fine, I can take on someone else too,' I said, remembering Valerie Jones from the café saying she'd like to work at the bakery if it ever reopened. I thrust the cake box at Kath. 'I made you a bribery cake.'

'You never have to bribe me, love.' Her eyes widened. 'Is it date and walnut?'

'Obviously.'

Milo was starting to stir, as if he'd heard the words date and walnut and wanted a slice of cake.

Kath released a sigh. 'Bless him, he's just done a poo.' I wasn't sure how she knew, but her knowledge seemed instinctive. She bent to tuck the cake into the basket beneath the pram and, straightening, cast a glance at Mum's bedroom window. 'You'd better go and find out what she's been up to.'

I looked back at the car, sorry to see it was still there. 'I'm not sure I want to.'

Kath patted my arm. 'You might want to let yourself in the back door, if you've got your key,' she said, making me suspect she'd considered doing the same thing. 'I've a feeling you're going to need the element of surprise to find out what's going on.'

Chapter Eighteen

As I walked round the side of the house, after promising Kath I'd call if I needed her, my bag vibrated. I pulled out my phone to see there was a message from Mum, but before I could open it my phone sprang to life.

Nathan. Heart leaping like a salmon, I answered. 'Hello?'

'Hi, you.'

His voice, warm and gentle, sent a spark of heat surging through me. Weak-limbed, I dropped onto a stripy sunlounger outside Mum's living-room window, noting the blind was closed so I couldn't see inside. 'Hi,' I said, striving for a businesslike tone. 'How are you?'

'I was wondering whether you'd signed the paperwork yet.'

'A couple of hours ago.' A smile unfurled. 'It's all systems go.'

'That's great, Meg.' His voice warmed further. 'Congratulations, again.'

'I've told Big Steve, and he's going to hand in his notice at Tesco's.'

'When will you reopen?'

'I was thinking this Saturday. I can't see any reason to wait.'

'It's going to be great, Meg, I know it.'

'Will you come over?' I said, hoping I didn't sound desperate. 'I mean, to see how it's going?' Sweat dampened my armpits. 'You can have a free slice of cake.'

There was a longish pause. 'Sounds tempting, but I'm actually leaving on Monday, so I'll have a lot to do,' he said. 'I'm not needed here now Charlie's mum's back, and the editor at the *Telegraph*'s given the go-ahead for a series called "Cool and Unusual Places to see in Ireland". I'm heading to a micro-valley, on the side of a mountain.'

'Oh.' A sour taste hit my throat. 'That's sounds fun.' *Hadn't he said he was done with travelling?*

'The itchy feet are back.' It was as though he could hear my thoughts.

'It's probably for the best,' I said in a perky voice. 'I mean, you might have ended up becoming an actual estate agent if you'd stayed any longer.'

'I'd never stoop that low.'

I laughed, though I felt like weeping. 'Well, I hope you have a good time,' I said. 'Maybe you could pop by to say goodbye before you leave.' *Let it go, Meg. You sound like a lovesick teen.*

'Maybe I will,' he said, after another brief pause.

'Uncle Nafan, where are my strangled eggs?' It was Charlie, in the background.

'Strangled eggs?' I said.

'I make the best ones, apparently.' I could tell he was smiling. 'He keeps asking when we can go back and see the witch and the cat at the café.'

In spite of everything, a giggle broke free. 'I'd better not tell Gwen.'

'He already did, apparently.' Nathan's voice was laced with humour. 'He said he'd asked her if she could make a spell for the cat's eye to come back, and she said no, but she could turn a car into a driveway. He didn't get it, bless him.'

'Gwen's sense of humour's an acquired taste.'

'UNCLE NAFAN!' roared Charlie. 'I've broughted you the eggs.'

'I'd better go, or they'll be strangled all over the floor,' said Nathan. 'Take care, Meg.'

'You too.' I sat for a moment when he'd gone, smile fading as I pictured him in his brother's kitchen with Charlie, making scrambled eggs, and was overcome with a sense of loss for all the things we'd never share.

Breathing deeply, I focused on the lavender bushes fringing the path to the tree at the end of the garden, where I'd once buried a time capsule that wasn't to be opened for a hundred years. I couldn't even remember what was inside, or whether it was still there, but I remembered Freya calling me a loser when I told her what I'd done.

As the urge to cry waned, I got up and went to Mum's back door and inserted my key in the lock. The door tended to stick, so I shouldered it gently until it gave, and stepped into the kitchen, which was small and bright, with a small oak table in the middle, and pots of herbs jostling for space on the windowsill.

Immediately, I sensed something was different. The air smelt different, and not just because the windows were shut, trapping the heat inside. The surfaces were scattered with crumbs, which was strange. Mum kept the kitchen scrupulously clean, and had done since finding a mouse one year, living off some cereal I'd spilt on the floor. The tap was dripping in the stainless steel sink and I turned it off, casting my eyes around. There were two plates on the side; the vintage, botanic-themed plates she'd bought off eBay, and only used on special occasions.

And what was that smell? It was like… *takeaway.* Chinese food. Mum and I used to treat ourselves on Friday evenings and, occasionally, I'd still pick up a meal for two from the nearby Chinese restaurant while Sam was out training.

I lifted the lid of the bin and, sure enough, there were several empty foil cartons inside. Surely Mum wouldn't be eating a takeaway if she had the flu? Kath had been right. Mum was seeing a man and didn't want me to know.

There was a sound upstairs and I froze like a mime artist. It had sounded like a yawn. A man's yawn, followed by Mum, speaking softly. As swift as a cat burglar, I slipped into the hall, back pressed against the wall. Shuffling along to the foot of the stairs, I peered up at the landing, shaded pink by the sun filtering through the curtains. The door to my old bedroom was slightly ajar, as it always was, a thin beam of daylight angled across the wall. Whoever was up there was definitely in Mum's room.

Bedsprings creaked, and Mum's footsteps padded out and along the landing to the bathroom. There was the sound of water running, and Mum humming as she brushed her teeth. It was a sound I'd heard often over the years, but now it was somehow spooky and out of time. I felt like a ghost, or as if I'd never existed – or as if I'd stepped into someone else's house.

Unsure whether to slip away, or make my presence known, I dithered, eyes skimming the cluster of photos on the wall, and was about to ease open the front door and make my escape, when I heard a muffled scream at the top of the stairs.

Twirling round, I saw Mum, wrapped in a towel, a hand pressed to her throat.

'Meg!' Her voice sounded strangled and panicky. 'I didn't hear you come in.'

She cast a terrified look at her bedroom door, as if warning whoever was behind it to stay put, and hurried downstairs, clutching the edges of her fluffy blue towel. 'I left you a message,' she loud-whispered, and I remembered it coming up on my phone before I'd answered Nathan's call.

'I know, I didn't read it,' I said. 'I mean, I forgot.' I couldn't stop looking at her face. Although blurry with panic, she looked about ten years younger. Her creamy skin was flushed rose-pink, her hair was messy at the back, and there was a light in her eyes I hadn't seen for… I didn't think I'd *ever* seen that particular light. It wasn't that she'd never looked happy before. She'd often told me how happy I made her, and the evidence had been in her smile. In spite of the tough times and tears – when she'd lost her job, and had to gather every ounce of courage to step outside, weeping on Kath's shoulder – I'd seen her helpless with laughter at times, and with joy in her eyes, and content at her computer as she sorted through her clients' accounts. Her face had exploded with excitement and happiness when I'd announced my engagement, but this… I wasn't sure I even recognised this look. My mind shied away from the word sex, though it was clear she'd had a man in her bed. Was she… was it possible she'd fallen in love?

'I asked you to come round later,' she was saying, glancing over her shoulder, as if whoever was up there might suddenly show up. 'We were going to talk to you over dinner. I – we – were trying to find the right words only, I don't know if I'm ready, I mean…' She reached out, and gripped my arm. 'Oh, Meg, the most wonderful thing has happened,' she said, as if she couldn't hold the words in a second longer. 'I can hardly believe it myself.'

There were tiny crescents of tears in her eyes, and my throat tightened in response. If she was in love – and what else could it be? – then it was *odd*, and unexpected, based on everything I knew about Mum, but how could I not be happy for her, if it was having such a strong effect? Except… it was so *new*. How could she feel this strongly so quickly? She couldn't have been seeing him long, or I'd have known, and although I believed in love at first sight, she hadn't had a relationship for years.

She might have fallen for someone who didn't have her best interests at heart, or was taking advantage of her, and how had they even met? Online dating was the only option, unless Kath had managed to drag her out… but Kath was as in the dark as I'd been.

My thoughts ground to a halt. 'I take it you didn't have the flu then?'

'Oh, Meg, I'm so sorry I lied.' She sounded traumatised, but before I could say I was only – sort of – teasing, as I tried to come to terms with how *well* she looked, she added, 'Although, at first, I was so shocked I was physically sick in the toilet. Isn't that awful? And then… well, I desperately needed some time to get my head around it all.'

Wait… *what?* Why would falling in love make her physically sick? Alarm swelled in my chest. 'Who is he, Mum?' I scoured her face. 'Why are you being so secretive?' A thought struck. 'Is he much younger than you?' I tried to picture it. 'Mum, he's not younger than me, is he?' I had an image of a waxed, broad-chested, tanned Adonis strolling out of her bedroom, with lustrous dark hair and big thighs.

'No, no, nothing like that,' she said, trying to laugh, but I had a feeling she almost wished that were the case.

'He's not someone's husband?' I whispered. Surely she wasn't going down that road again? 'Is he already married?'

'Oh, Meg.' She was clutching her towel again, biting her bottom lip, her eyes flicking around as if the right words were hiding.

'Mum, you're scaring me,' I said. 'I only came over to see how you were and to talk about the bakery, to ask if you'd do the accounts. I'd pay you, obviously, and…' I shook my head, as she gave me a blank stare. 'What the heck's happening? Kath said she heard music—'

'Kath?' Mum looked puzzled as if she'd never heard of her.

'She was worried, she looked through the letterbox.'

'It must have been Elgar,' Mum said tenderly. 'His cello concerto.'

'Is that his name?'

'What?'

'The man you're seeing.'

Confusion passed over her face. 'He's a composer.'

'The man you're seeing?'

'*What?*'

'You said he's a composer.'

'*Elgar's* a composer.'

'Oh, *that* Elgar.'

'Meg, you're not making any sense.'

'*You're* not making any sense.'

As we stared at each other, there was a groan of floorboards above. My gaze moved past Mum's shoulder as a man materialised, taking the stairs slowly, one hand on the banister as if worried he might fall down.

'No!' Mum spun round, reacting as though she'd seen a ghost instead of a medium-height smiling man with grey, tousled hair, thankfully dressed in a blue-and-white checked shirt and dark-blue jeans.

As he reached us, he was illuminated by a flare of sunlight through the square of glass in the front door, and I saw that his eyes were marine-blue, framed by laughter lines, and looked weirdly familiar. His skin was lightly weathered, and he looked to be Mum's age – maybe a couple of years older – and I decided there and then that I liked the look of him.

'It's OK, Mum, you don't have to hide him away,' I said, smiling. 'I'm Rose's daughter, Meg.'

He was looking at me with the oddest expression. I was briefly reminded of Nathan, the day before, breaking his news at the café. 'I know who you are, darling girl.'

Oh, he was Irish. I'd always loved the accent, although 'darling girl' was a bit strong.

I became aware of a peculiar stillness in the hall, and that the man's voice had sounded unusually emotional. *Odd.*

'I can't begin to tell you how wonderful it is to meet you.' He said it in that same, peculiarly charged fashion and I glanced at Mum, who seemed to have been struck dumb, and looked on the verge of crying. 'She's beautiful, Rose.'

'What's going on?' My heart had started to race.

'Oh, Meg,' Mum whispered, and pressed a trembling hand over her mouth.

'Meg,' the man repeated, looking at me as if he'd had a glimpse of heaven.

'Have you two been drinking?' I remembered the glass of champagne I'd seen on the table the day before. 'It's a bit early in the day, don't you think?'

To my astonishment, Mum's face was soaked with tears. 'I was only joking,' I said, trying to laugh. I felt like I was dreaming. 'Shall I go out and come in again?'

I dragged my gaze from Mum's face to the man's, and that's when I saw it: a tiny mole by his ear, just like mine. Everything seemed to slow down.

'Meg. A beautiful name, for a beautiful girl.' The walls zoomed in as the man held out his hands, a look of tender joy in his eyes, and even before Mum spoke, I knew what she was going to say.

'Meg, this is Mike.' Her voice cracked. 'He's your father.'

Chapter Nineteen

Mum caught me as I tilted sideways, her towel sliding to the floor, and Mike grabbed a coat off the hook behind him and hurled it around her shoulders.

'I don't understand.' It came out as a whimper. 'I thought my father was dead.'

'So did I.' Mum was still weeping, but smiling through her tears at the same time, which was horribly unsettling. 'That's why I nearly had a heart attack when he called me after seeing you on the show.'

'Show?' The word caught on an involuntary in-breath. *My father.* I looked at him sideways, trying to take it in. He was alive. He was here, looking as though he was meant to be – as if he'd been here all along, and I just hadn't spotted him. As if he'd just come home from work, or back from working abroad. 'You saw the show?'

I wasn't sure the words had made it out of my mouth, but they must have done because he nodded and said, 'It was my brother, actually,' and I registered his accent again, and remembered Mum saying *Your dad was Irish, Meg. His name was Mike, and he had a mole on his cheek, just like yours.* 'He's always known about me and your ma, and how much I loved her. He's lived over here for decades, and loves the show—'

'I have an uncle?' I felt disoriented, blood galloping around my head.

Mum's arm tightened around me. 'And cousins, and a grandfather who's still alive,' she said with a shaky laugh. 'Let's sit down, and we'll tell you all about it.'

Wobbly-limbed, I watched her fasten the belt of her ancient trench coat before taking my hand and leading me into the living room where we sat on the sofa as we had so many times – only this time there was a dad in the armchair opposite, eyes pink-rimmed with emotion, his face busy as if with all the things he wanted to say.

'Why didn't you tell me as soon as you heard from him?' I looked at Mum, feeling as if my eyes were going to dissolve. 'How could you have kept it from me?'

'Oh, Meg.' She picked up my hand and massaged it between both of hers. 'I was so shocked. I needed time to come to terms with it, before we told you.' Her voice wavered. 'Mike – your dad – flew over as soon as we'd spoken on the phone, and he came right here and…' She shot him a look that made my stomach tighten. 'All the old feelings were there,' she said, her eyes swelling pools of love. 'We talked for hours and hours, there was so much to say, and Mike wanted to see all the photos I had of you, and there are loads.' She paused, and our eyes gravitated to a photo above the fireplace of me aged four, wrapped in a dressing gown, face alive with delight as I delved into a Christmas stocking. 'I showed him your first baby tooth too, and told him about you having your appendix out when you were ten, and then we were just so tired…' Her flow of words halted, and I pictured them falling into each other's arms, and no doubt from there into bed, while I'd been blundering around, fretting about Sam, and worrying that Mum was ill. 'We were desperate to tell you, but were trying to work out the best way.'

'A phone call would have been nice.'

'It was a lot for us to take in,' Mike said.

I glanced at him and saw nothing but openness and warmth in his face but even so…

'How come she thought you'd died?'

'Because that's what my fiancée told her.' I watched his face darken and fill with memories. 'The night I was driving home to tell Patricia I couldn't marry her, because I was in love with your ma, my car hit a patch of ice and went off the road.' His voice was pitched low but clear, and his gaze held tight to mine. 'I was in hospital, unconscious, when your ma tracked down my parents' number, and Patricia picked up. I think she'd guessed by then there was someone else. She told Rose I'd been fatally injured, and to never contact the family again.'

'Oh my god.' I looked at Mum, and saw fresh tears on her face. 'That's awful,' I said, brushing her cheek with my thumb. 'No wonder you hated talking about it.'

'I blamed myself,' she said huskily, and I sensed Mike making a superhuman effort to not come over and gather her up in his arms. 'He'd been with me that weekend, and was driving back from the airport.'

'And it wasn't even true.' I looked back at Mike and saw pain etched on his face.

'I didn't know what Patricia had done,' he said. 'Almost as soon as I regained consciousness, Patricia told me she was pregnant. Her parents were Catholic, so there was no question of me not doing the right thing.' He rubbed a hand over his mouth. 'I tried to call Rose once I was home, but her housemate said she she'd gone back home to Plymouth. I guessed she must have thought I'd decided to stay with Patricia when I didn't come back, and wanted nothing more to do with me. I told myself it was probably for the best.'

Seizing a distraction, I said, 'You have more children?'

Mike gave a pained little smile and shook his head. 'It turned out Patricia wasn't pregnant at all, but we were married by then.' His eyes shimmered. 'Ironically, she couldn't have children.'

Mum brushed her face with the sleeve of her coat, and took the reins of the story she'd clearly been coming to terms with over the past few days. 'When they divorced, eight years later, Mike tried to look for me, but your granny had died and we'd moved out here, and, anyway, Mike didn't even know whereabouts in Plymouth I'd lived.'

'He knew your name though, it couldn't have been that hard.'

'I figured she was happily married and wouldn't want me turning up and rocking the boat,' Mike said. 'I decided to leave the past where it was. I even remarried, but that didn't last either.' His gaze dropped for a moment. 'I never forgot your ma, and when Stuart – that's my brother – told me he'd been watching the show and saw someone who looked like a younger version of Rose, talking about not knowing her dad who'd lived in Ireland…' He shook his head, as if he couldn't quite believe it. 'When he heard your surname was Larson, he called me right away, and I knew immediately you had to be my daughter.' He paused, as if struggling to contain his emotions. 'The programme's location gave away roughly where you were, so it wasn't hard after that to find Rose.'

They exchanged watery-eyed smiles, as if the wonder of it had hit them all over again. 'If I'd any idea your ma was pregnant, wild horses wouldn't have kept me away all these years.' His eyes searched my face as if looking for signs of upset. 'I honestly didn't know about you, Meg, and I'm so sorry. For not being there, and… for everything.'

Suddenly unable to bear the intensity, I rose and lurched to the fireplace. In the mirror above my face was the colour of glue, my eyes big with shock. I thought about Sam, and felt a dull thud in my chest. He should have been with me for this, not cycling past fields of sunflowers, hundreds of miles away, while my life twisted out of shape. I looked at my hands, and saw that my nails had dug white crescents into my palms.

'Meg?' Mum's voice was hesitant. 'I know this is a lot to take in—'

'Freya's left Don, by the way.' I spun round, expecting to see Mike still in the armchair, but he'd moved to sit next to Mum, as though now he'd found her he couldn't bear to leave her side. 'She's dumped Milo on Kath.'

'What?' Although Mum blanched, she still somehow radiated happiness. It was coming off her in waves, despite her tear-streaked cheeks. 'I'll call Kath later,' she said, adjusting the hem of her coat to cover her knees. 'We haven't spoken for a couple of days.'

'I know, she's been worried about you,' I said. 'We really thought you were sick.'

Reaching out, she gently touched my wrist. 'Meg, I'm sorry, I really am, but I hope you can understand why I needed a bit of time.'

A thought catapulted into my head out of nowhere. 'It was you!' I looked at Mike, who'd risen as if to approach me. 'You bought the bakery,' I said, staring at him. It made perfect sense. As soon as he'd watched the programme and realised I was his daughter – *his daughter!* – he'd made the offer that had blown Don's out of the water. 'It was you,' I repeated. It also explained Mum's flowery text, gushing her congratulations. Her beloved Mike had made up for not being a father for thirty years by buying his new-found daughter the bakery she loved so much. 'Well, you can keep it.' I was fighting a sudden, overwhelming urge to cry. 'You can't just come waltzing back and buy me a bakery and think that makes you my dad.'

'Meg!' Mum stood too. 'It wasn't Mike,' she said. 'I'm sorry, love.'

His look of confusion told me Mum was right. 'Rose told me about that, when she got your text,' he said. 'Believe me, Meg, if I'd had the means there's nothing I'd have loved more than to buy the bakery, but I'm not that well-off, I'm afraid.' His voice bulged with sincerity. 'I used to have money, but two divorces put paid to that.' He shot Mum an apologetic smile. 'I'm not broke,' he went on, as if to reassure me. 'I told your mum, I left my sales job after the second divorce and have a little antique shop now. It's not much, but it's a living, and I like it.' He cast his gaze around the room. 'Your mum has some lovely pieces,' he said proudly. 'She's got a good eye.'

'Does he know…?' I looked at Mum and she lifted her eyebrows.

'That I don't go out much?' She nodded. 'He knows everything.' She clutched his arm and gave a giddy laugh I'd definitely not heard before. 'And he *still* loves me.'

Love? My head swam. 'How come you were so thrilled about the bakery, when you wanted me to give up work a week ago?'

Her eyes flicked to Mike and back. 'Because it's your dream come true,' she said.

'But you told me that babies were what life was all about.'

'They are, of course.' Mum's face quivered. 'But Mike made me see that the bakery's important to you too, and it's not fair to put pressure on you to have a baby just because I want to be a grandma.' She really had told him everything. 'In a way, that bakery *is* your baby. But not as cuddly.' She gave another swirl of laughter, and squashed her cheek against Mike's arm, and seeing the eighteen-year-old version of Mum superimposed over the one I was used to, was unnerving. I had the feeling again that I'd somehow stepped back in time.

'I hear you're getting married in a few months' time,' Mike said. 'I can't wait to meet… Sam, is that right?' He looked to Mum for confirmation.

'Mike could walk you down the aisle,' she said, eyes glazing over as if picturing it. 'Won't that be wonderful?'

I looked at them standing side by side, like a team – like parents – and something close to panic started to build. It was too much, being presented with a dad like this. Mum and I had managed fine all these years, on our own. I wasn't sure I wanted a dad, and I didn't need one to walk me down the aisle.

'He's got some lovely photos to show you,' Mum was saying now, indicating a phone on the coffee table, next to her Edwardian silver teapot, and Mike smiled and scooped it up. 'He has a lovely little spaniel called Lennie.'

She took the phone off him, as if it was the most natural thing in the world, and held it out for me to see. I glanced at a liver-coloured dog with a tennis ball in its mouth, wearing a fluorescent green collar. 'And this is your cousin Ellen, she's a year younger than you, but don't you think you have the same eyes?'

I looked at the young woman on the screen, but it was as if she was a different species, and I didn't know how to respond. My brain felt ready to explode and I'd forgotten how to breathe properly.

'Anything you want to know about Mike, just ask,' Mum said. 'He's got a bit of arthritis in his left hip, he does a lot of walking, there's some lovely walks near where he lives apparently, and I've recommended a supplement. For his hip. Oh, and he reads a lot, mostly autobiographies, and he lives above his antique shop, which looks just lovely, there's a picture here somewhere, and he likes quiz shows—'

'I have to go,' I cut in. 'I told Kath I'd let her know you were OK.'

'Oh, Meg, you can't leave!' Looking horrified, Mum dropped the phone and grabbed my hand. 'We've so much to talk about, and your dad wants to know everything about you.' Her eyes were imploring. 'I'd planned for us all to have dinner, and was going to suggest you stay the night in your old room, and we could go out for breakfast tomorrow, and maybe show Mike the sights.'

It was as if she was trying to wind back the clock, to when I was a little girl, so my dad could read me a bedtime story and we could go to the beach together.

'It's too soon, Mum.'

'But we've wasted so much time already.' She looked ready to cry again. 'We've a lot to make up.'

A crushing tiredness descended, mingled with the sort of sadness I'd felt earlier, but this time it was for Mum, for all the time she'd missed with my father – and, maybe, a little bit for myself, too.

'I know, Mum, really, I understand, I do, but... I've got a lot to do,' I said. 'I'm reopening the bakery on Saturday and need to get organised.'

'But, Meg, this is much more important.' She appealed to Mike, who was watching me shrewdly as if he understood.

He laid a hand on her shoulder. 'There's plenty of time, Rose,' he said quietly. 'I think Meg needs a bit of space to let it all sink in.'

'But she'll be going back to an empty house.'

'Honestly, Mum, I'll be fine.' I stuck my palm out. 'It was nice to meet you, Mike.'

'Nice?' Mum tutted, as if she'd expected more, but a handshake was all I could manage.

'It's been wonderful meeting you, Meg. The best day of my life.'

When Mike took my hand, I felt again that tug of recognition – of having known him before – and the temptation to fall against him was almost overpowering. Instead, I let go of his hand and brushed past, managing a stifled, 'I'll be in touch,' before leaving the way I'd come in. 'She's OK!' I called, hearing Kath's concerned enquiry as I ran to my car without looking back. Mum was going to have to explain this one to her.

Chapter Twenty

Back home, the house felt cloistered, too small for the feelings I was struggling to contain. I made some coffee, needing a caffeine boost in spite of the heat, and went to sit in the garden with my phone. I checked Facebook first, and saw today's photo featured Sam and Chris, helmeted and goggled, arms slung round each other's shoulders, a ridge of mountains in the background.

> *Finally reached the Roman spa town of Lons-le-Saunie. Saving the real climbs for tomorrow, when we'll be crossing the Jura Mountains into Switzerland!*

Go Pedal Pushers, wish I was there :-(a group member called Ben had commented, and I remembered he'd broken his ankle and had had to drop out. Underneath Sam had replied *Miss you mate, you'd have loved it. Next year, you'll be here!*

I'd half-expected him to not have posted a photo, or to at least be looking upset after our conversation the night before, or to not be in the picture, too baggy-eyed after a sleepless night going over our conversation – then I reminded myself he probably hadn't remembered half of it. There was nothing in his grin to suggest he was out of sorts, and I wondered why I'd ever thought there would be.

I knew he'd still be cycling, but called him anyway and left a message. 'Big news, if you're interested. Turns out my dad's not dead after all. His brother saw me on television, and Mike flew over from Ireland, and he and my mum are back together. I've just met him. He seems really nice. Anyway. I thought you'd want to know.' I paused, then added, 'I really need to talk to you, Sam. Call when you can.'

I'd just hung up, and was contemplating my next move – a nap seemed like an attractive option, though the lawn needed watering too – when my phone rang.

'Christ, Meg, I can't believe it!'

'Sam?'

'We just stopped for a break and I got your message,' he said. He sounded a bit put out, as if he'd been having a great time and wished he hadn't looked at his phone. 'I mean, what the hell? Your dad's *alive*?'

'I know, can you believe it?' The tears I'd been holding back began to fall. In spite of everything, Sam was the one who knew my history; had listened to me speculate about the side of my family I'd never know, and comforted me by saying I was lucky to have Mum, and his family too, which was more than some people had.

'He couldn't have emailed you first, and given you some warning?' he said, and I heard it again. A tiny trace of impatience, as if my news had disrupted his day and now he had to factor in my messy feelings. 'So, what's his story?'

Tears drying on my cheeks, I gave him the potted version and when I was done, he said, 'Christ,' again, with a note of disbelief. 'I mean, I'm not being funny, Meg, but in a way it's a bit selfish of him to do this, don't you think?'

I frowned. 'Selfish?'

'I mean, it's such a *grenade*,' he said. 'You've been fine without him all this time, and now he turns up out of the blue, and you've got to get your head around having a dad.'

Despite thinking the same thing just an hour ago, I felt my hackles rise, but before I could process a response, he spoke again.

'I'm starting to think going on that show was the worst thing you've ever done, Meg.'

'Hah!' The sound rocketed out without warning.

'What?' Sam sounded startled, as though I'd burped. 'What's that supposed to mean?'

'It means… it just means…' I thought of Cassie, saying she'd known that going on the show would pay off, and Nathan letting me perform a pretend interview with him to calm my nerves beforehand, and people coming up to me in the café to say I'd done myself proud, and how – in spite of the way I'd blathered on – the show had not only brought me the bakery, but my father, and had possibly mended my mother's heart. 'It means, I thought you'd be happy for me,' was all I could articulate.

'I thought you were already happy.' He sounded baffled, as if he genuinely didn't understand why I wouldn't be. 'You've got my dad, you know he thinks the world of you—'

'Sam, that's hardly the point,' I cut in, watching a shuttlecock sail over the hedge from next door, almost surprised to see that the sky was still blue, and the sun was still shining when it felt like storm clouds were gathering. 'I didn't think I had a dad, and now he's here, and I want to get to know him.' I did, I realised. I wanted to get to know my dad.

'Everyone *has* a dad, Meg.'

It was a lame attempt at a joke, but I'd never felt less like laughing. 'Sam, do you remember our conversation last night?'

'What?' I imagined his forehead scrunching as he pulled on his powers of recall. 'Of course. You said that someone had bought the bakery.'

'They want me to run it,' I reminded him.

'Was it your dad?'

'I thought that too, but no, it wasn't him.'

'Well, that's weird.' I imagined him shaking his head, as if his thoughts had defeated him. 'Why would someone do that, and what do they want in return?'

I stared at my ring, glinting in the sunlight. 'Why are you so suspicious?'

'Suspicious?' His laugh was tinged with disbelief. 'I'm looking out for you, Meg. It sounds like somebody has to.' Someone called his name, and I guessed it was time for him to hit the road again.

'How's George?' I said, remembering the photo I'd seen of him looking at her admiringly, and how I'd automatically assumed that George was a man.

'Fine,' he said, after a miniscule pause. 'Why do you ask?'

'No reason.' I jumped as one of the twins burst through the hedge and tiptoed towards the shuttlecock as if trying to avoid triggering a landmine.

'We're all fine, just tired,' he said. 'I've got to go, Meg. We'll talk properly when I get back.'

'OK.' I couldn't edit the sadness out of my voice, but he'd already hung up.

'Why are you always crying?' said the twin, his nut-brown face screwed up in childish disgust. 'I *never* cry and I'm a child.'

I swiped a hand over my cheek, surprised it felt damp, and said, 'It's because you and your brother are so noisy and naughty it gives me a terrible headache.'

His face was a circle of shock. 'I'll tell my mummy on you,' he pronounced, folding his arms across his skinny chest. 'She says just 'cos you were on telly you think you're better than everyone, but all you do is bake cakes, and anyone can do that, even me.' He unfolded his arms and pointed to himself.

'Go on then,' I said, stalking back to the house. 'Go and bake a bloody cake, and stay out of my garden.'

Back inside I considered having a proper cry, but couldn't muster the strength. Instead I messaged Cassie and Tilly:

Emergency girls' night, cake and wine at mine xx

'Jesus, Meg, it's all happening.' Tilly had collapsed on the rug and folded her legs beneath her, while Cassie was ensconced in the granddad chair, a glass of wine balanced on the arm. 'You've had a sexy daydream, been on TV, found a buyer for the bakery, and your dad's come back from the dead.'

And that's only the half of it.

'Makes my life seems really dull in comparison.' Cassie hadn't touched her drink yet, she'd been so wrapped up in my retelling of the day's events, and I'd enjoyed my friends' reactions a whole lot more than I had Sam's. Through their eyes, I could see now just how amazing and arbitrary life was. How, if Mr Moseley hadn't passed away, and I hadn't been so 'wedded to that bakery' as Tilly put it, and Alice Denby hadn't been in Seashell Cove and invited me on the show, I'd never have known my father was alive.

'It's blown my mind to be honest,' I said, a bit tiddly on two glasses of Prosecco. 'I've never seen Mum look so… *happy*. Though obviously it's early days.'

'Well, I hope it works out for her, I really do. And she deserves to be happy.' Cassie drew her knees up and wrapped her arms around them. Her glass wobbled, and Tilly reached out and grabbed it before it fell. 'Do you think she always sensed deep down that he was still alive?'

'If she did, she never let on.' I thought about her collectibles, and wondered if they'd been a subconscious link to Mike all along. She'd known he'd had a fondness for antiques, all those years ago. Maybe it had been her own little way of keeping him alive.

'I was going to say, I'm surprised she never tried to look him up, but of course she thought he was dead.' Tilly took a sip of Cassie's wine. She'd emptied her own glass and nibbled her way through half of the cherry cake I'd hastily sliced and put out. 'I suppose it's a good job she never remarried. That could have been awkward.'

'I think Mike expected when he called that she would be, but I reckon Mum would have dumped a husband for him.'

'Your dad would still have wanted to see you, anyway,' said Cassie. 'It must have been so emotional, for all of you.' She rested her chin on her knees. 'Wasn't there a storyline in *Friends* about a dad turning up out of the blue?'

'You're thinking of Chandler's,' I said automatically. 'He and Monica went to find him to invite him to their wedding and he turned out to be a woman, played by Kathleen Turner.'

'Wow,' said Tilly, putting the glass on one of the coasters Sam insisted on using to avoid ring stains on the wood floor. 'I'm kind of sorry I never watched it now.'

'Oh, Meg!' Cassie's head shot up. 'Your dad can give you away at your wedding!'

'Mum did mention that.' I shifted position, easing my legs along the length of the sofa. Outside the sun was setting, staining the sky a deep orange, and the air felt sultry, despite the open windows. 'I don't know, though,' I said.

'How come?' Tilly gave me an astute look, her eyes catching the light so they looked especially green. 'You don't want your dad at your wedding, or…?' She left the question dangling.

'I would love him at my wedding,' I said, though I still wasn't sure about him walking me down the aisle. Or whether I even wanted there to be an aisle. 'I just don't think there's going to be a wedding.'

Cassie inhaled so sharply, she had a choking fit. 'Sorry,' she croaked when we'd finished slapping her on the back, and she'd swallowed half a glass of water. 'I thought you said there might not be a wedding.'

I smacked back down on the sofa and told them everything, including the kiss with Nathan, and Beverley telling me she'd never thought I was good enough for Sam. When my words finally petered out, the sky outside was navy, and Cassie reached around and switched on the floor lamp.

'I can't believe Sam's mum said that to you.' Her voice was tight with anger. 'What a bitch.'

'I can't believe you snogged Nathan and didn't tell us,' said Tilly, moving to sit by the granddad chair, her crop of dark hair gleaming in the pool of light. 'What was it like?'

'Tilly!' Cassie nudged her with her foot.

'It was amazing,' I said on a sigh. I shouldn't have had that second glass of Prosecco. 'It felt like my insides were on fire.'

'That's indigestion,' said Cassie. 'I'm just saying.' She raised a hand when I started to protest. 'Are you really prepared to throw away your wedding to Sam for a kiss with someone you hardly know?'

'Says the woman who dumped a millionaire banker for her old school crush.' Tilly grinned at Cassie's indignant look. 'Just saying,' she mimicked.

'I wasn't due to marry the millionaire banker,' she pointed out. 'I just think if Meg tells Sam about the kiss, and they love each other enough, they can probably get past it.'

'It's not just about the kiss,' I said, at the same time as Tilly said, 'I don't think it's about the kiss.'

'Go on,' I said, keen to hear her theory.

She pushed a hand into her hair and had a good scratch. 'Sam doesn't really support you, as far as I can tell. It's like…' She paused to consider. 'It's like, he's fine as long as you're good old Meg, doing whatever he wants—'

'It's what I wanted too,' I chipped in, sitting up straight, and wincing as my head began to thump. I grabbed a slice of cake off the plate on the floor and stuffed it in my mouth. 'I'm not a total pushover,' I said, spraying crumbs down myself. 'I mean, I wanted to get married and have a baby, I really did.'

'But now you don't,' said Cassie.

'Not with Sam,' Tilly corrected her, popping a cherry in her mouth.

I waggled my ring finger. 'I think he only gave me this so I wouldn't have a go at him about doing this cycling challenge.' My voice had risen to a wail. 'And I think he fancies George.'

Tilly and Cassie exchanged looks.

'She's a girl at the cycling club,' I said. 'But he never told me she was a girl, and I bet it was deliberate, so I wouldn't wonder what he was up to all those evenings when he was supposed to be training.'

'But why would he want to marry you if he was seeing someone else?' said Cassie. 'It doesn't make sense.'

'I suppose not.' I deflated. 'The point is, if I trusted him, I wouldn't even be thinking like that.'

'The point is, do you love him?'

A month ago – two weeks ago – I'd have said yes without really thinking. We were getting married, so it went without saying we must love each other. Why else did people get married?

'It sounds really strange, but I don't really think about love when I think about Sam,' I said slowly. 'Being in love's for films and books… other people, I suppose. We're just… Meg and Sam. I couldn't imagine *not* being married to him.'

'But now you can.' Tilly's gaze was deadly serious.

'Meg, you have to do what you think is best for you.' Cassie sat forward as if to make her point more clearly felt. 'If you don't love him, you have to tell him.'

'It's not that simple,' I said miserably. 'We've been together so long, I don't know what I'd be like without him.'

'Maybe it's time to find out.' She came over and sat at the end of the sofa, taking my feet in her lap. She was wearing a T-shirt I recognised as one of Danny's with a pair of rolled up combat trousers, her glossy hair flipped up in a ponytail – nothing like the person she'd been when she'd worked in London, with her purple hair and monochrome suits, arranging celebrity parties and meeting Kanye West. She'd believed for a long time she wanted one thing, when really she'd wanted something completely different. She just hadn't known it until she came home. 'What do *you* want to do next?' she said.

'It's such a big step to cancel a whole wedding, especially when we've booked the venue.' I half-closed my eyes at the heavenly feeling of Cassie's hands massaging my foot. 'And Nathan's leaving on Monday, so nothing's going to happen in that department.'

'That's no reason not to cancel your wedding, and you can't go ahead with it just to be polite.' Tilly sounded amused. 'Grow a backbone, Meg.'

My eyes popped open. 'What, and stop letting people tell me what to do, you mean?'

She raised her hands. 'OK, point taken.' She grinned. 'I just meant where Sam's concerned. You can't get married if you're not in love.'

'Not that I'd know anything about that,' we chorused. It was becoming Tilly's mantra.

'I don't want to talk about it any more.' I leaned over and helped myself to the last slice of cake. 'I think I'm going to focus on the bakery until Sam comes back, and then I'll talk to him,' I said. 'Could you do my other foot now, Cass?'

Chapter Twenty-One

True to my word, I spent the next two days getting the bakery ready for opening. On Thursday morning, I scrubbed and cleaned the shop after baking my cake of the day, while Tilly touched up the paintwork, and Cassie replaced the product boards behind the counter and drew some little loaves on them in chalk. Even Danny helped, coming over to clean the windows and take down the For Sale board, which I stashed in the downstairs toilet, and to touch up the sign outside so it looked as good as new.

'Sure you don't want to change the name?' said Cassie.

I shook my head. 'I feel like it should still be the Old Bakery. At least for now.'

Big Steve had popped in early to say Tesco had agreed he could leave his job after his Sunday shift, but he would make sure he baked some bread for the shop on Saturday before he went to work, and I'd given him a spare key so he could let himself in.

During a tea break, after checking Facebook – Sam had posted *This is the steepest hill we've experienced so far, so it's important to pace ourselves and not over-do it!* along with a photo of him hunched, red-faced and sweating over his handlebars amidst mountainous scenery – I emailed the local paper to ask if they'd run a story about the bakery reopening, which they happily agreed to do. It was the most significant thing to have happened in Seashell Cove since Mr Moseley's demise, and they were keen to report a happy conclusion to the story. *We'll send out a photographer on Saturday morning, and well done for flying the flag for local trade!*

'Local bleedin' celebrity, you are,' Gwen said at the café that afternoon, after numerous customers had congratulated me, and made clear their intention to start shopping at the bakery again. 'Lydia and Ed are gonna wonder what's 'appened when they get back on Monday and find you've gorn.'

'Cassie's already let them know, and they're pleased for me,' I said. 'And I won't have gorn far.'

Gwen tutted at my attempt to mimic her accent. 'Will Just Sam be there for the grand reopening?'

My smile faltered. 'He won't be back until Saturday evening.'

'You couldn't 'ave waited until Monday?' She threw me a perceptive look. 'Poor sod, I'm sure 'e'd want to be there on your big day.'

That was the problem. He wouldn't. Well, he would if he happened to be around, and wasn't doing anything more important, but it wouldn't be a priority.

'It's no big deal,' I said, affecting nonchalance. 'It's not like I'm flying to Geneva to watch him cycle across the finish line.'

'Why not?'

'Because…' *I wasn't invited.* 'It's – it's not the sort of thing we do, I suppose. He does his thing, I do mine. We tend to support each other in spirit.' I was getting sick of spouting that line, and could tell Gwen wasn't convinced.

'Sounds to me like 'e 'ain't interested in what you're up to, unless it's what 'e wants.'

'How can you say that, Gwen?' A spike of guilt pushed me to defend him. 'You don't even know Sam.'

'Exactly.' Her caterpillar eyebrows lifted. ''Ow long 'ave you worked 'ere, and 'e's been in, what? Never? I've never seen 'im. Why don't 'e wanna 'ang out wiv you, sometimes?'

'He's very busy. He works in Kingsbridge, and when he's home he likes to relax and go cycling, not come to the place where I work. I don't hang out at his office, do I?'

'Dunno, do you?'

'Well, I sometimes used to meet him for lunch, just after he started working there, but it's hard when we do different hours. We can't always coordinate and anyway, he goes out to price jobs, he's not always in the office. I can hardly call him and say,' I lifted an imaginary phone, '"Where are you, Sam? I'll come over and we can hang out."'

'All right, all right, point taken. Bleedin' 'ell, I'm just sayin'. Defensive, much?'

I recalled hanging out with Nathan at the bakery, and on the beach, and how I was certain he'd turned up because he wanted to spend time with me, but cut off the train of thought as my head began to buzz. 'You and your husband didn't do things together,' I said, without thinking.

'Yeah, and look 'ow that ended up.'

I'd walked into that one, and couldn't find a response.

As I was leaving, Kath collared me in the car park, flashing her gusset as she clambered out of a taxi in her denim skirt, to enfold me in a hug that smelt of baby milk. 'I can't believe it,' she said, rocking me from side to side in a tight embrace. 'Your dad's lovely! You must be made up.' She held me at arm's length, her eyes dancing over my face. I was pleased to see her false eyelashes were back, and she was rocking some fuchsia-pink lipstick. Kath didn't stay down for long. 'And shocked, I expect, you poor love.'

'Just a bit,' I said, smiling, though in truth, the shock had started to wear off a bit, and I was looking forward to going round to Mum's for dinner later. 'She told you then?'

'I was round there like a rat up a drainpipe once you'd gone the other day,' Kath said. 'I thought she must have shacked up with a toy boy from the way you rushed off, it gave me quite a fright.'

'I'm sorry about that.' I flushed. 'I hadn't got to grips with it all, but we've been texting, and they know I'm OK with it.'

'Oh, love, I completely get it.' Kath squished my arms. 'You could have buttered my bum and called me a biscuit once your mum had explained who the good-looking fellow was.' Her hair wavered as she shook her head in wonderment. 'You can tell they're made for each other, it's in their eyes,' she said. 'Can't keep them off each other, and he seems like a proper gentleman, too. The way he talked about you nearly made me cry.' Her eyes grew shiny. 'He said he felt reborn, like he'd been given a second shot at life and was going to do his best to make you and your mum proud.' She clutched her hands beneath her chin. 'And do you know what, Meg, I really think he will.'

'I do too.' I felt a burst of emotion. 'I know I went rushing off, but I think he understood it was because there was too much to take in, considering I'd thought Mum was in bed with the flu.'

'And now we know why she was really in bed!' Kath's cackle died in her throat. 'Sorry, my love, that was crude.'

'It's fine,' I said and it was – as long as I didn't think about it too deeply.

'Oh my love, I'm so pleased for you both.' I could tell Kath was genuinely moved –she'd come to Seashell Cove to tell me as much –

and I was sad and cross in equal measure that Freya couldn't see how special Kath was.

'How's Milo?' I asked.

'Oh, he's gorgeous.' Her eyes grew even shinier. 'He's with his dad, and I've been invited over there for Sunday lunch.'

'Oh, Kath, that's lovely.' I wondered whether Sam and I would be having Sunday lunch with the Ryans, once we'd talked when he came home.

'Don's sending a car to pick me up.' Kath ran a finger over her upper lip, where beads of perspiration were breaking out. It had been another glimmery, hazy, hot day, the sea in the cove dappled green. 'He said there's a room for me at the house, and I can stay whenever I like.'

Don was shooting up in my estimation. 'That's nice of him,' I said. 'Have you heard from Freya?'

'Only a text to say sorry, and that she's not cut out to be a mum.'

I felt a twist of disgust. 'Shame she didn't think about that sooner.'

'But then I wouldn't have Milo.'

I smiled. 'That's true.' I bent to give her a hug. 'He's so lucky to have you.'

Her arms tightened in acknowledgment. 'I don't suppose you've any cake, love?' She let me go, eyeing the inside of my car where I'd placed a box of leftover almond slices. 'I fancy something sweet for my pudding tonight.'

I nodded. 'By the way, Kath, can you start work at the bakery on Saturday?'

I woke on Friday after a night of turbulent dreams, in which I was either singing too loudly while a faceless person tried to shush me, or running along in clown shoes, but not knowing where to – only that there was something I needed to see.

By the time I arrived at the bakery just after seven, although I was tired, I'd reclaimed the glow I'd felt at dinner at Mum's the night before. Mike (I couldn't yet call him Dad) had cooked and served a surprisingly delicate Irish stew, while Mum laid out the 'best' cutlery (antique silver), emitting the kind of joy that only came from having a loved one return from the 'dead'. The conversation had been light too. Mike, with impeccable timing, had regaled us with amusing tales of the people he'd met during his antique foraging, and had talked about his wider family in a way that made me feel I'd love to meet them one day. Apparently, they were dying to meet Mum and me, and Mum was actually going to visit Mike's brother Stuart and his wife the following week. At their place in Yorkshire. I guessed with Mike by her side, she felt invincible, and, although I didn't think it would be that simple, I was happy she was even considering going all that way.

Sam, the wedding and babies hadn't been mentioned once, to my relief.

At the bakery, I propped open the door – the weather looked set to be hot again, the sun rising in a cloudless sky – and started making a couple of apple and raisin cakes and some ginger parkin, knowing they'd improve their flavour overnight. Then I baked some heart-shaped gingerbread biscuits with my new cookie cutters, which I planned to pipe with icing on Saturday morning, and give free with every sale, as a way of saying thank you to my customers (providing there were any). I found myself singing 'My Heart Will Go On', remembering how I'd been obsessed with the film *Titanic* for a while, and almost dropped the tray when I turned to the oven and saw a familiar figure at the doorway.

'Nathan!'

'Sorry,' he said, leaping forward to steady the tray of hearts as it tilted towards the floor. 'I should wear one of those bells, like a cat, so people know I'm approaching.'

Our eyes locked briefly, and my heartbeat doubled. There was a pillow crease on his cheek, and his hair was wilder on one side than the other, as if he'd just rolled out of bed and pulled on the clothes nearest to him – faded blue jeans and a grey T-shirt – and driven straight over. In other words, he looked gorgeous, and smelt of… rumpled bedding was the first thing that sprang to mind.

'What are you doing here?' Realising it sounded ungracious, I shoved the tray into the oven, hoping the billowing heat would account for my blazing cheeks.

'I couldn't leave without seeing you,' he said simply, holding out a paper parcel he'd had tucked under his arm. 'It's not much,' he said.

My heart was throwing itself against my chest as I took it and peered inside. 'What is it?'

'Um, maybe take it out and see?'

Catching the flare of amusement in his eyes, I said, 'Good plan.' I retrieved what felt like a piece of canvas material and after shaking it out, a smile lifted my mouth when I saw an apron with the words 'Meg's Kitchen' on a cream background, in pastel pink and green lettering, with a cake stand of cupcakes printed underneath.

'Oh, Nathan, I love it!'

He grinned. 'I know you want this place to keep its name, but I really think you should add "Meg's Kitchen" at some point.' It was the same name Big Steve had suggested, and was starting to grow on me. 'After all, it's yours now.'

Something about the way he said it made me look at him sharply. *Was he the mystery buyer?* I knew if I asked, he'd probably deny it and

I honestly didn't think he could have faked his excitement when he'd told me the news at the café, plus how could he afford it?

I pulled the apron over my head to mask a moment of confusion, almost dislodging my hairnet, which I smoothed back on. It wasn't flattering, but Nathan had seen it before.

'There's a couple more, for your staff to wear,' he said, adding, 'May I?' with an air of ceremony.

I gave a gracious bow and said, 'Of course, sir,' and he came and fastened the straps, his hands brushing my waist with a feather-light touch that made me ache for more. I sprang back, and made a fuss of smoothing the apron over my dress, touched beyond measure by the thought of him visiting websites and choosing the design. 'There's no pocket.'

'Ah, I didn't think of that.' He rubbed a hand over his chin. 'You'll have to find somewhere else to put your ring while you're baking.'

'Oh no, I didn't mean… it's fine, I mean, I don't need a pocket…' I trailed off as our gazes landed on my ring finger, the pale band where my engagement ring normally rested as obvious as if I was still wearing it. As if the sight had reminded him of Sam, Nathan moved away to the table where my cakes were cooling.

'These look great,' he said, clearly making an effort to sound merely friendly. 'Are they for tomorrow?'

I nodded, and ran him through what else I was planning to bake, from chocolate dipped flapjacks to strawberry and fresh cream tarts. 'I've a delivery arriving later, and Big Steve's coming in really early in the morning to prepare some loaves, so all I have to do is put them in the oven half an hour before opening, and Cassie's coming to help in the shop, because Kath needs to learn the ropes, so it's going to be all hands on deck.' I paused for breath. 'Alice is doing an update on her show this evening, and is going to thank the buyer for me, in case he's watching.'

'I'm sure he will be,' said Nathan, moving around the kitchen, stopping to peer in the sink at the dishes that needed washing, so I couldn't see his face. 'Do you want a hand with anything?'

'You could make some tea,' I said, determined to grab every second I could with him, before he disappeared from my life for good. 'White with one sugar.'

As he filled the kettle and rinsed the mugs, I got out the ingredients to make a cake for the café – carrot and orange – and tried not to think how natural it felt to be sharing the space with him.

'Are you all packed for your trip?'

'Not yet,' said Nathan shortly, and I had the sense he didn't want to talk about it any more than I did, so I asked about Charlie instead.

'He asked me last night why he can't see his own eyes,' he said, relaxing into a grin. 'Why do kids ask questions that are so hard to answer?'

Smiling, I went to remove my gingerbread hearts from the oven, while Nathan told me that Charlie had once asked his mum why she and daddy had some handcuffs in their bedroom drawer, and was mummy a policeman.

'Something pretty amazing's happened,' I said, when there was a natural lull, and while I grated the carrots for the cake, I told him about my dad, and he sat on Mr Moseley's stool, shaking his head now and then, and gave a low whistle when I'd finished.

'That *is* amazing.' He folded his arms and studied my face, which I guessed was shiny with heat. 'I can't even imagine how you – and your mum – must be feeling.'

'I know,' I said. 'It's been pretty intense.'

'Amazing, though. What an opportunity for you all.'

It was impossible not to compare his reaction with Sam's, and I had to remind myself Nathan wasn't invested in my future, and that there wouldn't be any ramifications for him. Although, the more I thought about it, I couldn't see any downsides to having Mike in my life. His biggest mistake had been to marry a woman he didn't love, but it wasn't as if he'd turned into some sort of addict (as far as I knew), or was heavily in debt, or an ex-con who'd been in prison, or had twenty-odd children to different mothers. He didn't even seem like he'd be an embarrassing dad; the type who told terrible jokes, or broke wind in front of guests (Mum had said her dad used to do that sometimes, finding it hilarious, to her mortification). Like Sam's dad, Mike seemed the sort of man who'd be a positive influence (already was, where Mum was concerned) – a dad with an instinctive feel for parenting. A man who deserved the title dad.

I said as much to Nathan, who nodded, seeming to understand. 'He's obviously ready to step up,' he said. 'It's all coming together for you.' He rose, his tea cooling on the worktop next to mine, and came over. 'It couldn't have happened to a nicer person.' He drew me into his arms, and I rested my head against his chest for a long, long moment, feeling his steady heartbeat through his T-shirt. I had to resist an impulse to push my hand underneath and touch his warm skin, and my breathing became unsteady.

'I hope everything works out,' he murmured into my hairnet, and I sensed him resisting impulses of his own.

'For you too.' A tight knot of tears gathered in my chest. 'And thank you. For everything,' I added, meaningfully, not daring to lift my gaze to meet his, knowing I wouldn't be able to stop myself kissing him again if I did.

'I didn't buy the bakery, if that's what you're implying.' Gently pulling away, he rested his hands on my shoulders. 'I can't work out now whether I wished I had,' he said softly. 'At least we'd be linked in some way.'

It was on the tip of my tongue to say that we would be anyway, because he'd worked his way into my heart, but I could hardly say it with Sam due home and anyway, Nathan was leaving, and I had a dad to get to know, and a bakery to take care of, which was more than enough to be going on with.

'I'd better go.' Nathan was moving backwards to the door.

'Thanks again for the aprons,' I said, wiping my hands on a tea towel as I followed him out, welcoming a light breeze on my boiling cheeks.

Nathan turned without warning, and took my hands in his. 'I hope you'll be happy with Sam.' His eyes probed mine. 'If you really want to be with him, then I'm happy for you.'

'Nathan…' I jumped as a car door slammed. Turning, my hands still laced with Nathan's, I saw a man walking towards us.

'Hey there!' Mike gave a friendly wave, his grey hair lifting off his forehead. 'Thought I'd come and see you at work in this amazing bakery I've heard so much about.' He smiled broadly, turning to Nathan who finally let go of my fingers. 'You must be Sam,' Mike said. 'I don't know if she's had time to tell you the story because I know you've been away.' He held out a hand. 'I'm Mike Byrne.' He clapped a mildly stunned Nathan on the back. 'It's great you've made it back in time for tomorrow. It'll mean a lot to Meg.'

'Dad,' I said, only registering I'd used the word when he turned to me with an expression of unfiltered joy. 'S-Sam's still in France,' I stuttered. 'This is Nathan Walsh.'

Chapter Twenty-Two

'So sorry about that,' said Mike, once Nathan had gone, after assuring Mike it was an easy mistake to make and giving me one last look, as though fixing me in his mind before leaving with a final wave.

'It's OK, don't be silly.' I felt oddly shy now we were alone, as well as bereft that Nathan had gone before I'd had a chance to say even a quarter of what was on my mind. 'How's Mum?'

'Oh, I left her and Kath having tea and a chinwag,' he said as I led him into the kitchen out of the sunshine. 'She seems like a good friend.'

'She is,' I assured him. 'I don't know what we'd have done without her, at times.'

He nodded with a sad, flat smile, no doubt wishing he'd been around for those times too. 'Looks like it's your mum's turn to repay the favour now the daughter's taken off.'

'Poor Kath,' I said, lifting the kettle, wondering whether he'd noticed the two still full mugs of tea on the side. 'Would you like a drink?'

He shook his head. 'I'm good, thanks. I'm drowning in the brown stuff, I've had that much since I got here.'

'Not just champagne, then?'

I felt bad when he flushed with embarrassment. 'I don't normally drink bubbly, but thought the occasion merited it,' he said, eyes scanning the kitchen, and the cakes on the table. 'It's not every day you find out that not only does the woman you've always loved still want you, but you've a daughter you never knew existed.'

'A sort of belated wetting the baby's head?' I said, thinking how odd it was that the baby in question was me.

'Exactly.' He smiled, but his eyes had settled on me, full of concern. 'Meg, I...'

He paused as the delivery turned up, continuing when I'd signed for it and the delivery man had gone, whistling cheerily.

'I know it's a bit much, me offering fatherly advice when we've barely met, but the way you two were looking at each other, I'd no reason to think you weren't madly in love.'

My heart did a big leap. 'Me and the delivery man?'

Mike gave me a look. 'You know fine well I'm talking about young Nathan,' he said, jerking his head at the door as if he might still be there. 'Why were the two of you holding hands, if you're not a couple?'

I glanced at the heap of carrots I'd grated and realised I wouldn't have time now to bake my cake before I went to the café. 'We're friends,' I said, my voice pitched slightly too high. 'We were actually saying goodbye.' I made myself meet Mike's gaze. 'He's going to Ireland, funnily enough. He does a bit of travel writing for the *Telegraph*. He's been helping look after his nephew, and the estate agency his brother owns.' I was talking too much – a sure sign of guilt. 'That's how we met, you see. He was handling the sale of the bakery.'

'And you've fallen for the fella.'

I stared at Mike, in his baggy white shirt and jeans, and sensible saddle-brown shoes, and felt as if something inside me was coming undone. 'Like I said, we're just good friends, not even that really, we've not known each other very long.'

'It only took me a night to fall in love with your mum.' Cupping my elbow, Mike guided me to the stool where Nathan had been sitting ten minutes ago, as if he thought I might faint. He tipped tea out of one of the mugs and filled it with water from the tap. 'It's not a crime, love,' he said, handing me the mug. 'These things happen, as I know only too well.'

I was breathing too quickly. 'All I ever wanted was to marry Sam,' I said, almost to myself. 'I've known him since we were at school.'

'I know, your mum told me.' He paused. 'Things change, Meg. Don't do what I did. Don't marry the man if you don't love him.'

He made it sound so simple – not like unravelling a whole life. 'I *do* care about him,' I said. 'At least… I did.'

'Meg,' Mike began, but I couldn't have this conversation. Not with Mike.

I stood up to curb further discussion. 'There's so much going on at the moment, my head's all over the place.' I whipped off my hairnet and shook out my hair as if to demonstrate, then tucked it back inside. 'And, like you said, it's a bit soon for fatherly advice.'

Whirling into action, I emptied the delivery bags, lining up bags of flour, sugar, cake boxes, cartons of blueberries, nets of lemons and oranges, and cartons of cream. 'I have to get this in the fridge,' I said, moving past him with my hands full. 'I'm heading to the café shortly, it's my last afternoon there.'

'You're not going to let me try this lovely cake?' His eyes were still touched with worry, but he'd clearly decided to back off. He probably felt glad that he hadn't had a lifetime of trying to advise and protect a daughter who wouldn't – or couldn't – listen.

'That cake's for tomorrow,' I said, 'but you can have a gingerbread biscuit, and I'll give you a tour if you like.'

I managed to keep my smile in place, and eventually he nodded. 'I'd like that very much.' He glanced at my apron. 'Meg's Kitchen is a great name, by the way.'

Big Steve was as good as his word, and when I arrived at the bakery at six the following morning, the kitchen was still deliciously warm and yeasty. There were several trays of freshly-baked loaves and rolls, waiting to go out on display, with a note to say there was plenty more dough in the freezer if I ran out.

There were granary, white and wholemeal loaves, a batch flavoured with basil and tomato, and one studded with sunflower seeds, as well as a tray of doorstopper scones and another note, wishing me luck.

It feels good to be part of team Meg! Rock and ROLL (!) S XX

Smiling, I pulled on my brand new apron and started work, trying to keep my mind empty of the previous day's events. My stint at the café had ended ingloriously with a massive sneezing fit after hauling Dickens away from a plate of crumbs on the counter, while Gwen tore a strip off Dom for chatting up Tamsin instead of working.

Back home, exhausted and puffy eyed, I'd checked Facebook to see Sam's latest update, which was a group shot somewhere high up, with a view of Lake Geneva in the distance, and the words *About to pass through the international border, then it's flat roads all the way! Big meal tonight, then time off to enjoy Geneva in the morning, before getting the Eurostar back to London!* He'd added a crying face, which had done nothing for my mood, and neither had the sight of George grinning up at Sam, who was resting his elbow on her shoulder. Ben had written underneath *You lot are making me sick now*, and didn't sound like he was joking. I'd switched off my phone then and watched *Britain's Hidden Gems* with a plate of cheese and a bag of Mini Eggs for dinner. Alice Denby had been visiting a remote but pretty fishing village in Cornwall, and before introducing the gifted guest of the week – a man who'd taught his dog to surf – she'd updated viewers about the bakery, passing on my thanks to the mystery buyer ('It's people like you, sir, who make this job worthwhile'), which led to me thinking of all that had happened since Sam had been away. I'd lain awake for ages, trying to process it all – and to digest the cheese and Mini Eggs – and had only managed to fall asleep after running through my mental database of cake recipes in alphabetical order.

Pushing aside a memory of Nathan fastening my apron strings (a memory Tilly would no doubt scorn, with its forties-housewife overtones), I got out my ingredients, and the pastry I'd made the day before, and spent the next two and half hours making blueberry muffins, some flapjacks dipped in dark chocolate, a variety of cupcakes thickly swirled with buttercream, and some apple and cinnamon pies. By the time I'd finished piping icing on my gingerbread hearts, I was hot-cheeked and singing along to an All Saints medley as Kath and Cassie arrived.

'I've got bunting!' Cassie came in brandishing an armful of cheery triangular flags. 'I remembered seeing some in the dresser at home,' she said. 'Nan said my parents hung it outside the café after it was refurbished, so I thought it might be nice to string it along the front of the building. There's some mounting tape, so we won't even need a hammer.'

'You lost me at mounting tape.'

She laughed. 'Have you got a stepladder?'

'There's one in the downstairs loo. Don't ask me why.'

As she went to get it, Kath hung up her bag and denim jacket, and the sight of her blingy shoes with bows and sparkle was touching. Her eyes almost popped out of her head as she eyed the wealth of baked products waiting to go out. 'They look marvellous, love, you have been busy.'

'Big Steve baked the bread.' Nerves were starting to kick in. 'Why didn't I think about bunting?'

'You've had enough on your plate,' Kath said, with an enviable lack of nerves, considering it was her first day in a new job. I guessed having a daughter flee the country, leaving behind a husband and a grandson, made selling cakes seem easy. 'You're coping ever so well with your dad coming back and sweeping your mum off her feet.' She patted her hair, which I doubted would fit beneath a net, but was at least piled out of the way. 'It's made me think about getting myself a nice Irish gentleman.' She faked a starry-eyed look. 'I might ask your father if he's got any single friends.'

Your father. It sounded nice. 'No harm in trying,' I said, handing her one of the aprons Nathan had brought. 'Do you mind wearing this?' I knew she didn't like covering up, and although she was dressed ultra-modestly by her usual standards, there was a considerable amount of cleavage visible in the dip of her leopard-print top. 'It's, er, to protect your clothes.'

'Oh, that's lovely,' she said, seeming tickled. '"Meg's Kitchen", I like that a lot.'

'Have I got one, too?' Cassie came back with the ladder, looking ready for business with her denim shirtsleeves rolled up. 'Good idea to get some new ones made.'

Flushing, I handed her one, deciding not to mention where they'd come from. 'It's a shame Tilly can't be here today, but I suppose she can't help being ill.' Tilly really had got the summer flu, and according to her text wasn't fit to be out in public.

'Let's just hope we don't come down with it,' said Cassie. 'We'll get this bunting up, and when we're done, I'll chalk up a list of your cakes. Do you have a cake of the day?'

'Apple and raisin,' I said. 'Or ginger parkin.' I was riddled with indecision, all of a sudden. I'd done it before, but this felt different. I was in charge now. What if I made a hash of it, or no one turned up?

'Stop fretting,' Cassie's voice cut in, as if she knew where my thoughts were heading. 'You've got this,' she said firmly.

'But what if I haven't?'

'You have,' said Kath, and their faith in me was both terrifying and heartening. 'We're rooting for you, love, the whole village is, and most of Salcombe too.' She winked so hard, her lashes almost stuck to her cheek. 'You'll see.'

While they got to work, bickering about who should go up the stepladder, and who should hand up the bunting, I snapped on a pair of latex gloves and started arranging the bread and cakes in wicker baskets, placing some in the shop window, another couple on the shelf behind the counter, and the rest of the cakes underneath the display area by the counter.

After placing my apple and raisin cake beneath a glass dome, I cut the ginger parkin into even squares and arranged them on a cake stand, then stacked my gingerbread hearts in a basket on the counter before standing back to admire the effect. With the sun pouring though the freshly-cleaned windows, giving the wood floor, counter and shelving a burnished glow, it looked like a picture worthy of Instagram. I was half-tempted to post some photos on Facebook, to show Sam what he was missing, but he was clearly having too good a time to be looking on social media, once he'd posted his update of the day. Instead, I took a couple of snaps on my phone and sent them to Mum.

Look what I did! X

Beautiful! I'm so proud of you she responded instantly. *We'll see you later. Mum XXX*

I wondered whether she meant dinner, or if she was planning to visit the bakery with Mike. Kath had persuaded her over to Seashell Cove a few times in the past, and they'd enjoyed a coffee at the café, but I knew Mum would rather be in the house, and still doubted Mike could get her up to Yorkshire.

I wondered whether the Ryans would put in an appearance, then remembered the way Beverley had ignored my news about the bakery, and how she only seemed to support me in things that involved her son. Like our wedding. Recalling the horror of the dress she'd had in mind, and my reaction, I doubted she'd want to speak to me ever again, and imagining how she'd react once I'd told Sam I didn't want to marry him made me want to retch.

Mind bubbling like a volcano, I tried to concentrate instead on making sure everything was ready for the opening, tipping the change I'd got from the bank the day before into the till, and making sure the card reader was plugged in.

By nine o'clock the bunting was up, the boards were filled with Cassie's arty lettering and cupcake drawings, and she and Kath were behind the counter with their aprons on, nudging each other in a giggly fashion.

Best of all, there was a queue outside, and everyone looked smiley.

I suddenly wished I'd had a proper opening ceremony, with a ribbon and scissors but I knew Mr Moseley wouldn't have approved of me making a fuss, so I took one last look around to make sure everything was perfect, and turned the wooden sign on the door from closed to open, and pulled it wide.

'Morning,' I said, nerves falling away as I scanned the bright, expectant faces, a lot of whom had been customers in the past. 'Welcome to the Old Bakery.'

Chapter Twenty-Three

By eleven o'clock, I was in the kitchen, pulling dough from the freezer as supplies were running low. The first raisin and apple cake had all gone, and there weren't many slices left of the second, and two people had been back for a second square of ginger parkin.

'Don't tell my missus,' the first had said, with a guilty grin. 'It's better than hers, and I thought *hers* was good.' Luckily, I didn't know his missus.

I'd had three orders for celebration cakes, a request for more specialist loaves, like sourdough (which I knew would thrill Big Steve) and a suggestion that we provide paper napkins with the cakes, which I hadn't thought of.

Cassie called the café and ten minutes later Tamsin hurried in with a boxful, her hair floating free from her bun on one side. 'Can't stop, or Gwen will murder me,' she panted, eyeing the cupcakes longingly, and I gave her one to take back.

After fumbling the first cake box into a peculiar shape, and dropping a flapjack on the floor, Kath quickly got the hang of things, and was proving as much of a hit with customers as Gwen was at the café – though Kath smiled a lot and wasn't rude, and called everybody love.

'It's just like being at Discount Clothing,' she said at one point. 'I mean the principle's the same, dealing with customers. Obviously you can't eat clothes, and you can't wear a cake.' She chuckled at her own joke.

Cassie was friendly and efficient, but I could tell she was reminded of her previous job, and that she'd be relieved to get back to her painting, so when Valerie Jones from the café came in and reminded me she'd liked to work there, I asked how soon she could start.

'Monday?' she suggested, a delighted smile stretching to her ears. 'Pity all interviews aren't that easy. When my son last applied for a job he had to do a group interview, and was so intimidated he forgot his own surname.'

The photographer from the paper appeared at that point and whisked me into the kitchen for a picture, posing with mixing bowl and wooden spoon, then snapped a few of me behind the counter, handing cake boxes to customers, and one outside the bakery where I was sure I was squinting as the sun hit me full in the face. A scroll through the shots on his display screen showed me looking completely at home, my eyes clear and my smile genuine. My apron logo showed up nicely and my hair, freed from its net, fell in shiny waves. My cheeks were a bit red, but the photographer assured me I looked wholesome, which was apparently a good thing for a bakery manager.

He asked emerging customers what they thought of it all, and the response was overwhelmingly positive. I'd just accepted my fourth handshake in a row – I would have to wash my hands for the umpteenth time – when someone said, 'There she is,' in an Irish lilt, and I turned to see a smiling Mike with Mum gripping his arm. She looked as flushed as I felt, but pretty in a soft blue dress that matched her eyes, and white, low-heeled sandals.

'Mum!' I wrapped her in a hug, thinking how much she suited being outdoors – that it brought sparkles to her eyes, and a brighter sheen to her hair – then I realised it was probably the Mike effect, rather than the weather. Either way, it didn't matter; she was here. 'I'm so glad you came.'

'I feel a bit breathless, but I'm sure it'll pass,' Mum said, casting a panicked look at the bakery over my shoulder. 'Let's have a look inside then, before I pass out.' She gave a nervous laugh, and Mike winked at me before leading her inside, where he handed her a gingerbread heart, and Kath came round the counter to give her a cuddle.

It had quietened down in the shop, and while they chatted, and Cassie tidied the cakes in the cabinet with a pair of tongs, I slipped into the kitchen where I froze, a tray of bread rolls poised half in the oven as a childish voice floated through.

'Please can I have a bwownie, I love bwownies, don't I? It won't spoil my dinner.'

Charlie! My pulse accelerated. Nathan was here! Trying not to think what it meant, I slid the tray into the oven and smoothed my hair and apron down, before hurrying back to the shop.

'Smeg!' Charlie cried when he spotted me, eyes lighting up like firecrackers. 'Can I have a bwownie?' He was wearing an orange T-shirt with a shark on the front, and was holding the same bucket and spade he'd had when we went to the beach. 'It's MEG!' he said, tugging the fingers of a man facing the counter. A man with a crutch and a cast on his lower right leg. A man who definitely wasn't his uncle. 'Daddy, *look!*'

I fought hard not to let disappointment wash away my smile as the man turned, fixing me with a curious gaze.

'Ah, it's the famous Meg Larson,' he said drily, twisting away from the counter, leaning on his crutch as he swung his way over, Charlie at his side.

'Hardly famous,' I said, blushing. 'You must be Nathan's brother.' As if he could be anyone else. Apart from the fact that Charlie had called him daddy, there was an obvious resemblance to Nathan in the shape of his face. He was a taller, leaner version, his wavy hair shorter, his eyes the same shade but slightly wider set. He was wearing baggy shorts with side pockets, and a pale-green T-shirt, but I could easily imagine him dressed in a suit and tie.

'Hugo Walsh,' he said. 'Good to meet you, Meg.' He said it in a speculative way that sent more blood to my face.

Charlie hopped from one blue-sandaled foot to the other, his eyes beseeching. 'Can I have a bwownie, *please*, Meg?'

'Actually, that's ginger parkin,' I said, realising where he was point-ing, unable to stop a smile at the sight of his sun-flushed face.

'What's parkin?'

'It's a cake like my granny used to bake, made with oatmeal and black treacle, and I think it might be too chewy for you,' I said. 'What about a gingerbread heart instead?' I looked at Hugo for confirmation and he nodded.

'Go on then.'

I took down the basket so Charlie could help himself, taking his time even though there weren't many left and they looked identical. Once he was nibbling round the edge, his bucket and spade at his feet, Hugo said, 'I thought we'd pop over so I could see what – or should I say *who* – has been keeping my little brother fixed in one place for more than a month.'

My heart seemed to lodge in my throat. 'I thought he was staying to help you out,' I said croakily. 'And to sell this place.'

'He agreed to stay a fortnight, tops.' Hugo adjusted the crutch under his forearm. 'Just until my wife got back from China.'

'Didn't she get back on Thursday?'

'She was back over a week ago.' There was an amused slant to Hugo's mouth, but his eyes were wary. 'He was looking for excuses to stay, and now I see why.'

Before I could answer, Mum touched my arm, startling me. 'We'll see you later, Meg.' She looked strained, and I could see she needed to leave. 'Bring Sam over for dinner, won't you? Mike would love to meet him.'

'If he's not too tired.' Aware of Hugo's critical gaze I kissed her cheek, which felt almost as hot as my own. 'Thanks for coming, Mum.' I smiled a thank you at Mike and he smiled back, casting Hugo a quizzical look. Mum wouldn't have cared if I was chatting to the Pope, she was so keen to get out.

'See you later,' Mike said, and looked for a second as if he might kiss my cheek too, but had second thoughts. We were still navigating the whole father/daughter dynamic, and I guessed it would be a while before it felt completely natural.

As they left, Cassie mimed getting herself a drink and I nodded, glad of a second's distraction from Hugo's attentive stare. 'Could you take the rolls out of the oven while you're there?' She gave me a thumbs-up and tilted her head in Hugo's direction, as if to say *who's he*? And I gave a tiny shake of my head.

'This is so yummy,' Charlie declared, causing Kath to look over, her face melting into a soppy smile. 'Can we go and see Mummy now?'

Hugo ruffled Charlie's curls, not taking his eyes off me. 'In a minute, Charlie.' His mouth had tightened. 'It's been a long time since I've seen Nathan like this over a woman. In fact, I don't think I ever have,' he said quietly. 'He got his heart broken last time he fell in love, too.'

Love? 'I… like him a lot.' My voice crumbled a little. 'It's just… I'm… I have some things to sort out. I'm getting married.'

'So I gather.' Hugo seemed to be waiting for me to say something else and I opened my mouth obligingly, but my words had disappeared. 'Anyway, I thought I should let you know,' he said, bending awkwardly to pick up Charlie's bucket. I dipped down to retrieve the spade, meeting Hugo's eyes on the way back up. 'My brother doesn't fall in love lightly.'

My heart turned over. 'Neither do I,' I squeaked.

'Good to hear.' He straightened, and handed the bucket to Charlie, who had icing round his mouth, and was feeding bits of biscuit to a soft-eyed terrier a customer had sneaked in. 'We were looking forward to having Uncle Nathan stay around, weren't we?' he said.

Charlie nodded. 'Uncle Nafan,' he repeated, and ate a piece of biscuit the dog had just licked.

I looked at Hugo. 'You can't blame me for him leaving.'

'I'm not blaming you.' Something like sadness settled around his eyes. 'We miss him, that's all.' He held out his hand to his son. 'You ready to go now, sunshine?'

Charlie nodded. 'Fanks for the biscuit, Meg,' he said as I slipped the spade into his bucket and tried to smile. 'It was d'licious.' He patted his tummy.

'Would you like to take one for Mummy?'

He nodded keenly, and Kath slipped one in a bag with a paper napkin without me having to ask.

As I watched them go, Charlie holding his dad's hand and chattering non-stop, Hugo manoeuvring more easily away from the confines of the shop, I found myself wishing we'd met under different circumstances. Hugo seemed nice (hard stare notwithstanding) and so was Charlie, and I wondered what Mrs Hugo was like – what her name was – and whereabouts they lived, and what Nathan and Hugo were like together; whether they bickered like Cassie and her brother did and whether—

'It's a nice age,' Kath's voice broke in, with an unusually wistful edge, and I moved back to the counter. I guessed she was remembering

Freya when she was four – though I couldn't picture Freya ever being as happy-go-lucky as Charlie seemed to be. 'I'm already looking forward to Milo being able to talk,' she said, as Cassie came through carrying the tray of rolls.

'Just caught them before they burnt,' she said.

Another flow of customers kept us busy, and most wanted a chat with me about my TV appearance, and to ask if Alice Denby was as nice in real life, and to tell me how lovely it was to see the bakery trading again, and how Mr Moseley was much missed.

'You're a worthy successor,' said one, an accolade I felt I hardly deserved, but it was nice to hear, and by five o'clock all but one cupcake had sold, and I'd finally stopped expecting Nathan to turn up and surprise me.

Chapter Twenty-Four

The front door was ajar when I got home, and I caught a glimpse of Sam's bike parked in the hallway. The sight of it made my heart leap and my stomach roll over with nerves.

I crept into the house like an intruder, eyes flicking over his rucksack on the bottom stair, and his cycling shoes on the floor. Just like at Mum's, before I'd met Mike, the air felt somehow disturbed.

'You're back!' I called in a sing-song voice, hearing movement in the kitchen, hovering by the coat hooks to delay the moment I'd see him again. All the things I'd wanted to say suddenly seemed either too much or not enough, and I had no idea where to start.

'Come and look at this!' Hearing trapped laughter in his voice, I was transported back to him seeing his cycling itinerary online for the first time. It felt like a lifetime ago.

'Coming!' My mouth felt desert-dry as I put down my bag and kicked off my sandals, and I had to work hard to summon a smile before entering the sunlit kitchen. 'What is it?'

With a feeling of déjà vu I saw that his eyes were trained on his laptop at the breakfast bar, and he smiled and held out his hand without looking up. 'Chris posted a photo of me on the Eurostar this morning, the cheeky sod.'

He'd changed into his usual T-shirt and joggers, but his skin was a shade darker from being in the sun, which made his hair look lighter, and he was sporting a prickly-looking layer of pale stubble. It was like seeing a stranger wearing Sam's clothes, and I had the sense I was seeing him properly for the first time.

'I fell asleep and he thought it would be hilarious to do this.' He chuckled, pointing at the screen.

I slowly moved over, and he drew me to his side as though we'd never been apart, and as if nothing between us had changed, and I stiffened before peering at a photo of Sam on his back, along the full length of the train seat. His legs were stretched out, his cycling shoelaces undone, and Chris had positioned the back page of a magazine over Sam's face, so he looked to have the head of a grizzly bear.

'That's funny,' I said, unable to match his chuckle as I pulled away. 'Typical Chris.'

Sam tugged me back and squashed a kiss on my hair. He smelt foreign – of trains and sunshine, and a hint of garlic and beer. I wondered what I smelt of.

'It went well then?' I eased away again, wishing he'd face me. I needed to look at his eyes, and read what was in them, but he crossed to the fridge and stuck his head inside.

'It was brilliant.' He threw me a smile as he pulled out a carton of orange juice. 'Toughest thing I've done, but totally worth it.' He took down two glasses, and poured us both a drink. 'Ben met us at the station. He's gutted he couldn't make it.'

I felt like saying *I know, I've seen his comments online*, but instead took the glass of juice he was proffering and said politely, 'What was Geneva like?'

Sam emptied his glass before replying, head thrown back, and I watched his Adam's apple as he swallowed. 'We didn't see much of it, to be honest,' he said when he'd finished, turning to rinse his glass.

The evening sun glanced off his hair, turning it almost white, and I had a vision of us, thirty years from now, in the exact same place, having the same conversation.

'We were a bit hung-over from celebrating last night.' A smile creased his cheek, as if revisiting a good memory. 'Chris threw up in a bin this morning, and Dom's legs ached so much after the descent yesterday, he could barely put one foot in front of the other.' He shook his head, as if he couldn't fathom it. 'I told him he should have put in more training, but he wouldn't listen.' He bent to open the dishwasher, his head snatching back when he spotted the unwashed plates, mugs and wine glasses inside. 'Forgot to switch it on?' he said with a grimace.

'I haven't had much time for housework.' It was a cue for him to ask about… *everything*. He didn't take it.

'I'll have a quick clear up,' he said, scanning the worktops as if they were coated with grime, eyes lingering on the empty Mini Eggs bag and crumpled cheese wrapper I'd forgotten to throw away. 'We don't want mice, like your mum had once, do you remember?'

I nodded, but he was already squatting to pull some disinfectant wipes from the cupboard under the sink, his joggers riding low to show a strip of bare back, and I felt an urge to tug his T-shirt down.

'I thought my brakes were going to fail at one point,' he said, bouncing up and starting to rub at the worktops. 'I had visions of myself flying over the handlebars and breaking my nose, but managed to slow down in time. I had to fit a new cable.' He paused, wipe in hand, face twisting violently, then released a huge sneeze and simultaneously farted. 'Pardon,' he said, turning his attention to the stove, even though I hadn't used it all week. 'You should have seen some of the hairpin bends we had to get past on the way to the Col de la Faucille.'

I slid onto a stool at the breakfast bar, with the curious feeling I was watching Sam from a distance, as he scrubbed at a particularly stubborn stain – I must have spilt a drop of wine when Cassie and Tilly were here.

I wondered what Nathan was doing at this very moment.

'How did it go at the bakery?'

At last. 'It couldn't have gone better,' I said stiffly as he finally stopped scrubbing and turned to look at me. 'We took lots of money.'

He folded his arms, fists wedged under his armpits and fixed me properly in his gaze. 'I'm glad it went well.' He sounded genuine, which was confusing. 'Tell me about it.'

I cleared my throat. 'Big Steve made some bread before he went to work this morning, and Kath and Cassie helped out in the shop, and Valerie Jones, you don't know her, is going to be working there too, and a photographer came, so I'll be in the paper, and Alice did an update on the programme yesterday…' I paused, aware of trying to paint as positive a picture as possible – even though there hadn't been any downsides, apart from my aching feet. 'Oh, and Mum turned up with…' I stumbled. 'With my… with Mike.'

'I'm still not sure about this mystery buyer,' Sam said, zeroing in on the part he disliked the most. 'I think you should try to find out who it is.'

'Why does it bother you, if it doesn't bother me?' I shifted position, and had to grab at the breakfast bar to prevent myself shooting off the stool. 'Would you feel the same if Mr Moseley had left me the bakery in his will?'

That seemed to throw him. 'I suppose not.' He scratched his forehead. 'But then, he knew you. It would have made sense for him to do that.'

'I really think he would have, you know. If he'd got round to making a will.'

'It's academic though, Meg, because he didn't.'

'But someone saw its potential, and mine, and wanted to give us a chance,' I pushed. 'Isn't that a nice thing to do?'

'I just can't believe there are no strings attached, Meg. What if it doesn't work out?' A persuasive tone had entered his voice that I recognised all the more clearly for not having seen him for a week.

'If it doesn't work out, he can always sack me and get another manager in.' My pulse throbbed with annoyance. 'Which won't happen, because I'm *not* going to fail.'

'I'm just looking out for you, babe.' His voice was softer, as if calming a temperamental retriever. 'It's risky, that's all, and also you're going to be there all the time, and I suppose I don't want to be fighting for your attention.'

Like I fight for your attention with your bloody cycling.

'I was thinking,' he said, before I could react, whipping a clean disinfectant wipe from the pack. 'What if we have our honeymoon in Geneva?' He shot me a smile. 'It's really beautiful. I think you'd like it, and we wouldn't have as far to travel, which means we'd get to spend more time there.' *Tell him now.* 'Meg?'

'Sam, I—'

'Listen, I know I've been an arse about everything, but you know what it's like when I'm training.' His eyes had filled with remorse. 'The challenge is over for this year, so I'm all yours now, babe. I'm going to make it up to you.'

Oh god. 'I – I don't know,' I said, mind frothing. 'What about George?'

'George?' A jumble of emotions crossed his face, gone before I could pin any of them down. 'What's she got to do with us?'

I thought about the photo, but it was hardly proof of anything. 'I…'

'Look,' he said, with a rueful smile. 'Emotions have been running high with one thing and another. You've had all sorts going on back here, and I'm sorry you had to go through all that with your… with your *dad*, on your own.'

So, he hadn't forgotten I now had a dad. 'It was a shock,' I admitted, as the memory of finding out about Mike came flooding back. 'I honestly thought I was going to faint. Mum had to catch me.'

'I'm looking forward to meeting him,' Sam said. 'I need to give him a good grilling about his intentions.'

'Sam!' Anger gripped my chest. 'I've already told you, he's not like that.' I pushed aside my untouched orange juice and slid off the stool. 'Why are you being like this about him?'

'Being like what?' He threw down the wet wipe and caught my hands, pressing them to his chest. 'Your mum's vulnerable,' he said, as if he knew her better than I did. 'And you are too, Meg, you just can't see it.'

I pulled away, catching a whiff of disinfectant, and wiped my hands down my dress. 'You nearly lost your dad, Sam. I thought you of all people would understand how amazing it is to know that mine's alive.'

Disbelief crowded his face. 'Having a brilliant dad in the first place meant I knew exactly what I'd be losing if he didn't make it,' he said passionately. 'It made me appreciate everything so much more.' He reached for my hands again and I let him take them this time, wishing I hadn't brought up Neil's near-death experience. He looked at me with faint disappointment, like a favourite jumper I'd shrunk in the wash. 'You've never known your dad. It's not the same.'

'I know, I'm sorry, I shouldn't have said that.' I released his fingers. 'I just wish you'd give Mike the benefit of the doubt, like I am.'

He pulled me close, tightening his arms around me as he pressed his face into my neck. 'Let's not argue,' he murmured. 'We never argue.' The light was lowering, sharpening colours and shapes. I looked at the hot-dog-shaped clock on the wall, as if I'd never seen it before. It looked so... *phony.* 'Let's go to bed.' Sam pushed himself even closer and I wrenched away, feeling an urge to test him.

'Mum's invited us round.' I tugged my mouth into a smile. 'Mike wants to meet you.'

All at once, tiredness shrouded his face and he gave a theatrical yawn. 'God, I'm shattered,' he said. 'I've barely slept in the last twenty-four hours.'

'We don't have to stay long,' I said. 'Just show our faces, really.'

He gave an understanding smile. 'I doubt I'd make a very good impression at the moment.' He cupped my cheek. 'You go if you want to, Meg. I think I need to crash out.'

His palm felt clammy and I tilted my head away. 'But, Sam, it's my dad.' I couldn't believe he wasn't prepared to come with me. 'He won't care if you're not on form.'

'I care.' His smile dimmed. 'I'm just not up to something so... *major* right now.'

Again, I had the feeling that I was spoiling the natural order of things; that a long-lost dad simply wasn't on his agenda. 'It's important to me, Sam.'

He squeezed my shoulder. 'If he's as nice as you say he is, I'm sure he'll understand.'

Chapter Twenty-Five

I didn't go in the end. I couldn't bear to turn up on my own when Mum and Mike knew that Sam was back in the country. After he'd hauled his rucksack upstairs and jumped in the shower – seeming to have miraculously revived – I texted Mum to say we were both worn out and having an early night.

She replied that she understood with two winky faces, which made my heart drop, adding *Kath said today was a great success! We're all very proud of you XX*

I shot into the garden, wondering how long Sam had been back and whether he'd noticed the patchy grass, and that I'd forgotten to wind the hose up. I stood for a moment, as the sun dipped over the rooftops, the smell of barbecue smoke so strong I could almost hear the spit and sizzle of steak fat on the grill.

'We're having sausages, you're not having sausages.' It was the twins, back on their trampoline, sunburnt faces almost feral. 'We're having sausages, you're not having sausages,' they chanted, more loudly.

I wished they would bounce into the nearest tree and stay there.

'We've got cake for afters, from your shop.'

'That's nice,' I said, when they bobbed up again.

'I bet it tastes like POO-POO!'

I sighed and went indoors, closing the windows so I couldn't hear their taunts. My thoughts were darting like startled rabbits not knowing where to settle, and I realised I was starving. I went into the kitchen and took some cooked chicken from the fridge and buttered one of the tomato and basil rolls I'd brought back from the bakery, eating quickly standing up. I heard Sam moving about upstairs, no doubt unpacking, probably still dripping from his shower, a towel wound round his waist.

Why hadn't I told him straight out that I was having doubts about the wedding? I'd had plenty of opportunities. I went through to the hall – imagined marching upstairs and saying it – but the words seemed stuck in my head.

'I'm in bed if you'd like to join me,' he called down, in his seducer's voice. I could almost see him flipping the sheet back and patting the mattress, a look of intent in his eyes, no doubt raring to go now his cycling challenge was over. 'Meg?'

I backed into the living room, a buzzing feeling in my head. 'I've got some paperwork to sort out,' I called back.

'OK.' Another loud yawn. 'I'll keep your side warm, although it's pretty hot in here.'

I'll tell him tomorrow. First thing.

I curled into the sofa and switched on the television low. I didn't need the volume high. I knew every episode of *Friends* almost word for word.

'Mum sounded a bit weird on the phone,' Sam said, as we drove to his parents' house the following day. I couldn't believe we were actually going – that I still hadn't talked to him.

'Maybe she felt guilty after what she said the other night.'

'I'm sure she didn't mean it, especially if she'd been drinking.' He rested a hand on my knee and I pretended I'd spotted a loose thread on my skirt as an excuse to shift away.

'Young children and drunk people always tell the truth. Isn't that what they say?'

He gave a small shrug, and I let it drop. He was still miffed that I'd fallen asleep on the sofa in the end, and wouldn't join him for 'a cuddle' earlier, because I'd given myself a stiff neck.

'I'll give you a massage,' he'd offered, when I took him a mug of coffee, pretending to pout when I wincingly declined, wishing he'd go training as usual, and as if he'd read my mind, he'd sprang out of bed and headed out with his bike.

He'd refused breakfast when he came back, saving himself for lunch, and had spent the next couple of hours tinkering with his bike in the garden and FaceTiming Chris – as if they hadn't seen enough of each other – while I put on a wash and tidied the house, practising saying *I don't want to marry you* in my head, but unable to form the words. It was as if, now he was back, I'd fallen straight back into our Sam and Meg rut, and couldn't claw my way out.

A vicious headache started to pulse behind my eyes, not helped by the sight of Sadie, hanging out of an upstairs window as we arrived at the Ryans'. She vanished as soon as she saw the car pull up, and I felt sick with the realisation that, by not talking to Sam, I'd probably made everything worse.

My palms were sweating as I got out, far too hot even though I was wearing a thin cotton dress and the temperature had dipped to slightly less than stifling.

Beverley was already bringing food to the table when we got inside, the smell of roasting meat making my throat close up.

'Ooh, I thought you weren't coming for a moment,' she cried, putting down the roast potatoes, and bounding over to bear hug Sam. 'Look at you, my lovely, you're so *brown*!'

She encompassed me in her toothy smile, but her eyes barely grazed mine, and I knew she'd remembered our last conversation and had meant every word.

'How was it, son?' Neil came through and there was more bear hugging with added back-slapping, as though Sam had been gone for six months and we hadn't just seen them last week.

He filled them in as we settled ourselves at the table and filled our plates, and I noticed with a surge of relief that Maura wasn't present.

'Your sister's got this summer flu, but sends her love,' said Beverley, opposite Sam, folding in her voluminous white top as she sat down so it didn't dip in the gravy boat. 'She'll catch up with you soon.'

She slid me a look of thinly veiled contempt, as though it was my fault that Maura wasn't well, and I realised they must have discussed me, and that Maura was firmly on her mother's side. The thought was deeply depressing, and I wished I could get up and leave – go to the bakery and make a cake or… go anywhere, really.

My thoughts felt like tangled vines, when a day ago they'd been straight lines, and I was increasingly furious with myself.

'Meg was busy while you were away, weren't you, love?' said Neil, once Sam had finished going through his itinerary, which I knew Beverley would have avidly followed online. 'She's got that bakery up and running again.'

'Yes, I did know,' he said, briefly resting his hand on mine, as though he fully supported my decision and hadn't more or less told me I wouldn't succeed. 'She's amazing.'

'Could you please pass the gravy?' Beverley asked me, clearly keen to deflect the topic, and I had another Groundhog Day feeling as I handed it over and watched her tip half the liquid on her roast lamb. 'The meat's tender, don't you think, sweetheart?'

I nodded. My appetite had fled, and I knew I was going to struggle to eat even half of what I'd put on my plate. Sam, sitting beside his mum, was having no such trouble, forking a floret of broccoli into his mouth.

Sadie came in and sat next to me, casting me a look that I couldn't read. She didn't seem hostile, but wasn't smiling either.

My heart rate doubled. 'How's, er, make-up college?' I fumbled over the words, feeling as if I had no right to talk to her, especially when I hadn't called to 'speak' like I'd said I would.

'It's cool.' She speared a pea with her fork. 'We're doing prosthetics at the moment, so we've been making each other into monsters.'

Her gaze flickered to me and her eyes widened. I dropped my fork. Was she saying I was a monster? Maybe I was. Sweat broke out on my brow, but when I looked at her again, she was watching Beverley squash a Yorkshire pudding into her mouth as if she'd never seen anything quite so repulsive.

I ransacked my brain for an inoffensive topic of conversation. I couldn't face bringing up Mike, and dealing with their reactions, and it didn't look as if Sam was going to either. He was still talking about his trip to Neil, at the end of the table, pausing only to swallow food, or take a gulp of water.

Beverley was sticking to water too, and I wondered whether she'd made a conscious decision to stay sober. Perhaps she didn't trust herself not to lunge at me over the table and rip my hair out.

'Had a word with your mum yet, about buying your dress?' she said brightly, folding a slice of lamb onto her fork.

I poked a nugget of sweetcorn, which shot onto the table. 'No, I haven't.' I risked a glance at Sadie, in time to see her eyes dart back to her plate.

'I probably won't be coming over every week in future,' she said, unexpectedly. 'My friends…' She paused, perhaps arrested by the panic on Beverley's face, and remembering the way Beverley had cried about losing her family, I almost felt sorry for her. 'We'd like to do things together sometimes on a Sunday.' She cast an apologetic glance in her dad's direction. 'Sorry.'

'Of course you do, love.' A drop of gravy splashed the front of his shirt as he lowered his fork. 'You don't want to hang around with the old folks every week, you want to be out having fun!'

'You're saying Sunday lunch isn't fun?' Beverley looked bewildered, her cutlery hitting her plate. 'What could be more fun than this?'

Almost anything.

The unspoken words hung over the table, and Sam laughed into the silence. 'I don't think it's meant to be fun,' he said, wagging his knife and adopting a grandfatherly tone. 'Sunday lunch with the family's about tradition, not about having fun.'

'That's horrible, Sam.' Beverley's chin quivered.

He looked alarmed. 'I was only joking, Mum. I'm having a great time.'

Sadie's lip curled. 'You're so stupid, Sam.'

'Sadie!' Beverley grasped her chunky necklace, as if it might offer protection. 'Sam's not stupid. He's just cycled from Paris to Geneva on a bike, and he went to university. He's far from stupid.'

'Oh, Mum.' Giving up any pretence of eating, Sadie tapped the tip of her nails on the table. 'You haven't got a clue, have you?'

This was it. She was about to tell them what she'd seen at the café. A pulse throbbed at the base of my throat, and the room strobed in and out.

'What's that supposed to mean?' Sam leaned across to get a better view of his sister.

'Yes, what *does* that mean?' Beverley sounded almost scared, tugging her necklace hard enough to break it, her dinner abandoned.

'What's going on?' Neil's face was creased with confusion, and I couldn't bear it any longer.

'I kissed someone,' I said to the dish of honeyed parsnips. Out of the corner of my eye, I saw Sadie open her mouth to speak and rushed on, 'Sadie saw us, I'm sorry, I should have said something, but I… I didn't, and I'm sorry.'

There was a brief, stunned silence. 'Sorry you didn't say anything, or sorry you did it?' Beverley rushed in, sounding positively gleeful, as though I'd made her day.

'You kissed someone?' I turned to see Sam staring at me, slack-jawed and incredulous. 'You *kissed* someone?'

I nodded, relieved to have got the words out, as if I'd sicked up something that had disagreed with me.

'A man or a woman?'

'Does it matter?' I frowned at him. 'A man.'

Beverley was up and pacing now, one hand in her curls the other on her hip. 'I always said she wasn't good enough for you.'

'You never said it to me,' Sam said, still looking at me with open disbelief.

'Or me,' said Neil, and his look of quiet betrayal was almost worse than Sam's wide-eyed incomprehension.

'I can't believe it.' Sam elbowed his dinner plate out of the way as though it disgusted him. 'I'm away for a few days, and you kiss another man?' He narrowed his eyes. 'Is that all that happened?'

'Isn't that enough?' squawked Beverley. 'After everything we've done for you, welcoming you into this family—'

'Hang on,' Neil said, holding up his hands. 'We don't know the whole story. I think we should let Meg explain.'

'What's to explain?' Beverley sat back down, and leaned towards me. 'How could you do that to my Sammy, and come round here all sweetness and light?' she said, spittle gathering at the edges of her mouth. 'I knew when I saw you on the telly, something wasn't right, and Maura saw it too.'

I was crying now, hot tears dropping onto the table. 'Sam, can we please talk privately?'

He was pale, like a man who'd been dealt a terrible blow he was trying to process – which I supposed he had. 'Sam?'

'I never thought you'd do something like that, it's not you.' His brow was furrowed, as though he was slotting a new, cheating version of me over the old Meg he knew. 'I thought it was the bakery you were into, not another man.'

'I always knew she'd let you down,' said Beverley, her hand shooting across the table towards her son. 'We're here, my darling, you're not alone.'

'Oh for god's sake.' Sadie pushed her chair back and stood up. 'You shouldn't feel too bad, Meg,' she said, clasping my shoulder. I looked at her through a puddle of tears and saw sympathy in her eyes. 'I meant it, you know. I wasn't going to say anything.' She looked at Sam, and when she spoke her voice was loaded with disappointment. 'Not after seeing him kissing another woman.'

Chapter Twenty-Six

'Meg, please just get in.'

Sam had slowed the car to a crawl, eyes begging me across the passenger seat.

I looked away. 'I'm good, thanks.'

'It's hot, you'll get heatstroke. You know what you're like in the sun.'

'Oh, now you know what's best for me?'

'Meg, this is silly. Just get in the car and we'll talk.'

'I've nothing to say to you.'

'Meg, please!'

I focused on putting one foot in front of the other – left, right, left, right – not caring that the sun was lancing across my shoulders, or that I couldn't possibly walk all the way back to Salcombe. I just wanted to put as much distance between Sam and me as I could.

'Meg, please, come on.' His voice was cajoling, and I knew he thought it was only a matter of time before he talked me down.

'If I need a lift, I'll call someone.' I slowed to take my phone out of my bag, and almost fell as the toe of my sandal caught in a crack in the pavement.

Sam pulled the car up ahead, and popped the door open.

I strode past, powered by something even stronger than anger. It felt close to relief... no, not relief. Justification. Because I'd known.

Not the details, obviously, but I'd known on some deeply buried level that I wasn't Sam's true love. That, whatever had brought him back to me when his father nearly died wasn't as simple as that.

He'd lied to me. And, perhaps, to himself, all these years.

And maybe I'd lied to myself too.

'Meg!'

Something raw in his voice prompted me to turn.

He was on the pavement, holding open the car door, and with a sense of mounting fury I marched back. Resisting a strong urge to slam the car door on his fingers, I threw myself into the passenger seat. He jogged round to the driver's side and leapt in, the grim set to his mouth softening a little. He thought he had me. That, within the hour, we'd have forgiven each other our silly transgressions, and things would be back to normal. He'd have to forgive me, now I'd found out that he'd kissed someone else too.

Clutching my bag in my lap I said tightly, 'Admit you only asked me to marry you in the first place because *George* turned you down.'

Because, of course it was George he'd kissed. George, who he'd been admiring in the photo. George with the strong thighs, flashing eyes, and gold trophy.

It turned out the cycling group had been in Paignton, where Sadie was at college, and she'd seen them in the park on her lunch break with her friends.

Sam and George had been apart from the group, talking under a tree, and he'd suddenly cupped George's face in his hands and kissed her tenderly, as though taking a long drink of something delicious. That was how Sadie had described it, the romantic in her leaping to the fore, though she'd apologised to me afterwards for saying it like that. At first, she'd thought it swoony, like something from a film, then realised the gravity of her big brother kissing another woman. After the woman had broken away and returned to the others, Sam staring after her as if his world had just ended, Sadie had rushed over and thumped him, she said. Not hard, because she wasn't strong, but she'd wanted to really hurt him, and he'd looked upset and said it didn't even matter, because George had just told him she was in love with Chris – womanising Chris, who didn't deserve a decent woman. And it had sounded as if George was quite decent, after all, because she'd seen Sadie attack Sam and caught up with her to ask her not to say anything to Sam's girlfriend, because the kiss had been a mistake, and the last thing she wanted to do was to cause any trouble.

And all this had happened about a week before Sam had proposed to me.

'It wasn't like that,' he said now, twisting in his seat, a determined slant to his jaw, and it was almost funny how hard he was prepared to work to get me to see sense. 'It only made me realise how much I wanted to be with you, Meg. That's why I proposed.'

It made me realise it's you I want to be with. That's what he'd said when he came back from Edinburgh – after Andrea broke up with him.

'You only wanted me when no one else wanted you,' I said, the truth finally dawning. It wasn't that he didn't care for me (surely he couldn't have faked it all this time?), but there was no longer any doubt in my mind that Andrea had been his true love – or maybe he'd thought George would be. 'If George had wanted that kiss as much as you did, we wouldn't even be sitting here right now.'

'Meg, that's rubbish,' he said, leaning towards me, as if he could change what was in my head by the sheer force of his presence. 'I don't even know why I did it when I had you at home. It was wrong, of course it was, but it led to me asking you to marry me, so, in a weird way, it was a good thing.'

I laughed, because I could see he really believed that, or at least that was how he'd justified it to himself.

'That kiss didn't mean anything,' he said. 'I doubt you can say the same about yours.' His gaze darkened. 'Yours was worse in a way, because I know it's not the sort of thing you would do.' His gaze darkened. 'Did he force himself on you, Meg?'

I recoiled. 'Of course not! I don't even know who kissed who first, but I wanted it as much as he did, if not more.'

There was a long silence as the impact of my words hit home. 'Right.' Sam dipped his head. 'So, your kiss really was worse, because you wanted it to happen.'

'It's not a bloody competition, Sam, about whose kiss meant the most. And you clearly wanted your kiss to happen with George because you instigated it!'

He chose to ignore that. 'But, if you had a choice, you'd rather kiss this Nathan than me?'

'Wouldn't you rather kiss Andrea, if she came into your life right now?'

'I thought you said it wasn't a competition.' He raised his eyes and now there was a hint of humour there. He was letting me know he was ready to turn the whole thing into a joke; something we'd look back on and laugh about in months to come. 'I'm invested in our future, Meg.' He traced a fingertip down my forearm with just the right amount of tentativeness. 'Nothing like that will ever happen again.'

'I suppose I was a safe bet.' I pulled away, determined not to be deflected. 'Good old Meg, always there like a faithful Labrador, never complaining. Meg would never cheat, or break up with you, or break your heart.'

'Or so I thought,' he said, and I knew I'd hit a nerve. Then his face relaxed again. 'Look, no matter what you think, I *am* invested in our wedding, in having a baby with you, in living the rest of our lives together.'

I wished he'd stop saying invested, as if I was a savings account. 'Until someone better comes along.'

He snatched his hand back and gave a short laugh. 'OK, maybe I deserve that,' he said quietly. 'But the truth is, I'll never find anyone better than you.'

I could see he really believed that, and tears distorted my vision. 'It won't stop you trying though.' I glanced at the sun-filled street outside, the colours blurring together. 'And, the stupid thing is, Sam, I was going to call off our wedding anyway. I wish I had now, before all this came out. Except if I had, I'd probably have never known about you and George.'

His head jerked as if I'd slapped him. 'Meg, I—'

'I don't love you any more,' I butted in. 'I don't think I ever have, or not for ages. Not in the way I should have done.'

'Meg, you don't mean that.'

But I did. Tears slipped down my face as I recalled how I'd let Sam call the shots in our relationship from the moment he'd told me we were breaking up because he'd met someone else in Edinburgh. He was the one who'd finished with me, and he was the one who'd decided we were going to get back together. It was what I'd dreamed of for so long, I hadn't questioned it, and had let him set the pace ever since. I'd convinced myself I was happy to let him take the lead, when really I'd been scared to initiate anything in case I drove him away. It wasn't as if he'd coerced me into buying our house, or getting engaged, or having tests to determine whether I was capable of carrying his children. I'd thought I loved him, and sometimes it had been easier to go along with what he wanted rather than challenge his decisions, but I supposed I only had myself to blame that he was shocked that I'd so much as look at another man, let alone kiss one, when I'd given him every reason to think I'd never want anyone but him.

I wiped my face, which was slippery and hot, and a memory struck, of Mum, reading in bed one Sunday morning, while I baked mince pies in the kitchen. It was nearly Christmas, a month before Sam came back, and Mum had finished her bookkeeping course and was looking forward to setting up her little business in the New Year. Kath was coming round later, to talk strategy – and to update Mum on her latest blind date – and I was going Christmas shopping with a friend. Happiness had flared as I rolled out pastry and made plans for the year ahead – a better job, more money, a savings fund. Maybe my own kitchen, one day. Four weeks later, Neil fell out of a tree, and Sam came back from Edinburgh.

A week after that, we were back together.

He tried to hold my hand, but I yanked it away.

'Look,' he said, back in persuasive mode. 'You kissed another man, and it hurts, but I get it. I was away from home, and I might have been training a bit too hard for the challenge, but I'll be around more now. We can put it behind us and focus properly on the future. You've got the bakery to think about and then there's the wedding—'

'I've just said, there's not going to be a wedding, Sam.' I twisted my ring up over my knuckle, tugged it off and dropped it in his lap.

'Now you're being dramatic.' He attempted to put it back on, but I wriggled my finger away.

'Please, Meg.' His smile was tight with determination. 'Let's not do this, OK? We've both made mistakes, so let's call it quits—'

'I've just told you I'm not in love with you.' I shoved the car door open. 'It's over, Sam.'

'Wait!' Fright skidded over his face. 'Where are you going?'

'I don't know,' I said, my breath quickening at the enormity of it all. 'But don't wait up for me.'

'Meg, I—'

I slammed the door and started walking, not slowing as he finally drove past, slowly at first, as if hoping I'd change my mind and beg him to come back, then speeding up before finally disappearing out of sight.

With every step my breathing grew easier. I began to feel stronger, as if he'd taken something heavy with him that I hadn't known I'd been carrying, but soon I was panting with heat exhaustion, and my sandals were rubbing my heels.

I stopped and got out my phone. 'Are you busy?' I said when Cassie picked up. 'I really need a lift.'

Chapter Twenty-Seven

'Jesus, Jumping Jack Flash!' Big Steve stared as I entered the kitchen the following morning, not through the back door as he'd have expected, but via the crooked staircase leading to the rooms above. 'Meg, what the *heck*?'

He dropped his dough scraper and took in my puffy face, his eyes stretched to maximum. 'Sam,' he guessed, immediately. 'Conscious uncoupling?'

'You could say that.'

'Oh, Meg, I'm so sorry.'

'I couldn't think of anywhere else I wanted to go.'

I'd asked Cassie to drop me at the bakery in the end, and she'd pulled away with a smoky chug after extracting a promise to call her and Tilly if I decided I wanted some company, or a shoulder to cry on. She'd nodded with understanding when I told her the wedding was definitely off, and, after I'd falteringly explained, said it was better to break up now, than get married and end up divorcing. She didn't bad-mouth Sam, which I was grateful for.

Tilly had shown no such restraint, phoning half an hour later as I attempted to clear a space in the cramped living room above the bakery kitchen, saying Cassie had called to tell her what had happened (Cassie really was terrible at keeping things secret these days).

'I *knew* he wasn't a keeper,' she'd said. 'And he didn't like me, because he knew I could see straight through him.'

'But how?' I was genuinely curious that she'd seen something I hadn't.

'It was the way he always wanted you to himself when we were at school, taking you fishing at weekends, implying that hanging around doing girl stuff was for girls, as though that was a *bad* thing. He never supported Legal Mystics and didn't come and see us when we performed at Cassie's house that summer.'

'He found it a bit embarrassing, that's all.' I'd leapt to his defence out of habit. 'It's not like he ever liked All Saints. It might have been different if we'd formed a Green Day tribute band.'

'I felt like he isolated you a bit,' she'd said. 'Probably because he didn't want anyone else to make a move on you. You couldn't see how gorgeous you were.'

'He didn't isolate me, Tilly.' I'd started crying. 'I liked being with him.'

'I know, and I'm not saying he didn't like you a lot too, I just think he knew you'd fallen for his whole family set-up and would be the perfect girlfriend.' I'd sensed her choosing her next words carefully. 'I think he knew he could play around with other women, and come back to you if things didn't work out.'

'Which is exactly what happened.' I'd slumped on Mr Moseley's velvet sofa, sending a cloud of dust into the stuffy room. 'I suppose I was the sort of girl you take home to Mum, not the type that men feel passionate about.'

'Er, does the name Nathan Walsh ring a bell?'

I hadn't let myself think about Nathan until then. 'It was probably just a chemical thing, like you said.' Hugo's words flashed into my head. *My brother doesn't fall in love lightly.* 'And, anyway, he's leaving tomorrow.'

Even though she was still feeling rough, Tilly had volunteered to come over with a bottle of wine, but I'd been hit by a tidal wave of exhaustion, and couldn't even respond to a text from Mum, asking if Sam had enjoyed his cycle challenge.

'Listen, I know it's bad timing, but I don't want you to worry that I'm going to let things slide,' I said to Big Steve, who'd come over to wrap a flour-coated arm around my sunburnt shoulders. My hair was frazzled from tossing and turning all night, and I was wearing the dress I'd had on the day before, which I'd also slept in. At least I'd tried to sleep, on top of Mr Moseley's unmade bed, repeatedly sneezing into the pillow, which was filled with feathers. I knew I looked a state. 'And by the way, I'm so glad you're here.' I stretched my arm as far as it would go around Steve's waist, noting the heaps of proving dough, waiting to be turned into loaves. 'We sold out of everything on Saturday.'

'So I heard,' he said, a twinkle of satisfaction in his eyes. 'Are you living upstairs now, then?'

I thought of home, with its perfectly polished floorboards, and the kitchen that Sam had chosen, and the garden Neil and Beverley had lavished so much attention on, and knew I couldn't go back. 'Actually, I think I am.' Something stirred in the pit of my stomach. A chink of hope – or maybe it was excitement. Or maybe I was coming down with Tilly's flu. 'It needs a lot of sorting out, and I'll probably have to clear it with the solicitor's,' I said. 'But it's… well, it's vacant, so I suppose it'll be OK.'

'And you'll be on the premises, so won't need to drive to work.'

To my astonishment I found myself high-fiving Big Steve. 'And you'll be right next door,' I said.

'We can shout to each other out of our bedroom windows.' He grinned so hard his eyes almost disappeared.

'And I won't need to set my alarm because you can just shout up the stairs.'

'And you can make your cakes whenever you like, even in the middle of the night, if you want to.'

'We can have midnight baking sessions!'

Suddenly we were doing another Highland fling, then reality hit me and I stopped mid-turn. 'I'll need to go and pick up some things,' I said. 'And I'm going to have to break the news to Mum and…' I nearly said Dad, and realised there was a lot Big Steve didn't know, and decided to leave that explanation for another day. 'I'll wait until this evening.'

The thought of bumping into Sam filled me with trepidation. He hadn't tried to contact me and I knew, deep in my gut, however upset he was now, that once he'd got his head around us splitting up, he'd package it away and put me in the ex-fiancée zone. He'd move on. Sam was good at that.

Telling Mum wouldn't be easy; she'd always liked Sam, and it meant there wouldn't be a wedding to look forward to, or babies on the horizon, but I knew she'd support me, no matter what, and having regular access to baby Milo would help fulfil any grandmotherly urges. Plus, she had Mike now, and a chance to experience the sort of love she thought she'd lost forever. Nothing was going to match that feeling, right now.

'Is there a shower upstairs?' Big Steve comically rolled his eyes in the direction of my armpits. I had a sniff and winced. 'It could make all the difference to this homeless vibe you've got going on.'

'Actually there is,' I said, clamping my arms to my sides. 'It looks older than me, but must still work. Mr Moseley always smelt nice and clean.'

'He didn't die in that bed up there, did he?'

'I'm not even going to think about that,' I said.

'OK, well I suggest you spruce yourself up and get to work, Miss Larson. You've got cakes to bake for the masses.'

I had one foot on the bottom stair, when someone knocked at the back door. My immediate thought was Nathan, but when Steve answered the door it was a tired-looking Sam standing there, surrounded by bin bags and a couple of suitcases I recognised as mine.

'I thought you'd be at your mum's but I suppose I should have known that you'd come here.'

My heart tipped over. 'You saw Mum?'

He shook his head. 'She was in the front garden watching a man paint the front door, so I guessed you couldn't be there and I didn't want to ask in case she didn't know anything.'

'Thanks,' I said, thinking how odd it was that I could talk to him as if he was just an acquaintance, when we'd been sharing a bed until a week ago, and were planning to spend the rest of our lives together.

'I've brought your car,' he said. 'I'll cycle home, my bike's in the boot.'

He ran a hand over his hair, and I noticed he was wearing his cycling shorts, with his work shirt. No time off nursing heartbreak for Sam. 'I've been away for a week, I have to go in,' he said, seeing me checking him out. He looked a lot better put together than I did, and I wondered whether he was gratified to see evidence of my sleepless night. 'There's no point me moping at home, if you've really made up your mind.'

When I didn't respond – there was a lump the size of a tangerine in my throat – he nodded, as if to say *I thought so*. 'I'll cancel the wedding venue.' His voice was clipped. 'We'll divide up the savings, and you'll have something to live on. I'll probably sell the house.'

'Sam, I—'

'I might go back to Edinburgh.' His gaze didn't quite meet mine. 'It's going to be too painful, staying.'

My heart felt like a rock. 'And there's an outside chance you might run into Andrea.'

He shook his head, as though greatly saddened by my comment. 'I know people up there,' he said. 'The company has an office. It would be an easy relocation.'

Less than twenty-four hours, and he was planning an alternative future. 'What about Chris, and the cycling group?'

'There'll be cycling groups up there, and we'll stay in touch on Facebook. Chris can come and visit, once I've found somewhere to live.'

He must have been up all night, thinking it through.

'I've packed as much of your stuff as I could find.' He gestured at the bags, hand on hip. 'Shall I bring them in, if you're staying here?'

'You can just hand them over,' I said, not wanting Sam to come inside the bakery. He'd never shown much interest, and had only seen me at work once, before Mr Moseley died, when he'd had a day off and popped in to meet the old man he'd heard so much about, because I'd tentatively suggested he might like him. (He hadn't. '*He should have retired at least a decade ago, Meg. He's running that business into the ground.*')

'Fine,' he said, smiling quickly as if to neutralise his feelings. 'They're quite heavy.'

He handed each bag over wordlessly until the narrow space at the foot of the stairs was crowded with all the things I'd accrued over the last few years. 'If there's anything else you'd like, any pictures, or maybe that rug you chose for the bedroom, just call and I'll bring them over.'

'There won't be.'

'I didn't know if you'd want photographs of us.' He raised an eyebrow.

I thought of the one by the bed, of us at Sadie's eighteenth. Had he been thinking of George then? *How long had he wanted to kiss her?* 'No, thanks.' Hurt and confusion flared across his face. 'Do what you want with them.'

Recovering, he said, 'Dad and Sadie are upset,' as if it was all my fault. No mention of his mum, and I guessed Beverley was thanking the heavens that her son had had a lucky escape – even if it meant him moving away again. 'They want you to promise you'll stay in touch.'

In fact, I'd already had a message from Sadie.

I'm sorry I won't get to be your bridesmaid. I love my brother, but you're better off without him. Let me know if you'd like a makeover, love you, S xxx

I'd cried then, big fat tears, remembering Sadie's sixth birthday picnic on the beach at Seashell Cove, when Sam had picked her up in a fireman's lift and run with her into the sea, dunking her under the surface, while Maura shrieked at the water's edge and Beverley, in a turquoise one-piece, tried to get a photo, and Neil fell over trying to escape a wasp.

'I will,' I said. 'And I'm sorry dinner was ruined.'

'OK, well, I'd better…' He looked behind him, as if seeing his office and all the things he had to do once he returned to work. 'I thought I'd go in early and catch up.'

'Right.'

'And you've probably got baking to do.'

I nodded.

'I am proud of you, Meg.'

'Thanks,' I said. I didn't need his approval any more. I never had really, even if I'd thought I wanted it. 'Good luck with everything.'

'You too.'

We looked at each other a moment longer, then he turned to the car to get his bike in the cycling shoes that made him walk as if he'd strained his groin. I waited until he'd gone, then stepped over the bags and went upstairs to have the most unsatisfying shower of my life.

Chapter Twenty-Eight

There was no time for reflection as the next few hours flew by, my attention trained on replenishing the shelves in the shop, as Big Steve finished his first batch of loaves and shot next door for a shower.

'Back in an hour,' he sang, looking – for the first time in ages – like a man who was happy with his job.

When Kath saw the three-tier strawberry and cream cake I'd made, she gasped. 'That looks am*aaa*zing.' She lifted the glass dome for a closer look, as if trying to absorb it through her eyes. 'Can you make one of those for my sixtieth?'

'I thought you wanted a rainbow layer cake.'

'I did until I saw this.' She mimed salivating, which wasn't a good look.

'It'll be a lot easier,' I said. 'It only took me about half an hour, once I'd baked the sponges.'

'You're a natural, love.' She made herself at home behind the counter as if she'd been there for years. 'I don't know how you've done all of this, with what you must be going through.'

'What?'

'Your break up with Sam,' she said, face crumpling.

I wondered why she'd given me an extra tight hug when she'd arrived, but I'd needed to get some scones out of the oven before they burnt, and by the time I'd finished transferring them to a cooling rack, she'd gone through to the shop.

'I'm sorry,' said Cassie, turning from the wall where she was hanging a painting she'd done of the bakery – though I suspected she'd really wanted an excuse to come check up on me. 'I thought you might have said something.'

'It's OK.' I tightened my apron straps, wondering whether Nathan was on a plane, or already somewhere in Ireland. 'Everyone will know sooner or later.'

Sooner, at this rate. I hoped no one would tell Mum before I'd had a chance to. I'd thought about calling, but felt it was a conversation I needed to have face to face.

'How are you coping, love?' Kath's face was one big furrow of sympathy. 'You two were together so long, you must feel really weird.'

'Actually, I'm not too bad.' I poked around my feelings to check if it was true. I was tired, and felt a bit like I'd had the flu, but seeing Sam earlier had only confirmed I'd been right to call off the wedding. 'I need some sleep, but that's partly because the bed upstairs was so uncomfortable. And I don't have any bedding.'

'Didn't the old man die in that bed?' said Kath.

'It doesn't bother me,' I said. 'Is that weird?'

'It is, love, yes.'

'You should ask Tilly to give the flat a makeover, once things have settled down a bit,' said Cassie.

'Good idea.' Kath smiled. 'You can have a little shopping spree, treat yourself to a new bed, and some furniture now you don't have a fancy big wedding to pay for.' She smacked a hand to her mouth. 'Sorry, love, that wasn't very diplomatic.'

'It's OK,' I said again, imagining the rooms cleared of junk and cosied up, with lamps and throws and pictures on the walls. 'I probably will buy new furniture, but first things first. Let's get the shop opened up.'

'About time,' said Gwen, bustling past the waiting customers to the front of the queue, before I'd even had a chance to wedge open the door. 'Day orf, now the Maitlands are back from their 'oliday,' she said, seeing my befuddled look. I couldn't recall ever seeing Gwen outside the café, though she was still wearing her Maitland's shirt and clumpy boots, her thighs pushing the seams of her denim shorts to bursting point. 'Thought I'd get me and Dickens a tasty treat for breakfast.' She tugged me to one side. 'Cassie told us about you and Just Sam,' she said, not lowering her voice one bit.

'Cassie!' I turned to see her cringing, as she positioned a picture hook on the wall. 'I thought she'd want to know,' she said over her shoulder. 'Mum and Dad send their best wishes.'

Was there anyone left in Seashell Cove who didn't know?

'When I left me 'usband,' Gwen said, folding her arms, her head jutting forward as if about to impart some great wisdom, 'I did a lot of shaggin' abart, and I mean, a LOT.' She raised a meaningful eyebrow. 'It got 'im out of me system,' she said, 'even if I ended up breakin' a few 'earts in the process.' Her eyes went faraway, as though seeing herself in the act, and I swiftly buried an image of her in lingerie. 'You don't wanna go darn that route,' she said at last, stroking her bottom lip with her thumb. 'You ain't cut out for that malarkey, so don't go puttin' it abart as if there's no tomorrow, or you'll just end up feelin'…'

'Bad about myself, I won't,' I finished, seeing people were straining to listen.

'I was gonna say, itchy darn below,' Gwen said. 'I ended up with terrible thrush, but yeah, you probably would feel bad abart yourself, you 'ain't cut out for shaggin' abart.'

I wished she'd stop saying shagging. A little girl was asking her mother what it meant, and a man with a hulking frame and tattooed arms was giving Gwen lustful glances and flicking his tongue over his lips.

Kath's face was red with suppressed laughter.

'I love working here,' she said, and I managed to loosen myself from Gwen's gaze and rushed behind the counter to help with the queue.

'That looks lovely,' I said, when Cassie had finished hanging her picture and the shop had quietened down. I studied the line drawing she'd lightly brushed with watercolour paint. It looked like a picture-book bakery, aglow with sunshine, and 'Meg's Kitchen' painted on a board outside. She'd even drawn a cat that looked like Dickens, and customers walking past, and I turned to the window as if they might actually be there and caught the eye of a man, looking in. It was Freya's husband, Don Williams. I wondered whether he'd come to talk to Kath about Milo, but when he saw me looking he turned and walked away.

On impulse, I ran outside. 'Don!'

He stopped and seemed to hesitate before swivelling round. 'Hey, Meg.' He smiled, looking expensive in his brightly patterned shirt and well-cut trousers, his silver plume of hair sweeping back from a widow's peak.

'Did you want to speak to Kath, because she's due a break?'

'No, no.' He held up a hand. 'I was just… looking.'

'Did you want a cake?'

He patted his flat stomach. 'Have to watch my weight,' he said regretfully, and I was struck again by his air of quiet kindness.

'I'm so sorry about Freya.' I moved closer. 'I sometimes think that if I hadn't told Kath about her wanting the bakery, and Kath hadn't called her, she might not have left you.'

He smiled in sad defeat. 'Oh, I think she would have,' he said. 'I love Freya very much, but I didn't realise just how headstrong she is.'

He tilted his head. 'I thought for a while that I was enough for her, and the baby would give her life meaning, but…' He shrugged. 'There's no fool like an old fool.'

I felt a strong wave of sympathy. 'She might come back.'

'And if she does, we'll be waiting.' He eyed the bakery, eyes crinkled against the sun. 'Looks like it's going well.'

'Oh, it is!' I was still having trouble believing it was open for business. 'I love it.'

'I know.' An odd look crossed his face. 'That chap was spot on about you.'

'Chap?'

'The agent who was here when Freya and I came to view.'

'Oh, er… right.' A frown settled on my face.

'When you ran off, Freya went to use the toilet—' *to snoop around more like* '—and Mr Walsh said to me, quite ferociously I might add, that if I was buying the bakery for someone to run, it should be you. That no one would love it more, or work harder to make it a success.'

I stared, dumbfounded. 'Nathan said that?' A feeling rose inside me, more exquisite than the rush of our first kiss. 'I didn't know.'

'I was very impressed by his passion, and yours.' A smile played around Don's mouth and his gaze was clear and bright. 'And I knew he was right, just like Kath was when she called to tear me off a strip for thinking about buying the place for Freya.'

He must have seen the show and was impressed by your passion. Wasn't that what Nathan had said, about the mystery buyer?

'It was you.' My heart seized with shock. '*You* bought the bakery.'

He slid his hands into his pockets. 'I heard the buyer wanted to remain anonymous,' he said.

'But I—'

'That he's someone who takes great pleasure in helping people realise their potential. People who deserve it.' There was the tiniest of twinkles in his eyes. 'I think Mr Moseley would be very happy to put you in charge of his bakery.'

'But, Freya…' I swallowed. 'If she knew…'

'Anonymous means just that,' Don said. 'Freya will find her own way, one day, I'm sure of that, but it won't be managing an ice-cream parlour in Seashell Cove.'

I knew I should say something, anything, but he'd turned on the heel of his shiny shoes and was striding away, marked out by his posture and the quality of his clothes, drawing curious eyes. A man with enough money to change someone's life, and not demand anything in return.

My bakery angel.

'Where did you go flying off to?' said Kath, when I returned to the shop, feeling as if I'd had a transformative experience – which, in a way, I suppose I had.

'I, er, needed some fresh air.' I stared at the window, where Don had been. If I hadn't seen him, would I ever have known? On balance, I was glad I did.

'I'm not surprised, love, after what you've been through.' Kath looked at what remained of the strawberry and cream cake. 'I don't suppose I could have a slice of that with a cup of tea, could I?'

'Go on,' I said. 'You've earned a break.'

'Are you OK?' said Cassie, when Kath had gone through to the kitchen.

'Isn't it your drawing day at the café?'

'I've cancelled,' she said. 'I thought you might need some help. And don't forget Valerie is coming in.'

I'd completely forgotten my newest member of staff would be here any minute.

'You didn't have to cancel your café day,' I said. 'I could easily have managed here.'

'Don't be silly,' she replied. 'That's what friends are for.'

I gave her a hug, wondering how I'd managed so many years without her in my life.

'Sure you're OK?'

I briefly considered telling her about Don, but knew she wouldn't be able to keep it to herself. 'I'm sure,' I said, just as Valerie turned up, eager to get to work, strapping on my old Star Baker apron with brisk efficiency. Once we'd had a little chat, I left her in the capable hands of Kath and Cassie and returned to the kitchen to start work on a celebration cake for an anniversary party, which the customer had requested be anything 'as long as it's lemon-flavoured'.

As I grated lemon zest and melted butter and sugar, my mind kept returning to what Nathan had said. Would Don have even considered buying the bakery if it hadn't been for Nathan?

My brother doesn't fall in love easily.

Had love prompted Nathan to say what he had to Don? If that wasn't love, then what was? I'd thought it was what Sam and I had had, but that seemed a paler, much tamer version. Not love at all, when it meant being second best, or wanting to be with someone else, or making a commitment because it's what you thought you should do.

I cracked eight eggs into a bowl, by mistake. I only needed four.

I couldn't think straight. I kept seeing Nathan's face as he'd burst into the café with Charlie under his arm. He'd run all the way from the beach to see me, to tell me the bakery had been bought. He'd thought about staying around – because of me. I remembered our kiss, and his face on the beach, watching Charlie – the tenderness in his smile.

I knocked over a bag of flour and it spilt across the table.

Was I in love with Nathan?

I picked up the lemon I'd grated. I'd taken off too much skin and knew the zest would be bitter. *Could I go the rest of my life without seeing Nathan again?*

I looked at the mess of egg yolks in the bowl. *What was I supposed to do next?* I was completely out of my depth.

'You look confused.' Big Steve was back, wearing a fresh T-shirt, his hair damp at the ends, smelling of coconut shower gel. 'Forgotten what you're doing?'

'Something like that,' I said.

Was it too soon to be thinking about someone else, when I'd only just called off my wedding? I thought about Mike and Mum and all the years that they hadn't known each other, only a short plane ride between them, but neither knowing it.

Life's too short, Mike had said. *When you know, you know.*

My heart was suddenly racing, as if I'd been running. 'I'm just popping upstairs,' I said to Steve.

'When you gotta go, you've gotta go,' he said.

'I don't need the toilet.'

'Did I say you did?'

I leapt over the bags, and almost shattered my tibia as I fell up the stairs, swearing and praying my phone still had some charge left. I couldn't be bothered to start rummaging around for my charger, providing Sam had packed it.

There was a single bar of power left in the battery, and I called Nathan's number with a shaky finger. It went to voicemail.

'Aargh!' He was probably in Ireland by now. I was too late.

I rang Mum.

'Oh, Meg, I was getting a bit worried that we hadn't heard from you,' she said. 'Mike was going to pop over to see if you were all right.'

'I broke up with Sam.' No point dressing it up, and if I didn't tell her now, she'd probably hear it on the lunchtime news. 'He kissed someone else, and I'm in love with another man.'

'Oh!' I waited for her to digest it, knowing a week ago she'd have had trouble handling the news, hoping now she had Mike she'd be able to bear it more easily. 'Does he know?' She didn't sound as put out as I'd expected.

'He knows I kissed him, but it turned out he'd kissed someone else, called George, from the cycling group.'

'Sam's gay?'

'What? No,' I said. 'She's a woman. Georgina.'

Silence. 'I meant, does he know you're in love with him? The other man.'

'No.' Tears slid down my cheeks. 'He's gone away.'

'Go after him,' Mum said. 'For god's sake, Meg. What are you waiting for?'

I couldn't speak through my tears but my phone battery had died anyway.

Back in the kitchen, I stared wildly at Steve.

'What?' He looked behind him, in alarm. 'What have you seen? This place is meant to be haunted you know, by the ghost of the smuggler who—'

'Can I borrow your phone?'

He pulled his head back. 'Er, sure.' He dug it out of his back pocket. 'Everything OK.'

'Not really.' I googled the number of Walsh Property Agents, crossing my fingers that Hugo would be there, and closed my eyes in relief when he answered the phone.

'Hugo, it's Meg. Meg Larson from the Old Bakery.'

'Hello Meg Larson from the Old Bakery.' He sounded droll, and a tiny bit pissed off. 'Nathan's not here, I'm afraid.'

'Has he left already? For Ireland, I mean.'

'He'll be at the airport now,' he said, voice sharpening. 'Why?'

I spun round on the spot. 'Oh… *poo.*'

'Did you want me to pass on that message?'

'I wanted to talk to him.' I was close to tears again. 'I'm not getting married now and I… I, oh, it doesn't matter.'

There was a pause at the other end. 'His flight doesn't leave until two. You might make it if you hurry.'

'Is it Exeter Airport?'

'It is.'

A surge of hope ripped through me. 'Do you really think I can make it in time?'

'I don't know, Meg, but getting off the phone and into your car would give you a fighting chance.'

I hung up and shoved the phone at Steve. 'I know I said I wasn't going to let things slide, but could you look after the place for a couple of hours, pretty please? I have to be somewhere.'

'So I gather,' he said, eyes full of curiosity. 'Go on then, or you'll never make it.'

Cassie came through, as I was rummaging my keys out of my bag. 'Valerie's got the hang of the till really quickly so I think I'll make a move.'

I looked up, feeling feverish. 'I'm going to the airport to find Nathan, to tell him I love him.'

Her mouth fell open. 'Oh my god, Meg!' She grasped my arms and gave me a little shake. 'You know what this means?' Her mouth widened into a grin. 'You're doing a Ross and Rachel!'

'Oh my *god*!' I looked from her to Steve. 'I'm doing a Ross and Rachel!'

Steve slapped a handful of dough down on the table. 'Someone should go with you, if you're going to be true to the episode. Phoebe and Ross turn up at the airport to find Rachel, and—'

'I know how the episode goes,' I said. 'I just hope Nathan won't already be on the plane.'

Chapter Twenty-Nine

I decided I didn't want an audience in the end, and Cassie and Steve waved me off with assurances that the bakery would still be standing when I got back, and a request from Big Steve to 'do something' with my hair.

It took too long to get to Exeter, thanks to three sets of roadworks and slow-crawling traffic, and then it took ages to find a parking space. I was sweating and panicky by the time I burst into the airport, praying that Nathan's flight had been delayed.

The lobby was swarming with people, and for a moment I felt paralysed. I began to run up and down, sandals slapping the tiles, scanning the display monitors overhead, and realised I had no idea which flight Nathan was even on. And was he landing at Belfast Airport or Dublin, before heading to… I couldn't even remember the name of the mountain he'd mentioned.

Maybe Hugo would know.

I scrabbled in my bag for my phone, then remembered the battery had died and that I'd used Steve's mobile to ring Hugo the first time.

Was there a public phone? There was, but I didn't have the number of the agency on me, and couldn't face wasting any more time trying to find it.

I scanned the monitors again, trying to see past the sea of heads, and to not trip over anyone's baggage, and saw that the Belfast flight was boarding, but the plane to Dublin had only just landed.

I rushed further inside, the air-conditioning icy on my sweaty fore-head, then realised that without a pass, there was no way I could get as far as the boarding area. If Nathan was bound for Belfast, I had no chance.

But if he was heading to Dublin, he might still be around.

I spent the next half hour scouring the area, darting into cafés, and shops, and WH Smith's in case he was having a coffee or looking at books, but couldn't see any sign of him.

I even ducked into the men's toilets and called his name, earning myself a few strange looks, then went into the Ladies to splash my face with cold water. I almost screamed when I saw my scarlet-faced reflection. I had a sliver of lemon zest stuck to my eyebrow, and was still wearing my Meg's Kitchen apron, and my hair was only half in the band I'd fastened round it that morning. I looked like a chef in the middle of a meltdown, trying to flee the country.

I patted my face dry and shot back out, looking around as if, by doing so, I could magically make Nathan appear. This was nothing like *Friends*, or any romantic movie airport scene I'd ever watched. There were just lots of people, either excited or bored, queuing or hurrying, and security guards milling about.

After locating the help desk, I asked if a Nathan Walsh had boarded his flight yet.

'I'm sorry,' said the man behind the counter, his heavily tanned face impassive. 'We're not allowed to give out that information. Data protection.'

'What about a loudspeaker thingy, where you ask someone to come to the information desk?'

His eyebrows lifted a notch. 'Is it an emergency?'

I hesitated. 'What would you class as an emergency?'

'Life or death,' he said flatly, perhaps assuming from the state of me that I meant to hurt someone. 'Has a loved one died?'

'Well, no. Thank goodness.'

'I'm sorry.' He raised a smile that didn't meet his eyes. 'I'm afraid we can't help.'

'But this is the help desk.'

'We don't offer the sort of help you need.'

What was that supposed to mean?

Knowing I was beaten, I retreated and sat on a bench, my bag between my feet, fighting an urge to cry.

I really hadn't thought this through. Nathan had gone, or was about to go, and there was nothing I could do to bring him back.

The drive back to the bakery was long and torturous, and I didn't even have a bottle of water to quench my thirst. My temples throbbed, and I couldn't find my sunglasses in the glove box. I remembered I'd left them in the kitchen at home. No, not home. Not any more. They were probably in one of the bags I hadn't had a chance to unpack.

Maybe it was as well I hadn't found Nathan, I reasoned. I should probably get settled into the flat first, and let him complete his assignment in Ireland, and then, when things were calmer, try and establish contact. If he really had feelings for me, they wouldn't just vanish overnight.

Tilly would tell me to wait. That I should be on my own for a while – but I had no problem being on my own, I'd just rather be with Nathan. And if it did turn out to be nothing more than a wild attraction, then maybe that was OK too.

It was gone four when I got back and the first thing I noticed when I stepped through the back door was that Steve had moved my bags upstairs. He was giving the kitchen a thorough clean, and his face lit up when he saw me. 'You're back.'

'So I am.' I dropped my bag on the floor. 'Is everything OK?'

'Perfect,' he said, and I realised he was suppressing some kind of emotion.

Cassie came through, Kath hot on her heels.

'It's OK, Valerie is solid, and the shop's not busy at the moment,' she said.

They were all wearing that same weird look. As if they had a secret I wasn't in on.

'I need a drink of water,' I said, filling a mug at the sink. 'It was so hot in the car, and there were so many roadworks, and when I got to the airport, I realised I didn't even know which flight he was on.'

I drank deeply, aware of the silence behind me.

I turned. 'What's going on?'

'You've got a guest.' Cassie's eyes were wide and bright, her lips parted in a smile.

'A guest?'

'Upstairs.' Kath's gaze hit the ceiling. 'Waiting for you.'

'He took your bags up,' said Steve. 'I made him a cup of tea and he's had a slice of your strawberry and cream cake, which by the way, has sold out, and if it's OK, I finished making that lemon cake you started and it's in the oven.'

'Guest?' I repeated.

Cassie turned me round and gave me a little shove towards the stairs. 'Go and see.'

Of course I knew who it was before I even reached the sun dappled living room and saw him sitting on the lumpy sofa, reading an old copy of *Little Women*, which must have spilt out of one of my bags.

'There you are.' He looked up as I reached the top of the stairs, and put the book down. 'I was really hoping you hadn't got on a plane to Dublin.'

'I knew it would be Dublin,' I said, my voice as light as air. 'How come you're here?'

'Hugo called. He told me you rang, wanting to talk to me, and happened to mention you were no longer getting married.'

'I did.' The look in his olive-green eyes was making me breathless. 'And I'm not.'

He smiled. 'I got a taxi here.'

'A taxi, all that way?' I took the final step, and then another, until I was standing in front of him. 'It must be love.'

'Oh, it most definitely is.' Reaching for my hands he pulled me onto his lap and we looked at each other for a long moment, and it didn't feel awkward at all. It felt lovely. I could have looked at him for hours. 'This sofa's really uncomfy,' he said.

'You should try the bed.'

'Oh?'

And then we were kissing, and it was just as good as it had been the first time, and every time that I'd imagined us kissing since.

'What about your assignments?' I said, when we'd finally pulled apart and had looked at each other some more, smiling as if we couldn't believe our luck, my stomach doing acrobatics. 'Won't you be sacked?'

'It's not that sort of job,' he said, fingers drawing circles on my back. 'It's the sort of thing I can do any time. I was thinking I might leave it for a few more weeks.'

'You know I'm going to be very busy with this place.'

'Of course,' he said. 'You've only just taken it on. I wouldn't expect anything less.'

'And it's early days for… this.' I gestured between us. 'I – I don't know what's going to happen.'

'That's OK.' He tilted my chin with his fingers. 'This is all new for me too.'

'Charlie will be happy if you're staying around for a while.'

He smiled. 'So will my brother, if it means free babysitting on tap.'

'Don Williams bought the bakery,' I said, unable to keep it in. 'After what you said to him.'

Nathan's head jolted back. 'He told you that?'

'More or less.'

He thought for a moment, then nodded. 'To be honest, I did wonder,' he said. 'He got this look… I don't know. And it seemed a bit coincidental that he withdrew his offer, then a mystery buyer came forward almost immediately.'

'Thank you, for saying what you did.'

He gave a tiny shrug. 'I meant every word.'

'Meg, sorry to bother you.' It was Big Steve, calling up the stairs. 'There's a customer wanting to know if she can have the recipe for your pecan and caramel tart,' he said.

'I'll be down in a minute!'

'You're already in demand.' Nathan's smile grew. 'I like it.'

I traced his lips with my finger. 'Gwen just tells them to mind their own bleedin' business.'

'But you can't do that?'

'I'm too polite,' I said. 'Too British.'

'A proper "hidden gem".'

I laughed and stood up, retying the strings of my apron. 'Will you wait for me?' I wanted to look at him a moment longer.

He leaned back on the lumpy sofa, his smile pouring through me like sunshine. 'As long as it takes,' he said.

A Letter from Karen

I want to say a huge thank you for choosing to read *The Bakery at Seashell Cove*. If you did enjoy it, and want to keep up to date with all my latest releases, just sign up at the following link. Your email address will never be shared and you can unsubscribe at any time.

www.bookouture.com/karen-clarke

It was such fun to return to Seashell Cove to tell Meg's story and revisit some familiar characters. I have to say, a lot of the joy came from dreaming up cake recipes, as I love both baking *and* eating cakes. My grandmother taught me to bake, as Meg's does, and my gran's date slices were a favourite of mine. My mum's a fantastic baker too, and some of my loveliest memories are of coming home from school to her home-made fruit cake, chocolate cake, teacakes and chocolate eclairs. It's amazing I was so skinny back then, but they were just a teatime treat!

I've included a recipe, in case you fancy trying Meg's Chocolate and Raspberry Cake, and if you do I'd love to see a photo of it.

I hope you loved *The Bakery at Seashell Cove* and if you did I would be very grateful if you could write a review. I'd love to hear what you think, and it makes such a difference helping new readers to discover one of my books for the first time.

I love hearing from my readers – you can get in touch on my Facebook page, through Twitter, Goodreads or my website.

Thanks,
Karen

karen.clarke.5682

karenclarke123

www.writewritingwritten.blogspot.com

Meg's Chocolate and Raspberry Cake

Ingredients

* 200g self-raising flour
* 25g cocoa
* 1 teaspoon baking powder
* 225g butter, at room temperature, plus a little extra for greasing
* 225g caster sugar
* 4 eggs

Filling

* 300ml double cream
* 200g white chocolate (optional)
* 1 teaspoon vanilla extract
* 300g fresh raspberries

Method

Preheat the oven to 160°C/Gas Mark 3.

Sift the flour, cocoa and baking powder into a bowl. Cream the butter and sugar together in a mixing bowl with an electric mixer until pale and fluffy.

Beat in 1 egg, then a spoonful of the flour mix. Continue adding eggs and flour alternately until it has all been added and the mixture is smooth.

Spoon into 2 lightly buttered 23 cm (9 inch) cake tins lined with a circle of non-stick baking paper. Smooth the tops so they're level then bake for 15–20 minutes, or until the tops feel firm and a skewer comes out cleanly.

Leave to cool in the tin for 10 minutes then loosen the edges and transfer to a wire rack to cool completely.

Whip the cream and vanilla extract and spoon half over one of the cake layers, then sprinkle with half the raspberries. Add the other cake half, top with the remaining fresh cream and raspberries, then sprinkle over icing sugar to finish.

(OPTIONAL: Melt most of the white chocolate in a bowl set over a saucepan of simmering water, then fold into the whipped cream before filling and topping the cake, and shave the leftover chocolate on top).

Cut into slices to serve.

Acknowledgements

A lot of people are involved in making a book, and I would like to thank the brilliant team at Bookouture for making it happen. Particular thanks to my wonderful editor, Abi, for her clever and insightful guidance, to Jane for her seamless copy-editing, Claire for her eagle-eyed proofreading, Emma for the gorgeous cover and Kim and Noelle for spreading the word.

As ever, I owe my lovely readers a massive thank you, as well as the blogging community, whose reviews are a labour of love, and Amanda Brittany for her tireless feedback and friendship.

And last, but never least, thank you to all my family and friends for their constant encouragement, my children, Amy, Martin and Liam for their unwavering support, and my husband Tim for everything – I couldn't do it without you.

Lightning Source UK Ltd.
Milton Keynes UK
UKHW02f0309010618
323562UK00007B/437/P

9 781786 813657